HER TRUE LOVE'S CALL

The outline of his shape was hazy, as if a veil of fog had been flung over him, but there was no mistaking her guest's identity.

"Are ye coming soon, lass?" His lips didn't move, but she heard the question in her mind.

Vapor rose between them like mist off a lake and a salt tang filled the air. Behind it, she could see the piper's pupils expanding until the black all but overran the pale grey of the irises. There were reflections moving in those eyes, but they weren't of the inn's plain room.

He leaned forward, parting the hazy veil with his broad shoulders. Bits of vapor clung to his locks as he thrust his way through the mist that divided them.

He reached out an insubstantial finger to touch her cheek, and a shiver at the feathery touch of something half-recognized rippled through her skin. It was like velvet, only softer, and scorching to the touch; mist that was fire, fog that burned.

She could see more clearly now, the images moving in his eyes. There were trees and an altar with two figures embracing upon it; one small and golden, the other taller and dark.

"Are ye coming tae me, lass?" The voice asked again, demanding an affirmative answer.

"Yes," another voice answered. She dimly recognized it as her own.

Other *Love Spell* books by Melanie Jackson:
MANON
IONA

NIGHT VISITOR

MELANIE JACKSON

LOVE SPELL   NEW YORK CITY

To my parents, with love.

A LOVE SPELL BOOK®

March 2001

Published by

Dorchester Publishing Co., Inc.
276 Fifth Avenue
New York, NY 10001

ISBN 0-505-52423-6

Visit us on the web at www.dorchesterpub.com.

AUTHOR'S NOTE

The story of the piper of Duntrune is a true one and I have made an effort to convey the incident in a factual, if colorful, manner. As is common with incidents in the far past, especially less-noted ones, the documents chronicling this event are scarce. The accounts I have read insist that Dean Mapleton was a bishop in the Episcopal Church. This will seem odd to many people who have come to think of the Episcopalian religion as being an American one (an arm of the Anglican Church that has its roots in the American Revolution). But the reformed Episcopal Church was alive and kicking in Great Britain from 1844 onward, including in London where the heroine lived, and it appealed to people who did not entirely approve of rule by bishops. (It is an interesting side note that two-thirds of the signers of the Declaration of Independence were nominal members of the Anglican Church, and that they did not want to bring the episcopal—i.e. bishops'—rule to the States and that this is what laid the groundwork for the formation of the American Episcopal Church.)

It is a gross simplification of the events surrounding the Year of Miracles, but for the purposes of understanding the cast of *Night Visitor* there were four main power players at work in the area around Duntrune: the Anglicans (English episcopals), Covenanters (Scottish puritans), Catholics (loyalists to King Charles I including the piper of Duntrune, Colkitto, and the Irish mercenaries known as *Gallowglas*), and the Campbells (who were looking after themselves). Where possible, I have used characters' own words to describe thoughts and events, but when I could find no records I supplied them with opinions on a best-guess basis. This story is also peopled with entirely fictional characters, and I have invented terrain, geography, architecture—and even decor as needed. For a purely factual account of the events that took place during Montrose's campaign, I recommend the book *Colkitto* by Kevin Byrne.

As to the *stillfolk* in *Night Visitor,* there were probably faeries hanging about the castle, but sadly I have found no documentary evidence to support this supposition. All references to things magical are created out of my imagination, though every good Celt knows that faeries are as real as brownies or kelpies and must be treated with the same respect—which I made every effort to do.

Happy Reading,
Melanie Jackson

Prologue

Duntrune Castle
Fall, 1888

Though he had no previous experience with exorcisms, Bishop Mapleton thought that dawn seemed a propitious hour to conduct one.

It wasn't that he wished to perform this act. He was a kind man, a good master, a doting grandfather. And he was fully aware that the Episcopal Church frowned upon any unsanctioned practice of such unconventional ceremonies—but with the discovery of those handless bones under the dressing room floor of his castle and the renewal of the infernal playing, which is rumored to have been heard by the castle's owners in centuries past from the battlements above the master's

11

bedroom, he had to do something! The household staff was thoroughly sick of hearing those damned ghostly bagpipes playing *Piobaireachd-dhun-Naomhaig* to a bloody Colonsay Loyalist who had been dead for over two centuries. One hysterical housemaid had already resigned her position and now the cook was threatening to leave as well.

Mapleton had tried prayer, Christian burial of the bones, and even reasoned conversation with the entity that plagued his household. All to no avail. Every sunrise . . . every sunset . . . the piper's warning to his master floated out from the castle walls, the indictment of its faulty metre there for everyone to hear.

Well, he had had enough! The reproach was completely misdirected. None of the dead piper's ills was of his doing, Mapleton assured himself, casting an uneasy glance at the ancient banner of the Campbells that hung in his hall. The ugly boar's head, bathed in moonlight, seemed to glare at him with enraged little eyes.

"Utter nonsense," he muttered, walking hurriedly away from the tusked swine.

And if this playing kept up he would be made a laughingstock. He was a bishop! He didn't have to tolerate some damned Papist ghost rousting him out of bed every bloody morning.

Still, this was a sensitive matter, likely to provoke gossip with the locals who were sympathetic to the ghost. So, without explaining why, he had ordered a watch to be kept and that the chapel bells were to toll a death knell upon the first showing of dawn in the eastern sky. Fearful of oversleeping Mapleton had chosen to remain awake the entire night through, with only a decanter of brandy and a Bible for companions.

Now he waited nervously in the cold and dark. As soon as the solemn peal began, he lit the candles on his impromptu altar and opened his prayer book. It was too dim to read, but that was no hindrance; he had the passages memorized.

Feeling somewhat awkward, and hoping that he would not be discovered by his staff or congregation in what felt somehow like a vulgar act, Mapleton began reciting quietly and hurriedly:

Most Glorious Prince of the Heavenly Armies, defend us against the spirits of wickedness in high places. The Lord has trusted the souls of the redeemed to be led into Heaven. We offer our prayers to the Most High, that without delay they may draw down His mercy upon us, and take hold of this pipe-playing serpent and cast him and his bagpipes into the bottomless pit.

Mapleton looked about uneasily, but could see no one nearby to witness his actions. He blew a warming breath over his naked fingers and went on:

13

His enemies are scattered. As smoke is driven away, so are they driven; as wax melts before the fire, so the wicked perish in the presence of the Lord. We drive you from us, unclean, cacophonous spirits. Begone! I command thee!

His last syllable had not yet died away when the sun burst full over the horizon and the sound of mournful bagpipes could be heard droning to life up in the empty, gray battlements. Apparently, his application of the old ceremony to remove the ghost from the castle hadn't worked.

Mottled with rage and frustration, the bishop barely restrained himself from hurling his prayer book at the invisible spirit.

"Bloody, damned Papist! Don't you know you've lost the war? King Charles is dead! The MacColla's dead—and so are you!" Mapleton's voice trembled with outrage as he snatched up the brandy decanter, unsure for a moment whether to drink the contents or to throw them.

Reason prevailed. Brandy was expensive and the decanter was a particularly fine one, purchased in London by Mapleton's father when he was presented with honors at Oxford in 1857.

"Stubborn, bloody ghost," he muttered. "But there must be something that will silence you."

As Mapleton stalked toward his library, drawing deeply from the imported spirits, he began to wonder if some other unseen agent of greater and darker power was at work in his home. After all, *something* had prompted him to wantonly spend his hard-earned money to remove a perfectly sound floor in his dressing room and turn this most grievous ghost loose upon the castle.

Maybe it was time for him to consult with old Andro, the grave-digger. The man was a fool, but he knew more about highland lore than anyone in Kilmartin; drastic situations called for drastic measures, the bishop assured himself. Something had to be done!

Chapter One

Kilmartin, Scotland
Late Summer, 1888

Taffy Lytton knelt on a throw pillow, sweltering in the old, closed carriage that had been converted to a small but portable photographer's studio. She didn't notice the heat, being completely preoccupied with developing her plates. The gelatin emulsion of the dry plate formula was a great deal easier to control than other methods she had learned, but still required a high degree of care and attention. Her father, Davis Lytton, was already skeptical of the benefit of her presence at his archaeological site; she didn't want to make any mistakes that would have him sending her photographs off to Eastman Kodak for developing.

To date, he had nothing to complain of in her photographic skills, she thought proudly. Her images of the great linear cemetery at Dunnard Fort were excellent. The five-thousand-year-old tombs had never looked better. These new plates of the Kilmartin cemetery were also coming out well, though they were of too modern a date to be of real interest to her parent, whose passion was reserved for the Picts and the ancient Celtic tribes of Scotland, Briton, Ireland, and Wales.

His obsession with the old cultures was so great that he had insisted upon naming her Tafaline, a Welsh corruption of a Hebrew name. Corruption was right! She insisted on being called *Taffy*.

"And may the devil swallow it sideways," she muttered, then glanced about guiltily in case anyone was lingering outside the carriage's door and heard her unladylike cursing.

Taffy passed a sooty hand over her brow and burped delicately. The *spotted lumpy dick* she had been offered for breakfast by the well-meaning Mistress MacIntyre was not sitting well in her stomach. It was simply too hot for eating thick porridge. She would have to speak to the landlady about preparing some lighter fare in the morning until the hotspell broke.

In the back of Taffy's mind, there lodged a hope that her father would not drop by that afternoon to check on her progress with these less important photographs. He had been gone from the inn when she awoke, off to somewhere—or someone—important.

Since there was no one to frown at her, she was dressed in one of her plain broadcloth sport dresses—*sans* corset and bustle—and she hadn't bothered with braiding her unruly hair and tucking her somewhat pointy ears out of sight, but had rather twisted the mass up on the top of her head and pinioned it with combs. Such methods of toiletry never served for long, and a quick pat of the head confirmed Taffy's suspicion that her hair had long since escaped its carelessly installed moorings.

Her fingers and nails were also stained with lamp black, she noticed unhappily, while putting the last plate aside.

Slovenly, her father would call her. He had said the same thing when he had put an end to her attempts to paint.

Taffy sighed in exasperation. She would have to scrub herself before dinner. It was not just her proficiency at film that her father questioned, but the moral effect of living in the "wilds." He did not consider her long stay in America to have improved her any, and Kilmartin—in spite of its ancient barrows filled with fascinating artifacts and bones—was the last word in backward societies as far as he was concerned.

Admittedly, she had returned from the United

States with some unusual mementos: a Winchester repeating rifle—*a powerful 45–70 steel frame with brass sighting and smokeless, wetproof shells*—a velocipede—*two-wheeler*—and a camera.

Had they been gifts for him, her father wouldn't have been so distressed. But they weren't gifts.

And worse by far than merely owning these things, she had returned home with an unladylike acquaintance with how to use all of them.

Of course, Taffy's most grievous sin, in her parent's eyes, was returning home without a husband. Jonathon Goodner had been her father's choice for her, and in an effort to restore the lost familial harmony that had come with her sudden inherited financial independence, Taffy had allowed herself to be persuaded to stay the winter and part of the spring in New York with Jonathon's mother and sister, where she and Jonathon might meet in the society-approved version of *in statu pupillari*—though how that academic joining was to have aided in a romance, Taffy could not imagine.

New York in the spring had been wonderful and exciting; Jonathon had not. He was a nice enough man, but they had soon reached the conclusion that they would not "suit" one another. Jonathon could never support the idea of a wife who was a better shot and archaeological photographer than he was. And the final crown of thorns for the Goodners had been the day she graduated from the ladylike tricycle to a man's hard-wheeled bicycle—and had daily insisted upon riding it to his *dig*. Obviously, such a wayward wife would not be an asset to a young archaeologist just making his mark in the world.

Poor Jonathon! The velocipede had, in fact, become her preferred mode of transportation. As she'd explained to him, it didn't rear-up unexpectedly, or bite or kick as horses did. It didn't smell and make inconvenient messes in the middle of the street. And it didn't require a servant to feed or groom it. She could load her camera and tripod into the paniers and come to the site whenever it suited her. Its practicality seemed evident to her, but left poor Jonathon and his mother stunned and feebly remonstrating.

Then, one path leading to another, following the purchase of the bicycle had come the inevitable need to alter her wardrobe. Bustles, trains, and billowing skirts were a hazard to the chain mechanism that drove the gears of the velocipede. So, she had cheerfully forsaken more feminine fashions and redone her wardrobe over in the daring sport dresses shown in Harper's Bazaar—and one set of utterly disgraceful bloomers that she had yet to wear. Still reeling from the blow of seeing her on a two-wheeled bicycle, for Jonathon, the shock of the sport dress had been the fatal blow to his marital aspirations.

He hadn't seen the worst of her new wardrobe either, Taffy thought now with a small, impish smile. He had only glimpsed the one fancy dress done in a fine navy satinet with sweet, old-fashioned Carrickmacross lace butterflies appliquéd on the collar, but that had been dreadful enough.

She wore that dress now only on more formal occasions, which were thankfully few in Kilmartin. The rest of her gowns were either done in kersey or broadcloth; which she wore depended on the weather.

There was also a single, speech-stopping outfit made of walnut and fawn cotton jean, which was strictly for cross-country tramping, tucked safely in Taffy's trunk away from censurious parental eyes. The seamstress, Mrs. Astley, had nearly burst into tears when Taffy had ordered a dress made from the crude fabric, but the cloth was comfortable and practically indestructible. This was something to consider when one was spending a great deal of time in the thistles and gorse, which were apt to seize an incautious hiker and shred frailer fabrics to piles of loose thread.

Of course, things would be very different when she and her father left Scotland in late September to return to their home outside of London.

Taffy grimaced at the impending gloom. She would be faced with the corsets and bustles she had cast off, and to be fashionable in London, she would have to double the yardage in her slimmed-down skirts. The style would be suffocating after a summer of freedom!

But to London, she had to go. It was time for her to marry—and Taffy had to admit that it was not entirely her father's notion. Since her mother's death, she had been—*not lonely*—but searching for someone with which to share her thoughts and dreams. There was also a growing conviction that somewhere there was a man whom she could truly love and esteem. A man who, in return, would love and admire who she was—not her face, not her fortune, not *entree* to her famous father, but Taffy Lytton, a bicycle-riding photographer who liked shooting guns and hiking through lonely country.

She hadn't found what she needed in America—though she had dearly loved the raw bustle and energy of the people who made their home there and planned to return one day, perhaps to live.

She would have preferred to find a country gentleman to keep her company, but sadly, she was not being presented with any sort of an alternative here in Scotland. So far, her selection of men included an aging sexton, who wandered about muttering in Gaelic, and some local workers who, though very handsome, were longer on brawn than intellect. Too, they were distressingly short on conversation appropriate for a "sassan-ach lady."

Of course, what conversation she could lure them into was fascinating. Her mother had been born a MacLeod of Skye, but her northern accent had faded greatly after years in London, and it had never been as musical as this local dialect.

Her father would have fits if he knew that she had been socializing unchaperoned, but the temptation to learn a bit of the Scot and Gaelic dialects had proven irresistible. She could now wish people a *"madainn mhath"* when she rode through the village in the morning, and she had collected a colorful store of Celtic curses, which she *didn't* share with anyone.

Taffy looked up sharply as the sound of pounding brogues approached her workplace.

"Mistress Lytton!" A heavy fist landed upon the panel door. "It's Jamesy, mistress. Your father said tae come away sharp. And tae bring your picture box! They've found the piper's body up at Duntrune!"

Taffy hastily put her plates aside in a leather satchel and opened the carriage door.

"A body?" she asked with some surprise.

"Aye! 'Tis the ghost piper. The joiner's son found him when they took up the dressing room floor."

"Oh, it's a skeleton then?"

"What? Oh! Aye, 'tis just bones." Jamesy

23

grinned. "But he is missing his hands, so it's the MacIntyre for certain. Your father was with the bishop when the great stone come up and he sent me tae fetch you and your picture box straight away. I have the pony trap waiting on the road."

"I'll come at once."

Taffy, her mussed hair and rumpled dress forgotten, reached eagerly for her camera and tripod, and the box containing unexposed plates.

A dead body would not have been a pleasant thing to photograph, but a skeleton! That was another matter altogether. She had seen any number of human bones during her years at home and, much to her father's disapproval, was not distressed by them.

She was also rather pleased to now discover that her father didn't consider her such a blot on western civilization that he couldn't present her to the bishop. She hadn't precisely been pining for an introduction to the Mapletons, as her interest in religious things was tepid at best, but they were much respected in the neighborhood and a chance to expand her limited society was not to be lightly scorned.

Jamesy helped her politely into the trap, seeming not one whit disturbed by her stained fingers. The afternoon had warmed up, but she was pleased to discover that there was a gentle breeze beginning to stir off of the loch, which helped cool her flushed cheeks.

Taffy looked about eagerly as they headed for the large bay. There were some pretty fields on the way to the castle, small and studded with the odd white sheep, which would make for an easy hike if she could gain permission to walk there.

A stray strand of hair blew across her eyes, reminding her of her slipping coiffure. She quickly set about tidying her locks over her deplorable ears so her father would not be ashamed to introduce her to the bishop.

The land was not a heavily wooded country anymore and the outlines of Duntrune Castle soon came into view. It was a tall but narrow building of some three stories of piled ashlars, and quite ancient in style, though not a haunted-looking place like Dunnottar or Dunderave. There, the sad ghosts of long-past atrocities clung to the very stones that made up the castles' walls. Duntrune was not as sad or frightening. Instead, it had about it an air of tired patience.

After his initial burst of conversation, Jamesy had lapsed into his habitual amiable reserve, staring into the distance as Taffy fussed with her hair. Realizing suddenly that she was completely alone with one of the more colorful locals, and unable to resist the chance to advance her linguistic and folkloric education, Taffy lured him into further conversation by bringing up the subject of the newly discovered skeleton.

"You said that these remains belong to a ghost

piper? I didn't know that they had any ghosts at the castle."

"Oh, aye! A piper he was, a MacIntyre of a MacLeod mother, they say, and a Papist. He was left at the keep with a small band of soldiers by the MacColla, them not knowing that the Campbells were near tae hand. Slaughtered to a man they were, poor lost souls."

"MacColla? That would be the one they call Colkitto?" Taffy asked with genuine interest. This MacDonnell was either a folk hero or the devil incarnate—depending upon who you spoke to. The Irishman had fought under Montrose along with Patrick *Ruadh* MacGregor in the rising of the 1640s called *The Year of Miracles*. Montrose and his generals had come out in support of King Charles I rather than Parliament, and, had they had a few more months before Charles's surrender to Parliament, many felt that he would have carried Scotland for the Stuart king and changed British history forever. Sadly, he had died in an ambush less than a year after his return to Ireland.

The Campbells she'd met called Colkitto a ravaging butcher. There were others, however, mainly MacDonalds and MacGregors, who felt that if anyone deserved to be ravaged and butchered it was the merciless Campbells. They celebrated the Irishman's brave memory.

The warrior had lived nearly two hundred and

fifty years ago, but Taffy had long ago discovered that the bloody history of the highlands was not relegated to seldom-read books, but lived clearly in the descendants' memories, and in fable and song.

"But this piper was a MacIntyre, you said, not a MacDonnell?" she questioned, seeking clarification. The pedigrees of the clans and their constantly changing loyalties were often confusing.

"Aye. His chief, the MacIntyre of Glen Noe, had sent him with the MacColla tae help with the battle. The soldiers needed a piper, you ken? And he was the best, being half of MacLeod blood as well." Jamesy cast a quick look at Taffy's poorly concealed ears. "But when the Campbells retook the keep, all the MacDonnells were put tae the sword. The piper had his hands struck off with an axe for playing a warning to MacColla's ship and sending him away from the trap they'd laid. But they had no bubbling pitch laid on and they couldna stop the bleeding. Very bad luck that is, killing a piper. Since then, he comes on stormy nights tae play his pipes upon the wall."

Taffy shivered, in spite of the sun.

"My! What an extraordinary tale!"

"That it is, and you'll see his mortal bones afore long," Jamesy said enviously.

The trap lurched onto the narrow road leading to Duntrune, which was rather smoother than the track they had just abandoned. Closer now, she could see that there was a pair of dignified elk guarding the entrance to the castle, which was itself a relatively small affair, perched upon the rock promontory of the north side of Loch Crinan on the Sound of Jura. Like many of the medieval keeps in Scotland and Ireland, Duntrune had a slightly wild look in spite of being inhabited and well-kept.

There was a curtain wall of what was called random rubble construction, a postern—though the seagate no longer seemed to be in use—and crow-stepped gables over the walls, which were made of peculiar green sandstone that gave the whole building an aspect of being underwater. It also had the feel of great age. The stones actually seemed weathered, like old brass verdigrised by the sea.

As they passed by one of the outside cottages made of smaller ashlars, Taffy noticed another set of stag horns embedded in the wall over the door, which had been painted a faded robin's-egg blue that harmonized nicely with the green-and-gray stone from which the croft was built.

Taffy looked about in pleasurable anticipation. She had never been to Duntrune Castle and was thrilled to have the opportunity to photograph it, however odd the circumstances. She was gaining a nice collection of castle photos and secretly hoped to exhibit them one day—perhaps in America whose citizens had a great curiosity about British castles and manors. The fact that this keep had a ghost as well was simply added fortune, as castles with ghosts were by far and away the most popular of attractions.

As they passed beneath the shadow of the battlements, feeling herself to be under friendly observation, Taffy looked up at the tower window with a warm smile of greeting. The impression of someone waiting for her there was so strong that she had actually lifted her hand to wave before noticing that the castle's tall walls were, in fact, empty of life.

"*A bheil thu tighinn?*" the wind whispered. *Are you coming?*

Feeling suddenly fey, Taffy tried to shake off the notion that she and Jamesy were being carefully observed by hidden eyes. What an inopportune time for the legendary MacLeod second-sight to kick in!

Her father was waiting for her in the courtyard, but though accompanied by many workers, there was no sign of anyone who might be Bishop Mapleton. Taffy was keenly disappointed, but reflected—after seeing her father's horrified glance rake over her from rough boots to combs—that perhaps this was not the ideal social situation in which to be making new acquaintances.

"Tafaline—"

"Taffy," she corrected automatically. He usually remembered her preference, but lapsed when he was angry or agitated.

"Bring that contraption of yours and let's finish this task. A waste of time," he muttered. "The bones aren't more than two hundred—possibly three hundred years old. I don't know why they summoned me."

"Yes, but they are rather famous bones," she pointed out, accepting her equipment from a suddenly smiling Jamesy.

"Gaoth deas ort," he whispered. *A south wind on you.*

"Tapadh leibh." Thank you. Feeling bold, she dropped one eyelid in a wink. She raised her voice. "They belonged to Colkitto's piper. A MacIntyre by the name of—"

Malcolm.

"—Malcolm."

Davis Lytton turned to stare at her.

"I didn't realize that you were conversant with this legend, Tafaline."

"Isn't everyone? This was a rather pivotal moment in recent Scottish history."

Jamesy coughed suddenly into a neckerchief.

"Very true," Davis looked at her thoughtfully, approval beginning to form on his stern face. "I am glad that you have not completely abandoned your studies in favor of frivolous pursuits."

"Certainly not. Where are the skeletal remains?"

The space was a small one, and the flagstone taken up an uneven one. The bones were resting on their side as though shoved carelessly into the hole.

The lower forearms and hands were indeed missing and the grossly foreshortened ulna and radii were terminated in shattered stubs.

Unable to help herself, Taffy knelt by the open grave and reached in to touch the mutilated bones. A tiny pinprick from a razor-tipped shard lanced the end of her index finger.

"Definitely an axe wound," Davis said imper-sonally, apparently not feeling any of the horror—*and rage,* she realized with a shock—that she was experiencing while looking at the grave.

Feeling slightly lightheaded, Taffy rose to her feet. She quickly sucked away the single drop of welling blood.

Out of habit, she looked next at the feet. The toe bones that were in place suggested that all the digits had been of the same length rather than tapering from the big toe down. They were also long and narrow without the heavy growth of bone at the heel, which she'd seen usually an-chored the ancient Saxons' more pronounced heel tendon.

"Yes, I checked the feet. He was a Celt," Davis admitted impatiently. "Let's get this over with. Mapleton wants to move the bones as soon as possible."

"But—"

It doesn't matter. Let them be moved.

"As you wish," she murmured in absent-minded agreement. Then louder: "I shall place the camera here. Perhaps later, I might climb up to the battlements and try for an overview."

She took the measuring rod held out by Davis and placed it beside the grave. She was careful not to touch the shattered bones again.

"You are very thorough," Davis said, grudgingly. "I'm glad that some of my training took."

Taffy didn't answer, but set about arranging her equipment.

"Step back, please, Father. Your shadow is in the way."

Just as she squeezed the bladder to burn the plate, a stray sunbeam shifted to the flags and reflected directly into her eyes. Swallowing an unladylike curse, Taffy unhurriedly loaded another plate into the camera. She would have to assume that the first had been ruined by the flash of blinding light.

Once prepared, she looked around to be certain that there was no one nearby who might be carrying a reflective object that would spoil her work with a redirected beam.

Taffy didn't see anyone, but the feeling that she was being observed persisted, and she began to wonder if there was some disapproving prankster hanging about, waiting to play a trick on her.

Her second plate was exposed without difficulty, and her father kindly acted as guide and porter as they climbed up the sea wall so she could take an exposure from above. The feeling of being watched presently faded, but it might have been because she was growing accustomed to the sensation.

When her assigned task was done, Davis sent her away. Swallowing her annoyance at his cavalier dismissal, Taffy managed a polite farewell from the back of Jamesy's pony trap. She promised to have the plates developed the following morning.

And she had every intention of delivering the photographs to Bishop Mapleton herself. She would wear her navy dress—*and gloves*, she decided with a guilty glance at her begrimed hands.

It would probably annoy her father, but she could claim to have misunderstood his intentions and point out the fact that he was always complaining about being taken away from his work by frivolous socializing with amateur historians.

"And what did you think of the piper, mistress?" Jamesy asked curiously.

"I think that King Charles needed more backbone," she answered without thinking. "He could have won had he more resolution."

Jamesy grinned.

"Aye, that he could have. Montrose would have

rid us o' the Campbells forever, had he another four months."

"It wouldn't have mattered to Malcolm though, poor soul."

Jamesy swiveled about in his seat and stared at her.

"*Malcolm?*"

"Yes, didn't you say that was his name?"

"Nay, I did not know it. But whatever his name, he was surely past all care by then, poor laddie." The man cleared his throat. "Mistress, your father, did he by any chance touch the MacIntyre's bones?"

"I don't know. Perhaps. Why do you ask?"

" 'Tis nought of importance. Just an old legend."

"Well, let's have it," she said encouragingly, squinting against the glare of the afternoon sun so that she might better see her carter's face. "I enjoy hearing the old stories."

"Aye, well. It is just a belief that when the spirit is in a state of betweenity, it happens that it might attach itself to the person who first lays his hands upon the bones."

A slow, involuntary shiver worked its way down Taffy's uncorseted spine.

"And what happens—" She swallowed and then tried again to ask the question sticking in her throat. "What happens to the person the ghost attaches itself to? They don't die, do they?"

"Ach! No! 'Tis not some cursed Irish banshee after all."

"Oh." She smiled, feeling both relieved and foolish for her momentary alarm. They were discussing a silly *legend!* "Then what happens? How does one know that the ghost is there?"

"They dream, mistress."

"Dream?"

"Aye. The dream o' the ghost's death, over and over 'til they die or go mad." He smiled suddenly. "Unless they're a MacLeod."

Taffy cleared her throat, which had tightened again.

"What happens to MacLeods? Why are they not haunted like other folk?"

"Well, being that some of them are of faerie blood, they get called and go tae live wi' the still-folk at *Caislean na Nor*, of course."

"Well." Taffy swallowed again, then said lightly: "I hope the workmen were careful. We wouldn't want anyone getting 'called.' "

"They were careful, no doubt. *They* would know better than tae touch the piper's bones."

Chapter Two

Argyllshire, Scotland
Early summer, 1964
Malcolm stood quietly in the shadows of a tiny croft, disinclined to approach his chief, *Mac an t-Saoir* of Glen Noe. He was to be presented to their guest, MacColla of the Irish, son of the fanatical *Colla Ciotach* of the Isles, also known to the sassanach as Lieutenant General Sir Alistair MacDonald, and more commonly, as Colkitto.

The light was dim, but plainly the visitor was a large man, fully the tallest being he'd ever seen. Taller even than Malcolm himself was, which was towering enough to draw comment among the MacIntyres, the MacColla had a black presence about him that spoke of great power. Such men influenced destinies, and Malcolm did not particularly want to be influenced just then.

The piper shrugged uneasily, trying to dislodge his brooding mood so that he might look upon this man fairly. He had an unexplainable feeling, so strong that it might be called foreknowledge, that though they had never met, his and Colkitto's lives and fates were now somehow intertwined.

There remained to see in what manner they would mingle their mortality.

Some things about the future, he could guess. There was no escaping the fact that just as his father before him, this MacColla was a hard man, as the enemy Campbells had already discovered. There was a tale at large in the glen that the MacColla had herded together all the people of Argyll—excepting not even women or babes— and once they were secured in the town's great barn, had set it ablaze.

The story might even be true, Malcolm admitted. The MacColla hadn't been there in Argyll to pay social calls upon the Campbells, who had his father and brother held fast in some prison, and who were committing massive slaughters among his kin in Colonsay and Ireland.

Too, this Colkitto came from a long line of men who had never been inclined to let mercy season their justice. So it followed that in any meeting with Colkitto there would likely be violence and bloodshed.

However, in these times of unrest there was much violence and bloodshed everywhere. That fact alone should not have caused Malcolm to be so greatly disturbed by the man's presence.

He looked up at the smoked-stained rafters, as though the shadowed eaves might hold an answer to what troubled him. Unfortunately, none were there that evening. Perhaps they'd been banished by the great one's presence. It seemed Malcolm had nowhere to look but inside himself for understanding, and he had not yet discovered any happy solutions waiting there.

The tangled politics of the highlands were but part of the larger concern of all the politics of humankind—there was certainly no escaping it in Scotland. Some covetous Englishman's unremitting preoccupation with wealth and power was ever focused upon Scottish land, it seemed. Perhaps that would always be so. And the Scots who fought and died for their freedom, from Wallace on, would ever resist such occupation. Even when it meant killing other Scots.

The Lord of Heaven, avowedly all-merciful and forgiving, supposedly approved of such atrocities that had happened in this year past. However it didn't seem to Malcolm to be the work of God, but rather of avaricious men.

Malcolm detested the Campbells, their brutality and ever-shifting loyalties. But he was not certain that he liked this self-appointed *Hammer of the Lord* either, aiding the MacIntyres though he was by rebuilding that damage the ravagers had wrought in the Glen. Not even Colkitto's service under the charismatic and just Earl of Montrose against the clearly evil Parliament—and murderous convenanters who were determined to unseat their lawful king—was enough to cause great liking or trust in Malcolm's breast.

Of course, in all fairness, he had to admit that little did these days. Malcolm was a man marked by the spirit world and awaited events in a state of emotional betweenity.

Still, had it been Patrick *Ruadh* and the MacGregors who had come among them, he would have rejoiced, for though they were Catholics, they were also highlanders and true, fighting for the return of their stolen lands. They were not this uneasy mix of Catholics from Ireland and the isles, and English Episcopals united more in political hatred of Puritans and the Covenant's Solemn League than they were because of the king or family affairs.

The king. Malcolm could only think on him unhappily. Though Charles was an Anglican now, he had not forgotten his Catholic subjects. In the decade before, he had given a charter to a vast track of land in the New World where Catholics could go and worship unhindered.

But now, his Catholic subjects—those still alive—were asked to be grateful for his past tolerance and possible future benevolence, and to go defend him against the covenanters.

The Irish and Scots served their king, as poor men always had—not with patriotic words, but by watering the fields with their blood. And as all the English kings before him, Charles had accepted this as his due and without any thought for the widows and orphans left behind to die by enemy swords or starvation.

And it was all a great bloody waste!

Of course, Malcolm never said so. His kinsmen already thought he was quite odd. Had he not been their piper, doubtless they would have driven him away long ago, for they truly feared him now that he was grown—as they had his mother and two elder brothers. MacLeods, all of them, and reputedly tainted by faerie blood. Even his body, in the matter of his pointed ears and ambidextrous hands, lent fuel to their superstitions.

It was a dangerous thing to provoke fear in one's kinsmen. Death from without was always a danger, but one for which a man might prepare. That same danger was rather more difficult to avert when it wore a familiar face. Confronted with such growing hostility, Malcolm's own parents and siblings had gladly gone to Mary's land when the *Dove* sailed a half-score years ago, and had he not been training to be the clan's piper, he would have happily gone with them.

His father, *Calum mor*, was a simple man and did not believe all the talk of his wife's second sight. Too, he thought that this habit of governments—and even chiefs—of forcing religious worship on its subjects by fire and sword raised a stink in God's nostrils.

After the first atrocities done *"for God"* under the Act of Revocations, he had taken his family to live over the sea amongst the Quakers who did not compel uniformity of religion. In a letter sent home with the returning *Dove*, he had written to his son that the strange people of Mary's land even believed in equality for women and allowed them to preach the Gospel there!

It had to be a wondrous place, Malcolm thought, that land where no one showed their love of God by slaughtering other men and where his mother could work as a healer. He would love to someday visit a place where the strength of one's sword-arm and the ruthlessness of one's nature were not the only measures of a man.

"Malcolm!" the chief called. "Hoots awa' wi' ye, lad. Come away now!"

Malcolm sighed and stepped out of his dark corner. Once again, distasteful duty called him from his thoughts before he was ready to leave them.

"Welcome, piper! You've the highest of gifts,"

41

MacColla praised him as he joined the two men seated by the fire. The Irishman nodded over his tankard but did not rise to his feet.

Malcolm looked calmly into his watchful gaze, appraising what he saw by the flickering firelight. The Irishman's young face was stern, even when the lips tried to smile, and the eyes were cold and wary enough to disconcert even a man already marked by the spirits for some unearthly fate. If their illustrious guest was drinking whiskey from his cup, he was not plunging deep into it.

"I thank ye for yer praise. I had a good master in Black Anndra," Malcolm replied formally, but made no effort to curb his accent as many of the lairds did in august company.

"That is so. I had the pleasure of hearing him play that very song some years past. He taught you well. Most men cannot manage so flawless a passage. Perhaps it is because their poor hands are too small and cannot be used interchangeably."

"Mayhap."

"Or perhaps it is because they are not of the MacLeods gifted with special talents. I have heard some astonishing tales of one particular line of MacLeods."

Malcolm did not answer.

The MacIntyre cleared his throat and joined the conversation for the first time. The chief looked rather ill at ease. It could have been because MacColla mentioned Malcolm's mixed blood, but he suspected that there was some other, more sinister cause.

"Malcolm, a great honor has come tae ye. Ye've been asked tae go wi' the MacDonnell and his men. They've need of a piper tae play them intae battle when they go tae take Duntrune."

"We need some music to drown out the arrows whistling past our heads," MacColla added with an unpleasant smile. "I've had a sudden vision of you playing upon the castle walls. With your presence, we shall be victorious, I have no doubt. And I always make every effort to ensure victory."

So, too, did Malcolm have this very same vision every night when he dreamt, and it left him mightily uneased that Colkitto had chosen those particular words to express his expectations of victory. It suggested that there was some deeper purpose at work in this meeting. Deeper purposes could not be ignored.

"Malcolm, lad. Ye've been asked tae play the king's men tae glory."

"Aye. I heard."

Asked, the MacIntyre had said, not ordered. Still, he knew his chief well, knew what was required of him in this time of war. Such obedience was the backbone of a chief's power and the safety of the clan.

Still, Malcolm hesitated to volunteer. What if

43

his fate was to overtake him on this journey to Duntrune and endangered the other men? What if he left the glen and Fate couldn't find him?

"Malcolm," the chief prompted again, likely fearing that his increasingly fey piper would seem to MacColla to have lost his nerve and turned coward.

That wasn't the difficulty, Malcolm knew, but how to explain about the new portents he'd seen—the silvered reed left beside his pipes, and the wraith? He was nominally a Catholic, as was his chief. He knew the way such religions minds as Colkitto's worked. They would not understand that he still kept some of the old ways and knew the customs. They would not discern what the reed signified. And if they did, they would likely seek his death for being bewitched.

But *he* knew. After all, he was partly a MacLeod, and though he had tried to reject that part of his nature and live as his father did, he had always been aware that there were other, older beings that lived among them in this world of men. Most people never saw the old ones—his father never had! But Malcolm did see them. They were in the sly shadows that crept about in the darkened corners of certain glades, and behind the careless shiver of leaves when there was no wind to stir them. These things also influenced men's lives and had to be carefully considered and sometimes appeased.

If he hunted when it rained and killed a stag, he always left a portion of venison for the faeries. At other times, he left milk on the flags by the fire, but on rainy days, he knew that the still-folk ate venison.

And the still-folk were grateful. Where others might find magic barriers stretched across certain hidden ways in the woods, no bar to passage was ever raised against him. Malcolm always returned with game before other hunters. He could always find his way through the woods on even the darkest night.

And he owed his skilled playing not to Black Anndra, but to the blessing his mother's kin had received in that long-ago cradle where the first half-human, half-faerie child was said to have been born.

And now, Malcolm had been left the silvered reed for his pipes. The gift of the moon-metal and the vision from the still-folk meant that he was chosen for some arcane task or sacrifice.

But this was not something that he could explain to others. Not ever. Nor could he tell them about the *knowing* that came now when he stood close to certain objects of power. Usually, it was a holy spring, or perhaps an ancient weapon, that brought forth his intuitions. This time, the object of power was a man: the MacColla. A man who, like Robert the Bruce—and himself—carried the trait of ambidexterity.

Yet now, when he needed the inner-guidance most, his instincts had gone quiet.

Aye or nay? Should he embrace this man and swear his loyalty, or refuse, and finally so anger the chief that he would be broken and sent away? Malcolm would not regret leaving the glen, but neither answer was a desired one until the spirits gave him some definite sign of what was to come. Danger was near, but from this world, or the other?

"Are ye drunk, man?" the chief demanded, frowning in earnest. "Speak up!"

Putting his unease aside, Malcolm prepared to answer the men of war who waited impatiently for his reply.

Then, just as he parted his lips to say he knew not what to do, from the corner of his eye he caught a glimpse of the wraith that had lately been haunting him. All unwilling, he turned his head to stare at her.

The apparition was a strange sight. Female, certainly, but dressed in a manner he had never seen on mortal women. She had honey-colored hair and eyes the deep shade of late blueberries with the bloom of dew upon them.

She was not, he felt certain, of the true *Daoine Shi*—the still-folk who lived under the ground in the turrets of *Shian*. Nor was she a terrible Irish banshee, nor a ghost, nor an elemental spirit. Yet something about her spoke of magic.

The coming of an apparition was always a sign of change—nearly always for the worse, and most often of imminent death. Yet, he could not believe that this shadowy girl he ofttimes saw from the corner of his eye was any portent of evil.

All she ever did was walk about, with a box mounted on sticks through which she peered from time to time before disappearing in a lightning flash. She had never spoken to him, never looked into his eyes, or given any sign that she knew he was there. Yet this time, when he needed to choose a path, she was staring in his direction, waving her arm in languid farewell.

Farewell. Not greeting.

"Malcolm," the chief prompted in a desperate voice. "Ye've returned no answer tae our guest."

Malcolm reluctantly turned away from the apparition and found the MacColla watching him intently.

"Have you the sight, piper?" he asked softly in Gaelic, leaning forward, those cold eyes avid as he sent a quick glance to the empty air where the girl had stood. *"Knowest thou the future? Hast thou seen the evil priest of the Campbells who is said to hunt thy kin? He is even now at Duntrune."*

"Nay," he denied automatically. It was true that his mother had been a MacLeod, and from a family of wise women, but he had never had the true sight—didn't want it! Yet . . . He had been born on the day of Saint Columba's birth,

47

and those born at the time of that holy saint were said to have the way of turning the riddle come upon them in later life.

And he had heard of this defrocked priest who hunted the still-folk. It was said that he used evil sorceries to find his prey.

Perhaps this wraith was his answer after all. Had she not first appeared at the same time the MacColla's people had entered the MacIntyre lands? Perhaps she had been sent as a message that he would soon be traveling away from Glen Noe.

If that was the case, he realized with a pang, *then she would depart this night and be seen nevermore.* Odd that the thought of her leaving made him irritable and even a little sad.

"I am honored to go wi' ye," Malcolm said with a quick nod, wishing the conversation over. "Ye plan tae depart in the morn?"

"Aye, as soon after dawn as may be arranged."

"Then I'll go at once and see tae mine own preparations."

"As you like." MacColla nodded back, his eyes still speculative. "Perhaps there will be time for you to play for us again later."

"Mayhap."

Malcolm didn't wait for his chief's dismissal, but turned and hurried in the direction of the place where he had last seen the apparition walking. Perhaps he could catch a final glimpse of her before the moonrise. He never saw her later in the night, unless it was in his increasingly fevered dreams.

He traveled from Glen Noe with only his plaid, his pipes, and the sunshine as his load. He had a silver dirk and *sghian dubh*, but fortunately the MacColla had asked him to bear no other arms aboard the ship; his pipe song, the MacDonnell said, was his greatest weapon.

This was true, of course, but he had long made it a habit never to carry weapons made of cold iron because of the repugnance it held for the still-folk.

Though they were nearing Duntrune Castle where bloody battle would ensue, his thoughts were not upon the struggle ahead. Instead he contemplated the possible purpose of the golden-tressed apparition appearing in his life. By his estimation, she should have left him yestereve; yet though he had not found her in the dark of the night, she had again been out walking when dawn lit up the sky.

She had paced beside the MacColla's men as they approached the loch, hair loose and sparkling as if under a noonday sun, though the sky above was cast over with grey. Malcolm had needed every fiber of will not to stare at her openly as she strolled with her magic box toward the softly frothing water's edge.

He wondered if she would actually board their boat, but like all spirits, she seemed unable to cross over water. Instead, she had set her box upon its long-legged sticks and peered out over the shore as though enthralled with the wrack and spindthrift that gathered there. Soon, there had come the expected flash of light and then, to his great disappointment, she was gone.

Malcolm exhaled slowly. It was surely madness to think on her. If the MacColla knew of his distraction, he would likely order him bound to a holy stone until Saint Fillan saw to his release from delirium.

Ah! But what sweet madness had him in thrall! He closed his eyes and let the refreshing wind of the Loch Crinan blow over him, teasing his unbound locks and slipping beneath his belted plaid. It was more pleasant than contemplating what lay ahead. He did not doubt that the MacColla's machinations would win them Duntrune Castle, but what should become of him after, he did not know, except that he sensed his days in Scotland were numbered at less than a score. The senses that showed him the quickest path on a moonless night told him that another road awaited him.

He hoped that it was a way to a new and better life in some other land far away, but if it was the "low road" for him, he supposed he could bear it if this golden wraith walked beside him. Strange as she was in her manner of dress, it seemed to him that she left nothing to be desired in a female companion.

Malcolm grinned suddenly.

What lunatic idiocy was this? *Nothing to be desired?* He had to be mad. Everything about her was eminently desirable! He'd cast off his plaid to make them a bed in an instant had she been anything but insubstantial dreams and shadow.

"You seem in good spirits," MacColla said quietly, taking a seat on the deck beside him. The two of them were nearly a head taller than any of the men nearby.

"Aye." Malcolm turned to look at the man who was so surely bound up in his approaching fate. He still did not know if he liked or hated him.

"Think you that we shall have success in today's great venture?"

Malcolm shrugged, still smiling faintly.

"I believe ye'll take the keep," he said.

"Aye? Think you then that we shall rid Scotland of the bloody Campbells as well?"

Malcolm shook his head.

"The Campbells are like the poor; they shall be with us always."

"You are indifferent to them?"

"Nay. 'Tis just that I shall not be here tae see them feasting on our bones."

MacColla was finally disconcerted.

"You are *leaving* us?" he asked softly in Gaelic. One did not speak of dying in the lowland tongue. Nor did the Irishman likely want to speak of death before battle when it might vex the men. "You are called to *travel*, MacLeod?"

"Aye. Before the next full moon." Malcolm's voice was equally soft as he told his unwanted spirit-brother the truth.

"And for this you smile?" MacColla was evidently part-fascinated and part-disturbed.

"Nay. I smile because I am for the first time—and certainly the last—in love." Malcolm laughed and gave the man a look.

Colkitto stood abruptly, his fascination replaced with alarm.

"I pray that you are mistaken."

"Whyever? A good Scotsman should enjoy thinking on a bonnie lass."

"Not when he is nearing the time of battle and *travel*. What ails thee, piper, to think of laying the hand of Fate upon this lass? I tell thee, it does not serve to give hostage to Fate."

Malcolm nodded, knowing that the MacColla was thinking of his own family, ransomed in the merciless hands of Lord Lorne.

"Worry not about me lass, Irish. She's already walking wi' the spirits. In any case, 'tis late in the day for us tae flee our memories. The heart that truly loves a woman cannae forget her, and somehow I ken that she is bound tae me as well."

"God grant eternity," the other whispered, crossing himself hurriedly.

To that Malcolm didn't answer, and MacColla, no longer so curious about the future, didn't ask if he knew what his own end would be or whether his imprisoned family would be waiting at Duntrune.

That was best, Malcolm knew. It would be difficult to lead men in battle if one knew that grim Death was waiting impatiently nearby. It was hard enough to lead men when one's piper's thoughts were not upon the coming battle but upon his own nearing end.

Malcolm turned back to look out over the loch. He couldn't be certain, but there was a tiny rowboat coming their way, and as none of the other men were raising an alarm at the approaching vessel, he was led to hope that it was the apparition. His . . .

Malcolm closed his eyes, and for the first time, reached down inside to the forbidden place where he never allowed his mind to go. He wanted to see if he could name her, his blond wraith.

What is your name? he asked her.

Taffy, a soft voice whispered back.

"Taffy," he repeated, testing the foreign syllables and finding he liked their rhythm.

He opened his eyes, watching the boat draw near. Something golden and shining was aboard it, glistening under an unseen sun.

Mayhap he truly meant what he had said to the

MacColla about being blindly infatuated. For which of the great lovers had ever not loved— and deeply—at first sight True, it was daft. But there was no escaping that this strange new feeling he had was stronger than the call to duty, stronger even than the fear of dying.

But if he had only a score of days left to spend in this world, why should he not spend them in love with this beautiful apparition?

Patiently he waited for the skiff to approach, breathing deeply the salt air, which was gradually spiced with the scent of sweet woodbine and blackberries ripening under the sun.

"Come tae me, Taffy, lass," he murmured.

I'm coming, he thought he heard the wind whisper back.

Chapter Three

Kilmartin, 1888

The darkness's disquieting dreams had given way to the morning rituals, which included performing one's toiletries by a small lamp feebly aided by dawn's faint light. Taffy loved Scotland, but she found this to be one of the more discouraging aspects of rural life. She did not care for early hours, cold baths, or arranging her hair when she was still fumble-fingered—especially this morning, as she intended to call on Bishop Mapleton and wanted to put in a respectable appearance for . . . well, whoever might see her at Duntrune.

"My sainted aunt!" Taffy muttered in Gaelic as she wrestled with her hair—which was much too

cumbersome that morning. She began to ponder, as the hands on her timepiece swept past the new hour, if perhaps it was time to halve its length. Surely no one needed hair that reached past their shoulders.

After the long and difficult battle with braids and combs, she arrived at the breakfast table in a dead heat with the tea. Fortunately, her father was preoccupied with reading some repelling, moldy manuscript and did not note Taffy's near tardiness and suspiciously formal dress as she discreetly slipped into her chair.

It wasn't that she was unfilial, Taffy assured herself, but as she had gotten older, she found that she was not open to parental suggestions on how to improve her nature. Nor was she receptive to advice on the manner of her clothing—which, according to her parent, was practically an eyesore for any that had beheld her in "rational dress."

It was unusually ill-natured of her to wish to avoid one of her father's favorite mealtime topics, but she was not in the mood this morning to endure another lecture on the matter. She had come to the conclusion that she wasn't meant to live up to his ideal of womanhood, and anyway, she had greater thoughts on her mind this morning than her attire.

Fortunately, other than the ritual daybreak greetings with Mistress MacIntyre, not a word was spoken over breakfast, and Taffy escaped the morning table as soon as she decently could. She needed to be out in the open air where she could think without interruption.

She paused only long enough to grab a short cloak and then hurried from the inn. The morning air was bracing and filled with a salty tang and the scent of wild honeysuckle. She breathed the sea air deeply, already feeling less constrained.

In the distance was the distinct sound of bagpipes. Taffy listened carefully as she fetched her velocipede. She couldn't hear the tune plainly, but what snatches there were sounded mournful. It seemed that there was also someone else who didn't care for being up with the dawn! Mayhap he had spent the night having restless dreams as well.

The sun, just fully over the horizon, was bright enough that Taffy had to narrow her eyes as she set the velocipede on its lurching course toward the loch. She should have fetched a visor, but it looked out of place with her fancier dress and would mean returning to the inn and possibly encountering her father.

Her precious prints of Duntrune were secured between slender boards and stored in a mud-proof oilskin satchel, which she used for transport on the bicycle. She had not taken the time yesterday to develop the first plate she had exposed at the castle, suspecting that it was ruined, but after her dreams of the night before . . .

Taffy shook her head once, and then, recalling her recalcitrant hair, desisted.

Well, never let it be said that she was one to let the sun go down upon an interesting notion. She decided to take the time to see if anything *odd* was there on the undeveloped plate.

Like Malcolm.

Taffy flushed with a sudden surge of emotion the name brought and slowed her pedaling. It would not do to have an accident and arrive at Duntrune in a muddied state or unbecomingly flushed.

It was not amazing, she assured herself as the sound of pipes grew louder, that she had dreamt of Malcolm the night before, given the thoughts she had taken to bed with her. His story was a colorful one, and though skeletal remains were a fairly regular occurrence in her life, they were usually very old, partial skeletal remains, and hardly resembled people anymore.

But these things, even in conjunction, could not account for the content of her dream. She had seen a virtual re-creation of yesterday's events, except that at the moment when she went to expose her plate, an unusually tall man with dark hair and the palest gray eyes had knelt down beside the grave.

He had been dressed in the old manner wearing a belted plaid, secured at the waist with a wide belt and then wrapped over the shoulder where it was pinned with a silver broach. He had hand-stitched brogues that came up well over his ankles, and beside him on the stone floor were a set of pipes and a severed boar's head.

At the last instant, he had looked up from the bones to stare at her, surprise—and longing—written clearly on his weathered face.

There had been something else, too, something very strange. Her own ears were the tiniest bit pointed at the upper tips, but the piper's had been *very* pointed. In fact, he very nearly matched the locals' description of a faerie. Yet this man could not be the infamous still-folk patriarch Tomas Rimer; that great faerie appeared to mortals only as an old man.

Taffy pushed the thought aside. Her mind was filled with rubbish this morning! But she would develop that other plate as soon as she returned from the castle. She hadn't believed any of her friends' spiritualist nonsense when the craze swept through London last winter, but there had been some remarkable photographs of supposed apparitions caught on film, and she was willing to see if perhaps she had encountered such a—a *"technical flaw"* with her own equipment. It might be that she would be able to finally lay to rest all the silly rumors about ghosts and faeries appearing on film.

59

Melanie Jackson

Taffy dismounted her velocipede at the castle gates and leaned it against the rough gray wall. She removed her cycling cloak, and then smoothed her skirt back into neatness before walking boldly up the long drive to the castle's entrance.

On the top step she looked about once, sensing that she was being observed, but seeing no one and hearing no stirring from within, she reached out a nervous hand and let the ugly door-knocker—a hideous tusked boar with mean, little eyes—fall on its iron plate

After a time, a drowsy housemaid answered the summons and took Taffy through a great hall, where there hung a large banner with yet another boar's head emblazoned on it—this swine in profile and having a forked tongue as well as dagger-length tusks—into a parlor which, judging from the accumulated books and folios resting upon every flat surface, was serving as the bishop's study while repairs were being carried out in his home.

Bishop Mapleton took some time in joining her and looked as though he had hurried through his toiletries. But he welcomed Taffy politely, even though he was clearly surprised at her early arrival and so distracted by the ongoing renovations that he spent most of his time peering out of his study window and jumping nervously at every sharp sound. Even a workman's tuneless whistling seemed to irritate his tender nerves.

Perhaps it was her velocipede that had put him off; many people did not care for the whimsical design of the bentwood hickory frame, she thought, noticing that it was resting within plain view of the window. Taffy frowned. Or maybe he did not like that a female was riding it. She had been rejected at the Glasgow cycling club for precisely that reason.

Taffy was slightly disappointed that the bishop wasn't more cordial in his greeting, but she supposed that being reclusive—no doubt due to that clever, bulging head with its prominent brow-ridge that made him, in her opinion, *plug-ugly*— it would hardly be shocking if he didn't know how to turn out a real highland welcome when company appeared.

Although, he wasn't truly a highlander at all. She decided that that was most likely the problem. Courtesy wasn't bred into the bishop's blood as it was with the other local people.

Taffy's already low opinion of her ungenial host sank even lower when he accepted her beautiful photographs of the piper's skeleton with all the enthusiasm of someone being offered a long-dead fish, and she decided then and there that she would seek no more of his society. Disliking the velocipede was one thing; scorning her precious art was another. Clearly, man of God or no, the bishop was a Philistine!

It was also the height of unchristian heartlessness not to say something about the fate of Malcolm's poor, abandoned bones when she raised the subject of their disposition. The bishop was positively evasive on the topic of what would be done with the remains.

Nor was he willing to answer any of her inquiries about faerie lore. Taffy had some questions about the matter, for she had heard it said that those who went to visit the faeries died on the dawn of the day they returned to the world of Christian men. A single night among the still-folk supposedly took the same toll on a body as the passing of one hundred mortal years—and though time passed slowly in the world of Faerie, the earth's spun along as before. According to the legends, to remain with the faeries for the length of one dance or to hear one of Tomas Rimer's poems was to lose a year of one's life.

But at Taffy's questions the bishop grew even more abrupt. He would say no more than it was fortunate if such heathens did die when the sun's rays fell upon them. With those words, he wasted no time in hustling her out of his home.

Stunned by such heartlessness, Taffy left without protest. There would be no answers from Bishop Mapleton.

The castle, she noticed upon leaving, didn't feel as welcoming this morning, either. It was just a pile of old gray-green rocks, devoid of any personality or life. Some form of grace had been withdrawn since the previous day's events.

Certain that she was unobserved, Taffy gave into a childish impulse and stuck her tongue out at the ugly door-knocker before hurrying down the drive.

Back on her bicycle and away from cold Duntrune in record time, Taffy left no blessings behind for its rude occupant.

As always, cycling lifted her spirits, and she soon felt more cheerful. The air agreed with her, made her feel whole. It was a morning that brought the sort of companionship that she sometimes found when riding with a partner. She could almost pretend that someone rode beside her, enjoying the scenery in friendly silence.

Finally, Taffy admitted to herself that seeking the bishop out in the early morn and unaccompanied had not been a very mature scheme. Some men simply didn't approve of women having a profession. And, too, it was very early for a social call, even in the country where the inhabitants were awakened at dawn by bagpipes. She should have delayed her visit a while, let him get a little of the bacon and eggs and coffee inside his fat stomach before confronting him with pictures of skeletons. And she had forgotten to bring her calling cards! She had no doubt that he thought her mannerless.

"Well, it is no bloody wonder he didn't receive me with enthusiasm," she muttered.

But, she decided on her way back to her wheeled darkroom, it had been worth the trip simply to prove to herself that she could get on with her plans, even with her father doing his best to nobble her. Independence took practice; she would get better over time.

Her carriage workroom was not yet suffocating, so she set about her labors without removing her annoying collar, though she did roll back her cuffs to spare them from the stains of blackening.

By this time, Taffy had convinced herself that she had imagined all of yesterday's strange episode, and if anything actually appeared on the plate, it would be a white blot—some completely unidentifiable shape—caused by a stray beam of light reflecting off of a lost button or shiny pebble on the nearby flagstones at the castle.

It therefore came as a rather large surprise when she washed away the softer gelatin and discovered that there was, in fact, the image of a man in a belted plaid kneeling at the side of the piper's grave.

"Angels and ministers of grace defend us!"

In disbelief, she picked up the blacking and began to gently rub the print into stronger contrast.

"And Columba preserve me!" she whispered, rubbing away the last of the excess blacking with a cloth and holding the print before her.

The plate could not show her what color of eyes the figure had, but it did show his face—the one from her dream!—and also those amazing, pointed ears peeping out of his thick, dark hair where it fell around them. The only thing missing from her dreams was the severed boar's head on the ground beside him.

"It can't be," she whispered. But the image didn't change and an almost forgotten phrase presented itself to her stunned mind. This man was *Homo arcanus*, as a Latin scholar would say. *Daoine shi*, to the Gaels.

"Pronounced ear cartilage was not uncommon among the northern Gaels," she told herself.

Her shaking hands did not agree. That there was *anyone* in the photograph was a matter so uncommon as to rate the appellation of *miraculous*.

She was grateful that she had a witness to the fact that no one—*visible*—had been at the grave when the photo was taken, else she would doubt her sanity.

Not that she would call on her father to verify this happening. No! She could well imagine his reaction if this plate was ever made public and he was appealed to for support by the members of the spiritualistic movement. . . . He'd more likely support the *suffragettes*, and he detested those *pushy women*.

No, she could not tell her father—ever—about this Malcolm of Glen Noe.

Again, there came the strong feeling that she

was not alone. Paying closer attention this time, Taffy exhaled slowly and closed her eyes. Goose-flesh arose on her arms and her head swam giddily. Almost, she could hear pipes playing a mournful song.

Malcolm.

It took all her courage but she managed to call softly: "Malcolm? Piper, are you here?"

"Tafaline! Is someone in there with you?"

She nearly shrieked at the loud summons right outside her door.

"Father! Just a moment. Don't open the door!" Quickly, she stuffed her damning plate into an open satchel and, peril temporarily averted, opened the carriage door to her impatient parent. "Yes?"

He peered over her shoulder for a moment, searching the small interior for a visitor.

"Father? You wanted something?"

"Hm? Oh! Have you those blasted prints ready for Mapleton?"

"Why, no. I delivered them earlier. Did you need to see them?"

Davis transferred his gaze to her.

"*You* delivered them?"

"Certainly. I have the proper means of transporting the plates, which are fragile. And you are far too busy to deal with such paltry matters. Anyway, it isn't as if the bones are important to your work."

"Quite." But he still stared as if she had grown two heads, causing her to wonder if she were behaving strangely. He asked, with obvious reluctance: "Are you quite well? Perhaps I should open your windows and let some clean air inside. It would be most inconvenient if you fainted from the fumes and heat."

There were many who thought that females were of negligible intellect and unable to think calmly in a crisis, but Taffy had learned to use both initiative and resourcefulness when she wanted her way. And what she most definitely wanted was for her father to leave before he discovered her hidden plate, or before she fainted dead at his feet from the shock of the ever-louder bagpipes playing an alarm in her head.

"Certainly not. It would ruin my work. It is only a little warm inside and I have not been using any dangerous chemicals. Was there something else you needed? I am in the middle of working on—" Taffy tried to think of some plausible project, but her mind was fixated by the ululations of the wailing music and was unable to formulate a lie.

Fortunately, Davis was not interested enough to spare the time for any explanations.

"Yes, I can see that you are busy. Don't strain yourself. No one expects the delicately nurtured to labor as diligently as a male when it is so warm." On his lips, the term *delicately nurtured* sounded like a disease, making her wish to deny her gentility.

It was an irrational reaction, so she put it aside, just as she had with all the other self-doubts and unhappiness his disparaging comments awoke.

"I shall be done before noon," she lied.

Aye, lie. Anything to get rid of him!

"Very well then."

"I shall see you this evening," she answered, shutting the door on her last syllables.

"Shhh!" she scolded the song in her head. Immediately, the crescendoing music ceased, but there was a soft rumble of laughter.

She waited patiently for her father's footsteps to fade away before opening one of the workshop's carriage shutters and retrieving her plate from its satchel.

Nothing had changed. It was *him*. The ancient plaid, the brogues, the pipes . . . the ears.

"Ar dheas De go raibh a anam," she muttered, then frowned. *May his soul be on the right hand of God!* Where had she learned that bit of Gaelic? Mostly she had only greetings and curses in her repertoire, not blessings!

Carefully, because her hands were shaking, she secured the photographic plate she held between thin boards and left her darkroom to return to the inn. She would hide her photograph in her portmanteau until she decided what to do with it.

"I'm leaving now, Malcolm," she whispered bravely. "Follow me, please."

Again, she had the sensation that she was not alone on her ride to the inn. It was unnerving, but somehow not unpleasant to think that Malcolm might be with her. Indeed, the notion of riding through the country with a ghost up on the cruppers was exhilarating. It was possible that no one—in the entirety of history—had ever done so.

Ah! But was this notion true? Was this ancient Scot following her back to her accommodations? She frowned. This all might just be her wild imagination. Perhaps she had spent too many hours in the heat and chemical fumes with only herself for company.

Scientific experimentation—that was the key, she decided, dismounting her velocipede in the innyard and leaning it against a shady wall. A strange phenomenon, if real rather than imaginary, should be capable of repetition under like circumstances.

She plucked her precious satchel out of the panier and held it tightly to her breast. Her camera was within reach if she found need.

She had seen this "Malcolm" best when she was asleep. But for the moment, short of laudanum, there was no possibility that she could rest this early in the day.

But there was still meditation. Mystics had used that for centuries to contact the spirit world. Of course, she didn't have any rituals to aid her, but a closed shutter and a quiet room would surely be all she needed to concentrate. After all, the ghostly presence seemed very near.

Hopeful that the piper would follow her inside, she went into the inn. Taffy climbed the narrow stairs, grateful that the Mistress MacIntyre was busy elsewhere. She was fairly certain that meditating people did not speak about mundane matters—like linens—when they were preparing to visit the spirit world.

Taffy soon reached her room, which was shaded against the bright sky. A candle would have been nice, if she had one nearby, but rather than waste time hunting for one, she made do with an oil lamp, its flame turned low. She propped her astounding picture against the wall where she might study it while she attempted a meditative trance.

She had a momentary pang of regret that she hadn't attended a seance when the opportunity was offered. It would have been useful to have some firsthand experience of how this ritual was done.

Feeling a little awkward, she stretched out on her cot and tried to relax. At first, she was nearly as rigid as hardwood, but soon her limbs un-knotted and she allowed her eyes to lose their focus. Her breaths were slow and deep. She felt as if a part of her was floating—

Malcolm played as the Irish mercenaries came flying off the ship and fell upon the keep. Their fury allowed no acknowledgment of minor wounds, and the Campbell guards, slow and careless in their duties, were quickly annihilated. The flag-stones of Duntrune were soon covered with the Campbell dead.

Malcolm ceased playing as soon as the last en-emy had fallen. The sudden silence after the din of his war pipes seemed even more appalling.

Colkitto turned to Malcolm as the piper joined the men in the courtyard. The bloodlust was still upon him and the MacColla's face was as hard and merciless as an animal's. He ripped the Campbells' banner down from the wall, crushing the boar's face in his iron fist.

"You had the right of it, piper. The keep is ours. I wish the black bitch herself was here. I'd like Lady Dunstaffnage and her bastard cleric to be my guests of honor. But it seems we will have to wait for that pleasure."

"Is she so very evil?" Malcolm asked.

Hearing his voice plainly for the first time, Taffy stirred restlessly upon her cot. She was aware of her true surroundings, the wool blanket at her back, the linen coverpane beneath her head, and the scent from the low-burning lantern, but she was unable to shake off the other bloody images that had her mind in their clutches. The history of this place surrounded her.

The piper's voice was low-pitched, beautifully timbred, and rich with the musical rhythm of the Gaels. Terrified as she was, she still longed to hear more of it.

"Aye. That she is, evil and more. A more heartless—" *A low moan sounded from one of the men lying at Colkitto's feet. Without expression, he lifted his broadsword and—*

"No!" *a strange woman's voice cried out, causing Malcolm to look around.*

"Lass?"

Their eyes met and he started in her direction.

"No!" Taffy jerked upright, her heart pounding. The room heaved as though passing under an ocean wave, and it took a moment for the chamber to resettle itself in its proper place.

She looked about wildly, and in spite of what she half-believed, she was still shocked to discover that she was not alone in the small room.

"Dear Lord in Heaven!" She drew her knees up to her chest and stared round-eyed at the figure who gazed upon her intently from across the tiny chamber.

The outline of his shape was hazy, as if a veil

of fog had been flung over him, but there was no mistaking her guest's identity.

"Are ye coming soon, lass?" His lips didn't move, but she heard the question in her mind.

Vapor rose between them like mist off of a lake and a salt tang filled the air. She could see Malcolm's pupils expanding until the black all but overran the pale gray of the irises. There were reflections moving in those eyes, but they weren't of the inn's plain room.

He leaned forward, parting the hazy veil with his broad shoulders. Bits of vapor clung to his dark locks as he thrust his way through the fog that divided them.

He reached out an insubstantial finger to touch her cheek, and a shiver at the feathery touch of something half-recognizable rippled down her skin. It was like velvet, only softer, and scorching to the touch.

She could see more clearly now, the images moving in his eyes. There were trees and an altar with two figures embracing upon it; one small and golden, the other taller and dark.

"Are ye coming tae me, lass?" The voice asked again, demanding an affirmative answer.

"Yes," another voice answered. She dimly recognized it as her own.

"That is well." He smiled gently. So beautiful did he appear that he did not seem human.

The impatient mist stirred again, surging up in

73

a wave from the shaking floor, making her feel disoriented and slightly sick to her stomach.

"Make haste. Ye've little time!" he said, imparting a sense of the terrible urgency with his demand for her speedy arrival.

"Wait," she whispered, but already the veil was pulling closed. In another moment, he was gone, swallowed by the thinning mist, which disappeared into the cracks of the ceiling and floor. In two moments, not even the smell of fog remained as proof of her vision.

"Bless Saint Columba and all of the Gaels!" she whispered, laying a hand to her tingling cheek and then over her forehead to check for fever.

Was he a human ghost? Or something more? Could he truly be one of the legendary creatures she had heard about? *Homo arcanus*, the Gaelic *daoine shi?*

"Rubbish," she assured herself, unable to accept any other spiritual revelations. "He is just a ghost."

Then, hearing her words, she fell back upon the cot and laid an arm over her eyes.

Just a ghost? What on earth was she going to do?

Two hours later, Taffy closed the book of local history upon the picture of the Campbells' clan badge—the same evil boar's head that was embroidered on the banner in Duntrune's hall, and the same one she had seen in her vision of the taking of the keep.

Even allowing for familial sentiments for the author, one Iain Lom, whose father had died at Campbell hands, the picture painted of life in the village in 1644 was an appalling one. The armies of occupation, masquerading as the bringers of enlightenment, had stripped the land like a particularly savage brood of locusts.

There had been unspeakable atrocities on both sides, but always, at the very front of the swarm, had been Lord Lorne and Lady Dunstaffnage with her band of treacherous Campbells. This evil creature had ridden out with her *Mialchoins*—her hunting hounds—and tracked down humans like any other prey.

Taffy shuddered as she returned the book to its shelf in the neat parlor. It was entirely still in the inn at this hour in the afternoon, but she could almost hear the sound of ancient baying as the deer hounds rampaged through the glens, their mistress and her ravening pack swarming after their tiring quarry, waiting for them to falter so they might rush forward and dip their forked tongues in the helpless kill.

It was this creature who had captured and mutilated the piper of Duntrune, *Malcolm*.

Are ye coming, lass? whispered the voice in her head.

Yes. Soon. And she was. But she needed more

complete instruction. How was she to get there? What was she to do when she arrived?

She knew of only one way to ask.

Taffy glanced at the parlor clock. Three o'clock. There would be time for a nap before dinner.

Chapter Four

Duntrune, 1644

The dead stared at the sky with the blank, sunken eyes of men who had passed out of life unwilling to believe that the tide of treacherous Fate had overtaken them. Malcolm's own short life flowed past for review before his mind's eye. Like a blue river in spate, it was there from birth to approaching death. And like a mighty flood, death seemed impossible to seize, to stop, or to escape.

Around him, the Campbells rushed with a kind of wild gaiety as they rehung their singed and bloodied banner. They seemed not to realize that regaining the castle through lies and betrayal rather than skillful battle was not a thing of which to be proud.

The Campbells had reclaimed Duntrune the moment Colkitto had sailed off, quickly overcoming the contingent of men the Irish had left to defend it. King Charles's vastly outnumbered men had surrendered upon promise of their lives—but the pledge of surrender was broken at the behest of the black bitch, Lady Dunstaffnage. A Groach by birth, she was, and as wicked as her ancestress, Lady MacBeth, had ever been, and as uncaring of the odium she incurred. Foolish Lord Dunstaffnage had married her, no doubt thinking that he could cure her nature with a whip. But such was not the case when wickedness was bred into the bones. As with religion, goodness could not be forced into the heart, not even at the end of the sharpest sword.

Of course, she was not alone in her perfidiousness. Her personal advisor was ever in attendance upon her. Markham, her newly swaddled Puritan minister from England, defrocked by the true church and branded with the *M*, sign of his evil crimes, burnt into the brawn of his thumb, was hard at her side when she had entered the castle to view the battered prisoners. Malcolm had never seen him but instantly knew him for what he was—one of the new Puritans with a taste for torture, gladly sworn to *kill the Catholic anti-Christ*. He was also the one the MacColla had mentioned: the man who for pleasure hunted both the still-folks and all mortals who bore their blood.

Together, their hands worked against all clans—even her own husband's. The wicked creature had become a scarlet-handed reaper. A female version of the murderous Lord Lorne.

Malcolm watched, a bound captive, as the last of the Irish mercenaries left to defend Duntrune were dragged forward. Young Mudro was half-dead already from his wounds and in too much agony to know any more fear. He fell prostrate before his captress; his savaged legs pierced through with arrows were unable to hold him. It seemed impossible that any woman faced with such suffering in a boy of but fourteen years could still act the part of the butcher.

The lad looked up slowly. At the sight of his face, stained with welling blood, her lips curled up over her teeth as though she prepared to sink her fangs into the poor wretch's throat and rip it from him. In that moment, she looked the embodiment of the tusked boar that was the symbol of the Campbell clan.

She did not move, though, but simply gave an order. Like the other dead and wounded, Mudro was stripped of his meager clothing, usable arrows pulled from his flesh, and then dragged to the rubble wall where he was flung over to crash onto the boulders below.

His screams were agony to hear, but the Campbells near Lady Dunstaffnage went about unaffected, snuffling and snorting happily as they

79

rooted through the possessions of the slain. Horrible to think on it, but perhaps they were inured to such acts of brutality.

After a moment, Lady Dunstaffnage turned from her contemplation of the mound of death growing at the base of the wall and stalked Malcolm's way. Her skirts rustled like dead leaves as she moved. She seemed a man's worst nightmare given life.

"So, piper." Black eyes, hard as stones and as lifeless, looked into his own. In her ominous pupils, he could see his death; not that day or the next, but very soon. "What am I to do with you?"

Knowing his duty to Colkitto required that he sup with the devil swine, at least for a time, Malcolm made an astonishing suggestion.

The barrow's passage was narrow, darker than the night outside, and the floor treacherously uneven. But the air, uncommon for an ancient grave, was fresh and slightly chilled. Taffy found herself grateful for the lantern's warmth on her fingers. Without this small point of hopeful light, her mood would have been as black as a shroud. This trek into a burial mound was in its own way terrifying, but her dream had been very clear. This was the way to the piper.

Navigating the tunnel was difficult, laden as she was, but Taffy needed everything she was carrying. The lantern was critical, as were her rifle and ammunition belts, which she wore criss-crossed on her chest in the style of the Texas *banditos*. Nor could she visit another century and not take her camera and a supply of plates! Unthinkable!

"Bloody hell," she muttered as she again found herself wedged in the tight passage.

And then there were her bulky satchels divided between bandages, photographic plates, and sandwiches, fruit, chocolates—and a purloined flask of whisky.

Many women had a casual attitude about meals, but Taffy was not one of them. Hiking always left her ravenous, and assuming that she survived this rescue attempt, she suspected that fortifications of both solid and liquid varieties would be needed soon after.

There was one last item tucked down in a pocket: a small weapon she had picked up on a lark from a street vendor in New York. It was actually a piece of heavy jewelry worn over the four fingers of the right hand. The item was sometimes called brass knuckles by the brawling underclasses, but the ones in her pocket were an exceptionally pretty set, made of silver with a carving of a mermaid on the front. The part of the jewelry that rested against her palm bore the amusing inscription: *Savage-Trainer*.

At the time she had purchased them, they had been a curiosity; the notion of ever having occasion to use them had been a ridiculous one. After all, Taffy had always assumed that she would run a mile in a corset and high heels to avoid any violent situations where she would be called upon to defend herself in some physical manner.

The knuckles were less amusing now. There were places in the world where women had need of such weapons, or they would never have been made. And it seemed she was being called to one of them.

Taffy didn't feel much like the feast for the eyes she wished she might be upon the occasion of meeting the famous piper of Duntrune. She wore her dark jean dress and hiking boots because they were the practical choice, though under other circumstances, she would not choose to play ambassador to Malcolm and the seventeenth century wearing such undignified clothing.

She supposed that her attire was a minor consideration when weighed against the fact that she was either completely mad, or truly following an inhuman omen brought in a dream that she might travel to the long-dead past. Still, it bothered her that she was dressed so unbecomingly for the trip.

Two hundred and forty-four years! Could she really get there—and back—on the *low road* of ancient legend? Her father would give everything he owned—probably even his life—to have these questions answered. If such travel was possible, he could go and see his precious Picts and live among the ancient Gaels.

But she hadn't told him a thing. Not a word, because without more evidence than her dreams and a lone bizarre photograph, there was nothing to convince him of the truth. And she felt, also, that while the way was temporarily open to her because of some magical dispensation of Malcolm's, her father would never be allowed to pass through. Not while he still lived, at least.

Suddenly, before her loomed the door she had seen in her daytime dreams, a giant carven panel of black stone. The writing upon it was not that of Celts, not Ogham, not Pict, not Norse rune. Faerie-script, that was what she had to believe it to be; a permanent marker for those who would travel the way of the dead.

She stretched out a finger, but the door fell back before her hand ere she made contact. Darkness, thick as tar, yet not so still, lay beyond.

Exhaling slowly, Taffy summoned up her courage. This was it, a point beyond which she was committed to the course. The choice, in plainest terms, was a simple one. She could either intervene in history and attempt to save Malcolm— sparing him an agonizing death and herself a lifelong haunting—or she could hang out the black crepe and mourn for the rest of her dream-haunted days, which were likely to be few in number, if what Jamesy said was true, for those of MacLeod blood were taken away to live with the faeries.

Are ye coming, lass? the low-pitched voice in her head asked.

Was she coming?

"Yes," she answered for a third time, and with a last breath, she stepped inside the chamber.

Around her was immeasurable space, but space unlike that to be found in any ordinary cave or room. It was without direction. No east. No west. No north or south. No up. No down. The smoky lantern was her only guidepost, but it showed her nothing but more vast, dizzying emptiness. It was a place so blank it had not even human time within it, but all the eons flowing together in a giant, disorienting sea.

There was a slight wind at first, eddying about her feet, but it quickly gathered strength, pushing her into the void—into the black—into the past.

It was time streaming around her. Two-and-one-half centuries were fleeting by, pulling the pins from her hair, flapping her skirts about her legs like the snapping of an ocean vessel's sails.

Though she was not asleep, another image of Malcolm came to her mind. This time he was as clear as if lit by the sun at high noon on a summer's day.

*   *   *

Malcolm stood in the tiny ramparts, guards at his sides, watching the white sails fill the horizon.

The Campbells had been lulled by his lack of weapons, thinking he was harmless because he carried no iron. It had amused them—them and that black-hearted bitch!—to keep the Mac-Intyre's piper as a plaything, a jester to entertain them. On his promise that he would not try to escape the keep, he had been given the run of the castle, and there he had bided his time, waiting for Colkitto's return.

Now his foes muttered the MacColla's name like an invocation, for it seemed their curses had conjured the very devil to their door. The usually canny Irishman had returned! But he came at the castle boldly, unaware of the danger, his ship's sails plain against the blue sky.

Malcolm had borne no love for the MacColla when first they met, but he knew now why the man fought the Campbells so assiduously—and in that Malcolm would gladly give him aid. Malcolm was a dead man already, as he had known since before this assault. The faeries had marked him for it, and if the choice be his in the manner of his end, he had one last task to perform as the clan piper.

Colkitto was not meant to die this day. It was Malcolm's duty to see that he got away.

Colkitto's ship drew closer.

Melanie Jackson

He raised his pipes: the chanter to his lips, the lyart reed in place. He had his piece selected. It was the one he had played on the night he and Colkitto met. Both men knew it well, and like all great pipe music, its cadence was a rigid set of counts of eight. It would be easy enough to drop two counts every third line in the *urlar* and *crun luath*—was a trick that had been used before to save MacColla's father from a trap at Dunyvaig. The MacDonnell would ken his warning in the mutilation of the song while these lowlanders scratched their heads, wondering that their quarry was escaping their trap.

He played, and in the strains his message was clear.

> *MacColla, fliest thou from the castle.*
> *Go with the wind and make for open sea.*
> *We have been seized, we have been seized.*

The wind was abruptly gone, and another door was waiting before her. The script carved upon it meant nothing to Taffy's eye, but her heart knew where the passage led. This time, she did not hesitate to pass through the portal. Malcolm felt very near.

The day on the other side was pleasant and normal, though slightly cooler than the one she had left. The westing sun afforded her an adequate, but filtered light. She was in a thick copsewood of mountain ash, she realized with a thrill that fluttered in her slightly upset stomach. If this afternoon's dream was correct—as it had been so far—to reach the castle wall, she needed only to follow the stream heard bubbling in the distance. If that failed, there was the alarming music floating out into the still air to guide her. She had heard it before, on the morning when she had taken her photographs to Duntrune. It was the same mournful tune.

Malcolm.

Taffy swallowed, pushing down a burgeoning case of nerves.

After her flight through the magicked door, she found the solid ground beneath her feet very reassuring—its common, earthy reek of sheep and cattle dung, of peat smoke, and of green things growing in the rich soil. It upset her to think that she would have to face the awful void again when she returned home, so she pushed the thought from her mind.

Taffy extinguished her lantern, setting it carefully at the base of the hidden door to mark her passageway back to Kilmartin. She hid her satchels and camera, nearby in a hollowed-out tree. She did not allow herself to dwell on what would happen should the door refuse to reopen upon her return. Such worry would only aggravate her nerves and ruin her aim. Nothing could be allowed to interfere with this rescue.

Automatically, she began straightening her disheveled hair. There was no wind yet from the loch, but she knew from past experience that there would be one as the sun went down, and shooting straight was a difficult enough matter without her hair flapping around like a banner.

All day he had played, from sunrise to sunset, never ceasing though his fingers were near lamed. He wanted them so, lifeless and numb when they were stricken off.

He would die without his hands—thus had been the sentence of Lady Dunstaffnage. In another moment, he would go down the stairs and to the courtyard to the block, where the axe would strike and the blood would rush from his body. His eyes and ears would go dark and deaf and be pleased no more by earthly things.

He thought then of all the wondrous beauties he would never see again. The moon shining down on fields at harvest time, the quietude of the meadows on a summer afternoon, the drifts of luckengowen growing wild in a late spring blanket, which would thicken and darken as summer wore on.

But the most beautiful thing he had ever seen was his golden-haired apparition, and he clung to the thought—the hope—that his dreams were true and he read them aright. For if they were, she would very shortly appear and lead him on the "low road" to *Caislean na Nor*, the golden castle of faerie Elysium. He would be happy there, even if shut off from the heaven of man, were she there with him.

The area about the castle in this century was more thickly cloaked in woods, but the stones were the same and the stream had not diverted its course, so Taffy found her way to the tiny keep with ease.

Grateful for the dull brown of her dress, which matched both deadwood and earth, she crept up to the castle until she came upon a barrack of rock flanked by a thicket. It was the perfect place for her to make a stand; it had a perfect view in through the gate of the keep, boasted lots of cover, and the setting sun would shine directly in their eyes when the enemy turned her way. If only she could lure Malcolm's captors into the open courtyard, her plan would turn this into what the Americans called a *"turkey shoot."*

On that thought, the object of her interest obligingly stepped into plain view. *Malcolm*. She felt a sharp stab in her chest as he looked up and stared in her direction. His eyes were fey.

"Are ye coming, lass?" his still lips seemed to ask.

It was impossible that he could see her, of course, but perhaps, just as she thought she had sometimes read his thoughts, he sensed that she was near.

Taffy had already loaded her Winchester rifle, but she made a last check to see that she was truly prepared. The steel was cold beneath her hands.

"Yes, Malcolm. I am coming."

Absorbed as she was in the task at hand and Malcolm's steady stare, she was not aware of the rustling in the dry undergrowth behind her, as if the roots of the copsewood trees were being tran-shifted.

They stood in the courtyard, he and the Black Bitch, staring into each other's eyes. Freedom was only fifty strides distant had he the desire to strive for it. Through the gate, he could see the surrounding forest just outside the keep. Once in the magic wood, the secret ways would open up and he could disappear within them. He could escape Lady Dunstaffnage and her hatred.

The Campbells on the ramparts had not understood the MacColla's veering off at the last moment, but Lady Dunstaffnage had seen the Irishman salute the piper through her glass. Unfortunately, she too had recalled the trick that had once saved Colkitto's father. She alone kenned what had passed. And she had decided to exact her vengeance.

To harm a piper was to bring misfortune upon

one's clan, but ill-luck or no, the Black Bitch's wrathful punishment would fall upon Malcolm for her humiliation. Her pride demanded it, whatever the cost.

There was no time for lamentation. Malcolm had known he would not return from this assault on Duntrune. And should his death bring misfortune to Dunstaffnage and her men, gladly would he surrender the here and now for the better hereafter he believed would follow.

A movement in the woods caught his eye. It was only the smallest flash of gold, but he knew it well. It was his spirit lass come to guide him! He allowed himself a small inward smile.

"Are ye coming, lass?" he whispered.

She did not reply at once, and immediately he could sense that she was somehow altered. She seemed solid and not wandering in some fathomless way, but studying the castle with determined eyes. Alongside her cheek, the flesh now bleached pale as linen, was what looked to be one of the Sassenach's unreliable flintlocks.

"Yes, Malcolm. I am coming," said a soft, but determined voice in his head.

Malcolm stared in disbelief, a sense of odd dizziness overtaking him. Exhausted indifference fled. Seeing his apparition—suddenly made in vulnerable flesh and prepared to rush into mortal danger—he found a reason to take up arms and rejoin the fight. Alarm pumped strength and quickness into his tired muscles, and his desire to die took flight.

Suddenly there was an eruption of shots, louder than any he had ever heard. The man beside him leapt back, as though receiving a blow to the breast. His readied axe dropped to the ground.

Without hesitation, Malcolm snatched up the weapon in his bruised and bound fists and swung it into the nearest Campbell's chest.

The axe pulled away only with difficulty as it had lodged somewhat firmly with the force of his blow. Thereafter, reluctant to lose his weapon to a careless cleave, Malcolm spent some time in nimble avoidance of the other guards' dirks. Reversing his axe, he swung the blunted end up into his nearest captor's bearded chin.

There was another crack of flintlock fire followed by a sharp cry. Malcolm spun about, amazed that a path was being systematically cleared before him. Without hesitation, he sprinted for the gate, hands still tied in front of him, leaping over wounded Campbells with an agility born of sudden hope.

He felt the tug of an arrow as it passed through his plaid but did not look back to see how closely danger followed, rather he sprang like a wolf after a fleeing hart and ran with all his strength.

His eyes burning with some new inner fire that had slipped free of his control, Malcolm bared

his teeth in a feral smile that frightened the remaining Campbells into falling back from the
gates rather than face the strange, inhuman
power burning within him.

He did not know what manner of weapon his
golden savior carried, but it was more effective
and grievous than any Sassenach flintlock he'd
ever seen. And more powerful than anything he'd
ever recalled wielded by the still-folk.

The Campbells seemed confused by the repeated
gunfire, Taffy was elated to see. Doubtless, they
thought that a company of the MacColla's men
had come upon them through the covering forest.

Her first shot had sent the axeman staggering.
Her second and third went into Malcolm's nearest guards, wounding though not killing them.
The next would have been sent into the breast of
the woman responsible for Malcolm's torment,
but she had already fled into a doorway below
the now familiar and hated banner. Taffy had to
content herself with clearing a path for the
piper's escape.

She pumped the lever rapidly and brass
shellshot fell to the ground nearby with tiny
pings. She aimed for those nearest the castle gate
who were in the best position to interfere with
Malcolm's escape. The piper had felled two more
guards, she was pleased to see, but there were

still several more between him and freedom. Fortunately, they were now focused on the outlying threat to the castle and did not perceive the danger behind them.

The gun snicked without firing, telling her that she was out of ammunition and needed to reload. She dropped behind a large boulder and began to thumb shells into her rifle. The barrel was burning hot to the touch.

"Bloody hell!" she swore, as a new threat in the form of an arrow splintered against the boulder that shielded her. Another struck, quivering angrily in the ground, to her left. Pounding footsteps heralded Malcolm's approach—directly into the path of the archer's fire.

Taffy rolled to her knees, moving some distance to the right and began scanning for the archer. She had him in an instant, an arrogant silhouette with a crossbow standing against the reddening sky. He crumpled nicely when she put a bullet in his thigh.

All at once, there was a crash and then a rustle, as if tree limbs had been smashed violently together. Before she could bring her rifle around to defend herself, a battle-enraged Campbell was standing over her, slashing down with a gleaming claymore.

She had no time even to scream, for in an instant Malcolm was there, and the Campbell was swallowed by the nearby shrubbery, an axe buried in his chest. His wicked sword clattered to the ground beside her, slicing deeply into her skirt.

"Come wi' me," Malcolm ordered, jerking her to her feet with a single tug of his bound hands. He headed into the heart of the thicket where, miraculously, the seemingly solid wall of plants gave way for them.

"The claymore!" she suggested. But he did not bother to retrieve the sword.

"Never mind it! We've no time for a stirrup-cup."

A hound bayed loudly from within the castle walls, calling to Taffy's mind the tales of how Campbells had hunted down their enemies, letting their animals rip their victims to pieces when they had them cornered in the glen.

With that image in her head, Taffy didn't argue. Hearing the sounds of pursuit behind her, she put the Winchester over her shoulder and discharged a round in the general direction of the castle, hoping to temporarily deter their enemies.

For her pains, she caught a stray limb in her hair, which tugged painfully until Malcolm pulled her free.

"Dinnae bother, lass. They'll be skedaddled in the woods." Then Malcolm set his leather bonds to his lips where he bit down with hard, white teeth. In a flash, the binding was shed from his wrists and flung violently away.

The now free hand that towed Taffy also guided her, which was a fortunate thing as her hair was again loose and falling over her eyes. Through that golden veil, she thought she saw a wall of brambles fold apart and then, as she turned her head to stare in disbelief, weave itself together behind her. She had the uneasy impression that the very greensward around them was being rearranged as they passed through it, becoming denser behind, but she could not see clearly enough through her hair to know if it was true.

Presently, all noise behind them ceased, and Malcolm slowed their pace, which was fortunate as fatigue and sickness were finally overtaking her. Whatever battle-rage it was that had guided her into setting the bloody ambush was departing quickly, leaving a sort of lightheaded horror behind and her stranded in the middle of a nightmare.

Taffy bent over at the waist and took some calming breaths. She absolutely, completely, and utterly rejected her stomach's suggestion that she empty the remains of her supper onto the forest floor. But as a precaution, she removed the heavy belts of ammunition that were pressing on her chest. She took a few deep breaths.

* * *

Malcolm looked at the apparition—nay, the *lass!*—and felt some of the strange and awful power that had flooded his body folding back in on itself.

"Ye are real," he muttered, for human she certainly was, and doing poorly. Her face was pale rather than the pink it should be from their run, and she looked to be on the verge of gut sickness.

"Are ye ill, lass?" he asked gently, running his eyes over her slender form to see if she had been hurt from the Campbell's claymore. For one with even a hint of faerie blood, the simplest wound from cold iron could sometimes prove fatal. "Are ye wounded?"

"No." She swallowed and straightened valiantly. "Just . . . just . . . tired. I've had a busy day, shooting people, running through the woods. . . ."

Malcolm forewent a smile; such a mettlesome reply deserved better than teasing. Gently, he tucked her straying hair behind her lovely pointed ears. The expression on her face was one of confused disbelief and wariness.

He didn't know what aspect he himself wore. A strange but giddy mix of euphoria and desire beat at his temples and drove his blood fiercely through his pounding heart. Not all of the heady new power had left his head, though, and he made an effort to throttle it before it frightened her. Despite her brave attack upon the Campbells, he kenned that this lass was tenderly made.

"Ye're a MacLeod," he said softly, not terribly surprised. He put his other hand beneath her chin and tilted it up. "Of course, they would send someone tae me who shared the cousin-red."

She looked confused. "*Cousin-red?* Oh. Blood." She swallowed again. Color was beginning to flood her cheeks. Too much of it. "Yes, I'm a MacLeod. At least, my mother was."

"And what are ye called?"

"Taffy. Tafaline, really, but I prefer Taffy." She peered at him in the deepening twilight. Her breathing had not slowed and she was showing some signs of alarm at his fingers, which remained tangled in her hair and beneath her chin.

"Taffy," he repeated, tasting the syllables. He wasn't surprised by her words. They were as his inner dream had predicted.

"And you are Malcolm, the piper, aren't you?" It was just barely a question. "And this is really Scotland in sixteen-hundred and forty-four—and those were Campbells chasing us."

"Aye. You kenned that, did ye?" He reached out and caught a second tuft of her golden hair. He stared, mesmerized as it curled about his blistered fingers. He tugged experimentally and then started to wind the tress about his fist in the manner of a distaff.

"Yes. I saw their banner and—Malcolm?" She stepped forward a pace as he wound her hair tighter. This was no fairie, no apparition that had come to aid him. Unable to resist, he bent down to take a tiny taste of his beautiful, *human* savior.

As he suspected, she was sweet. She was also very near collapsing now that the battle rage had worn off, so he contented himself with only the smallest of touches before releasing his hold upon her. His body ached to do more, but Malcolm fought his baser impulses down.

"My gratitude tae ye," he whispered, suddenly thanking the still-folk for more than just his life.

Taffy knew that at various times in history, kissing had been used as an ordinary mode of casual salutation, rather than any special endearment between lovers. But she felt sure that wasn't the case in seventeenth-century Scotland, where Puritans had outlawed kissing, even between mother and child. A single look at Malcolm's face assured her that the piper was feeling anything but casual. The emotion there might be gratitude or excitement—or even something wholly different—but whatever it was, it would have to wait for another time. In spite of her determined struggle, Taffy feared that she was going to be ill.

"Excuse me," she gasped, dropping her rifle and rushing for the cover of a mountain ash. The trees limbs obligingly parted to let her pass.

"Lass?"

"I'm fine," she managed before being sick. She

added a moment later when the spasms subsided: "I'm just not used to killing people." *Or faerie magic. Or flying through time. Or kissing strange men.*

"Are ye not then?" At last he seemed surprised. Surely it was surprise and not amusement that colored his voice! "Ye've certainly a natural talent for it. Must be the MacLeod blood."

"So it seems," she muttered unhappily, thinking of the men she had shot without any thought, other than that they were an obstacle between Malcolm and freedom. *What had happened to her?*

"Well, they wrought long and difficultly for such an end. And 'twas a kinder end for the Campbells than any they ever gave an enemy. Dwell not long on the subject. They are traitors to Scotland and wished us dead—either they had tae fall in battle or we did."

Taffy didn't answer and after a moment there was a rustling of shrubbery and then a warm, and oddly proprietary hand rested gently on the back of her neck. Taffy fished out a handkerchief and wiped her mouth hastily as she gave her companion a reproachful glance.

Wasn't the day sufficiently cursed with bloodshed? Did Malcolm need to see her vomiting and wearing an ugly dress, with her hair all about like a birch broom? Why didn't the ground just open and swallow her?

There was a sudden trembling beneath her feet, as though the soil thought to oblige her with her request, but Malcolm lifted her up off of it. He set her on a flat-topped stone where her sliced skirt fell open revealing her white shift.

Malcolm didn't notice. He was frowning down at the earth, his grip tight.

Taffy swallowed. *What had they been speaking of? Oh yes! The Campbells and being morally stuck between the devil and the deep blue sea.* She found it very hard to concentrate with his hands upon her. All her senses seemed located beneath his burning palms where the flesh prickled with unnatural heat.

"There is that fact in mitigation, I suppose. Though I am not a Scotswoman."

Malcolm looked up from the now-calm ground and Taffy looked down at it. The quaking had hidden the evidence of her upset stomach, she was glad to see.

"Ye are Sassenach? Do ye regret saving me then?" Malcolm's voice was neutral, but the hands on her waist were not relaxing their grip.

"No. Those Campbells are a right pot of poison. Especially that she-devil who leads them." Taffy looked up from the mercifully barren soil into his face, and in the last of the daylight she saw his lips quirk, probably at her strange speech. Certain idioms did not translate well into Gaelic.

"I'm speaking Gaelic," she said aloud, surprised and pleased. She knew that she should have been shocked as well, but was too tired to manage any more astonishment.

"Aye. Though very strange Gaelic it is, too." Malcolm plucked her off of her rock, took her arm in a gentle grip, and led her back into the clearing. "If it is too difficult we may converse in the Latin, French, or *Sassan* tongue."

"What? The Gaelic is fine. Or Scots. I think I can speak in all of them," she answered without thinking. The plants *were* making way for them!

"Ah! We've had company," he said. "A pity that they couldnae fetch my pipes as well."

Newly alarmed, Taffy searched the darkening glen. Immediately she spotted her satchels and camera, which were laid down next to her discarded rifle.

"How did they get here?" she demanded.

"The still-folk brought them, of course."

"*Still-folk?* Where—the lantern, too! Oh no!" she exclaimed in a failing voice.

"What of it?"

"It was my marker. For the door home," she said hollowly. "I can find the copse, I think, but without a marker I don't know if I can rediscover the door. It was set so tight in the mountain face that there was barely even a seam to set it apart."

"Dinnae trouble yerself, lass. When the time is right, the road for us shall be revealed."

"And when might that be? I saved you, didn't I? The curse is broken. I have to go back now. My father will be worried. . . . They will let me go back, won't they?" she asked, as Malcolm guided her to her neatly stowed gear. Her movements were made clumsy by her sudden trembling. "I won't have to shoot anyone else, will I? Because I really would rather not do that again."

Malcolm picked up his weapons and stowed them away. "I cannae say. There is likely something that we must do for the still-folk before we can depart. They fetched us here for a reason— and I doubt it was tae kill Campbells. There are plenty of men tae do that work for them." Malcolm urged her down to the grass. "Set, lass. Ye're chittering in the knees."

"Oh, thank you. I think I had better sit. But I don't understand. What else could they want?"

"Is it possible that you have brought some bread somewhere in those great, bulging bags?"

Taffy blinked at the change of subject, for a moment completely uncomprehending.

"Of course. That one there has food—and drink," she added, relieved that she had thought to include a flask of whisky. She felt the need of a revivifier.

Malcolm grunted in pleasure as he untied the lacing and found the bounty within.

"I have no' eaten since the day afore last. And ye need some meat as well."

"I need a drink," she muttered, plucking out the silver bottle and bolstering her courage with a largish swallow. The fiery taste nearly shriveled her tongue. There was a moment when her twitching stomach threatened to reject the panacea, but it apparently had had enough upheaval for one night and let the Scots' *water of life* keep its place inside her.

She handed the flask to Malcolm and laid back on the grass. She closed her eyes on the encroaching darkness, as though she could wish the present away. Almost, that seemed a possibility.

"Ah! *Highland* whisky," he said with satisfaction after taking a hearty swallow.

"You can tell? By taste?" she asked, momentarily diverted.

"Aye, that I can. There's *heiland* scotch and lowland scotch, and like the men, there's no mistaking the character of either. Poor lowland villagers, weary of the mirky barley-bree they brew and living in their muddy huddles."

"I live in a huddle," she volunteered after a moment. "A large one. It isn't muddy, though."

"And the name of your huddle?" He took another swallow of whisky.

"London," she said baldly. "And recently, New York."

"London?" he stared at her and then shook his head. "You haven't the look of a true Sassenach,

104

lass. Too tall. Too bonnie. That ye are a Yorkshire lass I can more readily believe."

Taffy felt herself blush and was grateful for the dim light. She didn't try and correct his geography.

"What manner of thing might the still-folk want from me?" she asked again, ignoring his compliment since she couldn't think of how to respond. "Can I do it soon, do you think? Before morning?"

"From *us*," he corrected. "They need us both, I think, or some other event would have occurred."

"From *us* then."

When Malcolm didn't answer, she cracked open an eye to see what he was about. It was hard to observe clearly in the twilight, but she felt his steady gaze resting upon her, assessing her health and nerves.

"Well?" she demanded in a stronger voice, lest he think her too fragile for the truth.

"Mayhap a night's rest would be best afore facing any more difficult things," he said, apparently unimpressed with her tone, before biting into one of her sandwiches and chewing with relish.

"That is not an answer that will send me into comfortable sleep," she informed him. "I can't spend the night with you. It would be scandalous. What would people say?"

He chuckled softly.

"Nay. That it isn't, for ye cannae be wandering about wi' Campbells so close by. 'Tis my duty tae protect ye. Be sensible. There is no scandal in that."

"Duty?" Then, tiredly: "Bloody hell!"

He laughed again.

"Aye. Well then, lass, if ye want the truth, I can think of only one reason why I was spared the axe and ye were finally given earthly form—"

"Earthly form?" She blinked, the scotch beginning to creep into her brain and play strange games with its usually sensible thoughts.

"Aye, until this day I saw ye only as an apparition. A wee ghosty wandering about with yon box." He pointed at her camera.

"I'm not a ghost," she assured him. "Actually, *you* were the ghost. You've been haunting me since they found your body under the castle floor."

Malcolm considered her blunt words in silence, making her feel tactless and uncaring.

"I'm sorry, Malcolm," she said, sitting up and reaching out an apologetic hand. "That was not well said—"

" 'Tis nought," he said. But he allowed her to pat his knee with her soft fingers. As her hand touched his skin, he seemed to shiver with pleasure and he closed his eyes. Then he frowned and went on gently: "Ye come from the futurity then, not the dead. How many years have ye traveled, Taffy MacLeod, tae find me here?"

She didn't correct his use of her mother's name. In this instant it was the most relevant of her titles. It made them kin—even if of a very distant variety. That was somewhat reassuring.

"Two-hundred and forty-four years," she said softly, patting his knee again, aware that it was an inadequate gesture but uncertain of what else to do.

"They've had a long search then," he said absently. "A long wait for a woman of MacLeod-red tae find my bones."

"The— the *still-folk*, you mean? Faeries." She stopped patting him, but left her hand to rest on the crisp hairs that pricked her palm. *"Homo arcanus."*

He cocked an eyebrow, probably at her use of Latin. That she was educated in Latin would probably not make much sense to him in this time and place—it never had to her father in the present.

"Aye. That they would be called, I suppose, by a priest or scholar."

"Why did a MacLeod need to find you? Because of the guiding dreams?"

"A woman MacLeod, of a certain age and face, aye," he said again.

"But why?" she asked softly, frustrated by her ignorance, but also nervous of the answer, which she suspected might be large and ominous.

"Because I needed a reason tae live," he said cryptically.

"And I'm that reason?" she asked, baffled, flattered, and frightened by the idea of being that important to anyone. Since her mother's death, no one had claimed to have such value for her.

"Eat your supper, lass," he said gently, taking her hand from his knee and putting a sandwich in it. "The answer will present itself wi' time."

Deciding that she had been valiant enough for one day, Taffy accepted the somewhat stale food and ceased asking uncomfortable questions.

Malcolm dug deeper in her sack and discovered her chocolates and rather crushed berries. He consumed both with great enthusiasm and a blithe unconcern about putting anything aside for future meals. It seemed he was on a one-man mission to empty their larder. Apparently, the still-folk would provide food or else he felt a skilled enough huntsman that he could catch prey with only the short dirk he carried.

Darkness fell completely while they were eating. Malcolm rejected Taffy's suggestion of lighting the lantern, telling her that the new moon would soon be up. Perhaps, living as he had in the country, the thick darkness did not disturb him.

Taffy was less sanguine of sitting out of doors after night had fallen, but Malcolm's suggestion of a bath in the stream happily diverted her from thoughts of bears and wolves and the intensely desired bright light.

Again, she found her hand tucked inside his as he led her down to water. Having her wits about her this time, she was aware of his battered fingers.

"Malcolm," she said unhappily. "Don't they hurt?"

"They are a right soss," he agreed, not sounding particularly pained or upset. "But they are still on my hands, which are still on my arms, so I willnae complain about them."

"I'll bandage them for you when we get back to . . . to camp."

The gurgle of shallow water grew suddenly louder and soon Malcolm halted. The chuckling stream sparkled blackly in the shadows. It was impossible to know how deep or fast the water ran.

"There is a sand bar here where ye may safely bathe. I shall be but a few paces yon, so sing out if aught alarms ye."

"All right," she agreed after a moment, watching Malcolm's shadow retreat with a strange and unexplainable mixture of alarm and regret.

Once alone, Taffy gathered her nerve. For centuries, people had bathed in streams. Outside. Without clothing. She could do it, too.

But she wouldn't enjoy it.

What she truly wanted was to wash with lavender soap and then change into something more spectacular than a dirty dress of cut-up jean. Something that would be a bit more pleasing for the eyes. Something utterly frivolous, feminine, and impractical.

There came a tiny slithering from the bush behind her. She spun around.

"Malcolm?" she called softly.

"Aye, lass." The voice was somewhat distant—just far enough to allow her modesty on a dark night, she told herself.

"The still-folk aren't about, are they?" she asked, nervously pleating her thick skirt as she searched the woods with night-blind eyes. The thought of being observed by anything, dark night or no, put her off any notion of complete nudity of limb during this bath.

"Not that I can see," he answered, apparently amused at her timidity. "Nor are there any of the savage plague of locust Campbells about."

"Bears?" she asked. "Wild pigs?"

"Not even a wee mousie, but do ye need me closer whilst ye bathe, lass—"

"Nay! I'll manage, thank you."

Taffy straightened and dropped her mottled skirt to the ground. She needed a bath to cleanse herself of the sweat and dust of Duntrune. It would be best to wash her clothes, too, if there were some way that she might dry them before sunrise.

The notion, once conceived, was tenacious, but there was little she could do to further it. She hadn't planned on a prolonged stay in the forests of Argyllshire and had no change of clothing. And without a fire, the heavy jean would never dry before sunrise.

Hearing Malcolm move downstream, she set about removing her blouse. Fortunately, her rational dress had buttons in the front and did not require her to ask for assistance.

Malcolm watched Taffy carefully, his eyes able to see quite well even in the dark. She wore an expression that betokened a certain unhappy distraction of thought and—most amazingly—she blushed as she disrobed, even though, as far as she knew, no one could see her in the blackness.

He wondered if he should warn her to use caution in her wishes, words, and dreams while in the sacred glen. The old ones were close at hand and very good at guessing mortal desires.

Unfortunately, their gifts could be quite dangerous, especially for the unwary who did not realize the still-folk had complete control over this magicked glen.

His own wish and desire would be readily apparent to anywho watched. He would try to be discreet with his spoken words, however, until

Taffy was more used to being in his company.

It was unimaginable that a lass of her age—and so bonnie—could be a virgin still, but she certainly had the manner of it, blushing at the slightest touch and always looking away from his chest when her eyes strayed to his opened sark.

He was confident that with time she would perceive what was wanted of them. The still-folk would leave some obvious signs—which was fortunate, as he found himself unequal to the task of explaining his and Taffy's situation. But that still left the matters of her reaction to the still-folk's request—and to his own desires, for that matter—which were definitely better hidden for a time. Even a starving wolf would show more gentleness than the impulsive beast prowling inside of him.

Taffy was modest and reserved, but there was little question she was attracted to him. He didn't doubt that he could persuade her to bundling, but to start this courtship ritual without her knowledge of what he sought, would be dishonorable, since he was not the only one who wished this particular consummation from her.

He watched avidly as her heavy skirt and sark were shed. Beneath them she wore a sleeveless *leine* of white silk. It was unspeakably perfect in its stitchery, and he was glad that she did not heed the Puritan notion that silk was sinful when worn by women.

Perhaps in her time, the cloth no longer was forbidden, though her modest reactions to him—even when she obviously felt drawn to him by inclination and magic—suggested that the Puritans were still having their way with the ladies' upbringings.

There was little plumpness to her, he saw as she removed most of her undergarments and stepped cautiously into the stream wearing only the sheer *leine*.

But she was beautiful for all of being thin. Painted in the faint light of the stars, her skin was lustrous as fresh-drawn milk where it peeped over the nearly invisible dampened silk.

He closed his eyes on the breathtaking sight and exhaled slowly. Enough! He, too, needed to bathe. He plucked the brooch from his shoulder and set about unwinding his plaid. It and his saffron sark were quickly tossed aside.

Malcolm grinned suddenly. He had not wanted to enter the still-folk's realm, but now here he was and he would get one wish granted. He had thought to cast off his plaid to make a bed for them to lie in, and he would have to; they had no blankets. Of course, he had thought to lay her down in a drift of heather—

He lifted his head at the faint rustling back in the glen and then laughed silently. It wasn't birds that moved about, for no avians nested in the copsewood, perhaps put off by the ancient magic wrought for thousands of years within this heart-wood and sacred spring.

Well then, and if he was wishing for things, perhaps there might be a slight chill to encourage her to cuddle down with him—

A finger of cold air traced over his neck, causing him to shiver.

Later, he thought firmly. After they had washed the stench of the Campbells away. And mayhap he would sing her a wee lullaby. A night visiting song perhaps, to see if her blood could be stirred by such warm verses.

With luck, he would not need the faerie breezes at all.

Chapter Five

Taffy cast her wet shift over a shrub to dry and dressed herself quickly in her dusty jean skirts. She didn't dare move about the riverbank without Malcolm there to be her guide, even though her eyes were slowly becoming accustomed to the dark.

Fortunately, he was delayed only a moment before joining her on the sloping bank. This time she found his hand resting at her waist less unnerving, and she was grateful for its guidance along the glen's narrow trail, though she never actually stumbled upon a single root or vine.

Though the moon was by that hour well up in the sky, the thick arboreal cover kept most of its light from shining through. And what little light showed into the copse seemed pale, as though a curtain of fog had been thrown over them. It felt oddly protective to Taffy, a baffling shield against any who sought them.

There was enough light, however, to reveal the fact that Malcolm had stopped at the side of the glen and begun unwinding his barely anchored plaid. He was calmly spreading it on the ground.

"Malcolm? What are you doing?" she asked, in a whisper scarcely louder than the rustling cloth. His shirt was a pale shadow that fell only to mid-thigh. Even in the dark, it seemed indecent to watch the muscles ripple up and down the expanse of bared leg.

"The benefit o' hieland dress, lass. We always carry our bedding wi' us."

"Oh." She swallowed and looked away. Then, feeling stupid for her modesty, she allowed her gaze to return to Malcolm's long outline. His legs were tanned as leather and ropy with the hardened sinews of a man who spent his days climbing steep mountains.

"I smell heather," she said, surprised at the soft fragrance that tickled her nose and seizing on that safe topic the way a drowning person would grab at passing flotsam.

"Aye. We've a soft drift of it here. Come, lass." He reached out his warm hard hand and found her immediately in spite of the dark. He tugged her down beside him before she could voice a protest. Her hands encountered the soft wool laid over a floral cushion as she knelt at his side. More of the delicate highland perfume caressed her face, though it was mixed now with the scent of Malcolm himself.

"Ants," she suggested breathlessly. "They might be attracted to the flow—"

"Never say so, Taffy lass" he warned, sounding half-serious. "Come now. 'Tis growing chill. We must wrap up tight."

Now that he mentioned it, Taffy felt a nearly autumnal breath of wind passing over her nape and shoulders. Feeling painfully awkward, she nevertheless allowed him to draw her into his arms and roll them both into a cocoon of plaid.

"Your hands. I should bandage them," she suggested quiveringly, unable to manage anything but the shallowest of respirations.

"They are not so dainty as tae be humbuggit by a day of playing, lass. You are chittering like a baby bird. Come closer."

At first, Taffy's body held itself rigid, but as Malcolm's own limbs relaxed and his heat began to seep into her bones, and his scent began to fill her sleepy head, she allowed some of her wariness and embarrassment to slip away. Waiting nearby was a night's and day's and then another night's cumulative exhaustion. It blotted out such things as modesty and even fear of the dark or bears or Campbells.

117

*   *   *

Malcolm inhaled, taking in the scent of Taffy's hair and soft, white skin. Female, yes, but different from the others as well. She was, he knew, perfect.

She was also tense as a cat in a burlap bag at target practice. Clearly, she had not lain with a man before. This was a marvelous situation that he both cursed and was in genuine awe of. Virgins were not a species with which he was at all acquainted.

Uncertain if it was an aid or no, he began stroking her silky hair. The feelings of sensation had already returned to his hands. The healing waters had done their work. Her presence would finish the cure.

Then, recalling his earlier notion of a night visiting song, he began working a lyric inside his head. Once arranged, he tucked her securely into the curve of his body and began to sing a soft lullaby. His voice was barely stronger than the fall of feathered spring rain upon still water.

He didn't bother to order his hidden audience away. Nothing intimate would pass between him and his bonnie lass this night, and his order would be for naught; the still-folk dearly loved music in any form.

I've come back at long last, my love,
Through tempest, death, and war;

O'er mountains tall and lochs most deep,
Tae visit ye once more.

And here she rests on blanket warm,
Wi' her golden hair unbound,
While I wait, beyond her gate,
Kneeling on the stony ground.

To my lass, I softly call:
"Arise, love, and let me in,
For I must away wi' the dawning light
And have but an hour tae spend."

And o'er she turned in her blanket warm,
Shewing not the least alarm,
And op'd the blanket tae her love,
And tak'd him tae her bonnie arms.

Taffy sighed. As a troubadour, he was un-equalled. His voice was meant for song. Her heart—and likely that of every other female who had ever heard him!—was wheat before the sickle of his poem, she thought sleepily.

Gloriously male and talented . . . but those things weren't everything. What she truly wanted in a lover was . . . was . . . she screwed her eyes shut in an effort to concentrate beyond the spell of that dream-weaver voice, for some reason not in the least degree alarmed at the line of thought she was pursuing.

That's right! She wanted a *future*. And a future they would likely not have, for she would be returning home soon. She had to bear that fact in mind when her spirits were in such a turmoiled state that she might be inclined to do something extremely foolish.

As the song ended, she turned her head up far enough to see the pale triangle of his face.

"And will you be gone in the morning?" she asked, her voice slightly slurred by overcoming sleep.

"Nay, I'd not leave without saying farewell. It isnae in my heart tae be so cruel. Tae either of us."

"Ha! I bet you say that to all the women."

A soft, silent laugh shook him.

"Well, 'tis truth, after all. And there has not been sae many of them that it was an imposition."

She snorted, but it was a half-hearted effort.

"Such *clishmaclaver*, lass! I'd not say one thing and do another. You needn't worry that my morals are so malleable as those purse-proud, acquisitive Sassans ye've been living amidst."

"That's beautifully said . . . for a parsimonious, bloodthirsty highlander, but I still wager you spend your nights festooned with weak-willed wenches," she grumbled, nearly silently. A thick drowse was stealing over her words and notions that gave her a new freedom of thought at the same time they robbed her of the power of measured speech.

This time he laughed aloud. His soft chuckle was but another caress to her head where his fingers still stroked her tangled hair.

"Festooned? Not lately. Now, go on tae sleep, lass," he urged, his ancient accent growing more pronounced as he also slid toward dreams. "We'll speak more o' this on the morrow."

Unable to resist the pull of slumber, she rested heavily against his sark-clad chest and did as he requested. That night, she was untroubled by dreams.

She awoke gradually the next dawn, aware of the man who laid beside her, but undisturbed to find herself still wrapped in Malcolm's arms.

"Good morrow, lass," Malcolm's delicious voice said softly, and then something soft caressed her brow.

"It's so quiet," she murmured, unalarmed by the gentle kiss or the long breath that fanned her forehead. "I've never heard a morning so still. No roosters, no sheep, not people even."

"No deer come here tae graze unless invited. No birds feast on summer fruit. This is an old place, Taffy lass, and the still-ones bear the sway in these ancient, magicked lands."

Taffy lifted her chin and looked into Malcolm's eyes. For an instant, they were as they appeared in her dreams, pupils dilated and shadows moving in their depths. But he blinked once and the illusion was gone.

"And that's why the Campbells haven't found us either? Because this place belongs to the still-folk?"

"It is. Though 'tis less a case of this place belonging tae the still-folk than the still-folk belonging tae the glen," he answered. Looking up intently into the bower overheard, he narrowed his eyes.

Taffy sensed that Malcolm had more to say but was debating internally about whether it was best to speak to her of those thoughts in his mind.

"Are they still searching for us? The Campbells, I mean," she asked at last, not nearly as alarmed at the thought as she had been the night before.

"Most assiduously, I expect. And suffer we shall an they find us."

"But they won't find us, will they?" she asked, confident of his answer. No one would find them until they were ready to be found.

"Not so long as we remain here in the still-folk's sacred place."

Taffy sat up and looked about the glen. She had been unable to see much the night before because of the darkness and her distraction, but it seemed to her that it had changed in the night.

It was softer now and wore the colors of late spring rather than summer.

"We can't stay here forever, I suppose," she said regretfully and began hunting about for her hairpins. Finding them gone, she began braiding her unruly mop into a long chain.

"Na, 'twould no' be wise tae tarry over long within the glen."

"Why?" Taffy paused, a bit startled and dismayed. "Are we still in danger? Here? But I thought the Campbells couldn't find us."

"No from Campbells—let it be, Taffy lass." Malcolm reached out and threaded his fingers through hers and pulled her hand away. The braid unraveled along with her breath. "Why all this passion for pins and bindings in your hair? The breezes like it loose and so do I. Leave off the fussing."

"You won't like having to guide me about like a blind person," she warned, diverted from her earlier question, which somehow seemed unimportant, something she didn't need to worry about just then. "It gets everywhere when I leave it loose."

"Tuck it behind your ears. It'll stay."

"No, thank you. I prefer the untidy hair."

"Ye don't care for yer ears."

She shrugged carelessly.

"Others don't." She turned her head to look down at Malcolm sprawled comfortably in his heather bed. No man anywhere had ever looked so at ease. She could only marvel at his calm acceptance of their circumstance and try to emulate him. Worry served no useful purpose. And they were quite safe, she was certain.

"They fear them?" he asked with a small frown forming between his slanted brows.

Taffy reached out a finger to smooth away the frown marring his beautiful face.

"It isn't that. They are just unusual, and women are not supposed to be unusual. We are all supposed to be pretty—pretty ears, pretty noses, pretty feet. And be obedient and spiritless and want to be wives and mothers."

Taffy was a little surprised to hear the almost bitter words that spilled from her lips. She couldn't imagine what had possessed her to share such thoughts, even though they were true.

"And ye have no wish for these things?" The frown didn't deepen, but Taffy sensed that he was disturbed by her answer. She caressed him again.

It wasn't surprising that he would dislike her answer, of course, for women possessed even fewer freedoms in his time. Such opinions as hers were nothing short of heresy. She tried to reassure him.

"I do. It is just that I would like to be a wife and mother in my own way. I would like to ride where I want and wear what I please . . . I think

I want to be an American," she said daringly. "Though I wasn't willing to marry one to get there."

Malcolm blinked, and something moved about in his eyes.

"Ye wish tae go to the Colonies? But why should ye marry tae go there?"

"They are their own nation now—I mean, in my time," Taffy told him. "It's a wonderful place—brash and crude. But exciting. And there are many women there who have their own businesses and professions. As for the marriage, it wasn't my idea but rather my father's. And it was obvious from the first that the two of us would not suit one another."

"Ye kenned that he was not the one fer ye," Malcolm asked, a trace of satisfaction in his voice.

"Immediately," Taffy agreed.

"My own family is in Mary's land now. They live among the Quakers. They say that the light o' reason burns in the land o'er the sea."

"They live with the Quakers?" Taffy asked, fascinated. "Do they like it?"

"They do. My mother is allowed tae be a healer there." Malcolm sat up suddenly, bringing his face much closer to her own. His eyes were vivid. "I, too, wish tae be American."

"You do?" For some reason her heart had begun thrumming. Perhaps it was from being presented with a clear view of Malcolm's chest beneath his unlaced shirt when she dropped her eyes from his too intense gaze.

Uncomfortable with her response to his bare flesh, she made an effort at compromise, lifting her eyes as far as his mouth.

"I always longed tae go," the lissome lips said, and he lifted a hand.

Taffy turned her head and watched, mesmerized, as Malcolm's free hand reached out and tucked her locks back, exposing her pointed ears.

"I dinnae fear that others will see yer ears, or yer spirit. Spirits are of small worth if they are so retired as tae never be seen. Let yer thoughts and will come forth and never blush for them." The tone, if not the words, was seductive to her ears.

"You'll feel differently when I start hounding *you* for breakfast," she warned, her heart's wild beating now nearly painful in her chest. She had to put some space between them or she would faint. She knew that, but still she did not move. "Then you'll wish I was quiet and obedient. I'm sure of it."

"Hungry, are ye?" Those entrancing lips smiled. Taffy's poor heart protested the effect on its laboring and she raised her eyes a bit more to stare instead at his large scintillant eyes. They were gray and green and really a bit of every

126

color. A low roaring began in her ears. "Then up ye get, lass."

Nay!

"Up?" she repeated, still staring dazedly at his amazing eyes.

"Yer bundled in my plaid." Malcolm took her chin in hand and tilted her head down.

For a moment, she was still uncomprehending, but the sight of their nearly entwined legs finally penetrated the fog in her brain.

"Oh! Certainly. Excuse me." Taffy scrambled to her feet, both relieved and yet terribly disappointed to be away from Malcolm's warmth. Almost immediately, the ringing in her ears and the thrumming of her heart subsided.

The piper chuckled. He wrapped his length of tartan with skill of a lifetime, donning his apparel in only a moment and fastening it with a curious silver brooch. He kept his body and face three-quarters turned from her, for which she was grateful. Another moment of all but sitting in his lap and there was no knowing what might have happened! Something ruinous, most likely.

On the heels of that thought, Malcolm swiftly turned her way. Wisely, Taffy dropped her eyes and began counting pebbles on the ground.

"Let us go down tae the stream," he said, at last. "There is watercress and berries fat with the summer sun. And ye may see some of yer timorous kin."

"My kin?" Startled, she looked up again into Malcolm's eyes, which was what he had intended, she was sure.

"Aye. Tae my mind, you are one of the shy blackberry blossoms. Pretty and some day tae bear fruit if a lucky bee can make it past yer thorns."

Taffy turned away before he could see her blushing. This time she contemplated the trees. Some of them were more than passing strange. One actually seemed to bear the face of a bearded man with staring eyes and leafy branches sprouting from his opened mouth.

"Would you consider yourself to be a blackberry as well?" she asked, facing her eyes away from the disturbing tree trunk and searching for something—anything—safe to watch.

"Will ye spend the day blushing if I answer that I would rather play the bee?"

"Very probably," she muttered in a suffocated voice, causing him to laugh.

"Then I'd best say that I am a thistle, for I am no' so pretty as berry flowers, and e'en more likely to draw blood with my thorns."

"What you are is a flirt," she told him pertly, heading for the stream without a backward glance. "And I want more than watercress for breakfast, which it seems is all I can have and not be a cannibal."

"Lass?"

"What?"

"The water is this way."

"But—" Taffy stopped. She was absolutely positive that they had come from the stream in the direction she was walking. But a moment of silence presented her with the soft gurgle of a brook from the direction Malcolm was pointing.

With one of her forbidden Gaelic oaths, she spun about and headed for the sound of the stream. A quick glance upward showed her that Malcolm's eyes were twinkling, though whether it was at her poor sense of direction or her profanity that amused him, she could not say.

She spotted a tiny path winding through the shrubbery and stepped onto it without waiting for Malcolm. If he thought he wanted a spirited woman, then she would just let him have one.

The stream soon materialized, looking less placid than it had the night before as it rushed about a tumble of largish stones with tall sprays of white plume.

Malcolm's still amused voice spoke from behind her:

I stepped intae a sparkling brook
Tae cut and peel a wand.

Melanie Jackson

Tae catch a silvered fish
Of which my lady is most fond.

Taffy turned and watched as he suited his actions to his words. His silver knife quickly stripped the bark from a flexible branch. True to his prediction, there was a trailing vine of berries waiting at the stream's stony side from which he plucked a single piece of fruit.

> *I hooked a berry tae my stick*
> *And cast it softly out*
> *And in the blink o' an ee,*
> *I'd caught myself a trout.*

Taffy stared, amazed, as only a moment later Malcolm had pulled a silvery fish from out of burbling water.

"Ye've time for a bit of a buskit, lass, while I cook yer breakfast," he told her, eyes still twinkling as he went to fetch his trophy. "Go down stream a pace and you'll find the water calmer. And, lass?"

"Yes?"

"Yer willfulness is showing. Have a care, or some man will think ye spirited enough tae follow what's in yer heart and do it."

Taffy, recovering from her amazement, was suddenly aware that she was definitely feeling the need for a bit of privacy. Without saying a word about his provocative remark, she turned away and followed the curving stream until it bent out of sight.

"I know that he was just showing off—but how did he do that?" she asked the calming waters. "And can he truly read my mind? Or is that another trick?"

The water did not answer.

Feeling extremely vulnerable without the protection of her shift, she nevertheless decided to indulge in a morning bath. The previous night's dip had been a hasty affair and she had feared going too far into the water without a light to guide her.

The waters this morning were cool but not unpleasantly so, and they seemed slightly scented with heather. As the stream here was just a gentle eddy and clear as purest crystal, she decided that she would wade farther out where she might easily rinse her hair. Once wet, she could more readily arrange the wayward mass to be contained with a band or braid.

The water was extraordinary, infusing her body with vigor. She felt ready to cycle a hundred leagues or dance a reel at double-time—or even swim with silvery trout. Lowering her face into the pure liquid, she allowed it to ripple over her cheeks and forehead and to comb out her tangled hair.

As she rose up into the warming air, a movement by the stream's side tugged at the corner of her eye. Oddly unalarmed, she turned to look for Malcolm. He had likely come to see if she had drowned while bathing.

But there was no Malcolm waiting on the heathered bank. It was empty but for a few stands of bluebells, nodding gently under stream froth that fell upon them with a careless patter.

There was no jean dress on the bank either, she noticed with sudden alarm, dropping back down into the water's protective cover. She looked about with very attentive eyes.

Her attention was rewarded, for presently a flutter of white caught her gaze, and downstream a few paces, she saw the shift she had washed the night before was laid out on a rock warming in the sun.

Only it wasn't the same shift she had cast off the night before, she realized as she crab-walked downstream under the protective cover of water. The silk had been shot-through with silvery thread and tiny berry flowers had been embroidered upon it. The skirt had also been sundered in a dozen places and the edges knitted up with the tiniest bastings of silver. The whole garment was sheer as morning mist.

She looked about quickly. Not a branch or leaf stirred to betray passage.

Debating for only an instant, Taffy left the water's cover to come up onto land. The strangely softened heather branches crushed beneath her feet erupted with perfume at every step.

Beside the shift there were handkerchiefs, which she had brought to serve as bandages, laid in a neat pile. They were a bit small to apply as an effective towel, but she managed to dry off with alacrity. As soon as she was passably dry, she reached for the gossamer garment. It was surprisingly substantial as she pulled it on over her head. Not heavy precisely, but . . .

Protective armor.

"Ladies' chainmail?" she asked the heather with a smile. The expression froze as she saw the words written out in water rivulets upon the tabled rock under where the shift had lain:

> *Vast love, for whom he lives,*
> *For whom he died.*
> *Behold him, the warrior.*
> *The poet made lover.*

Even as she stared, the startling words evaporated with the glittering sunlight in a soft curl of silver mist.

Her gown settled against her, lying warmly next to her bare skin with an intimacy never accomplished by human silk. The only sounds were her thudding heart and the soft splattering of water drops that fell from her hair onto the bruised blossoms at her feet.

Still, Taffy was not surprised when Malcolm's voice spoke from quite nearby. She was growing accustomed to the fact that he always appeared when she was distressed, and that he moved in silence.

"Lass, are ye snared in the heather or gone away wi' the faeries?"

Away with the fairies? Yes, indeed, she thought with a small spurt of reasonable alarm, turning in the direction of Malcolm's voice.

She found his gaze intent upon her. He was smiling slightly and breathing hastily as though he had been rushing to reach her.

He stepped nearer, reaching out, as he so often did, to touch her dripping hair.

"Fell in the stream, did ye, lass?" he joked.

"I did not," she answered, sounding completely normal even though she knew that she was not. Somewhere in the last day and night, years of parental moral teachings had been stripped away, leaving a terrifying tendency to speak the truth.

"Nay? Well, let us grane this dry and then be away. I've a pretty trout wi' berry gansel for ye that would please a hungry Brownie."

"A Brownie? Are they here, too?" she asked as he twisted her hair into a rope and wrung the worst of the water out. This time she didn't bother to fight her attraction.

"Donnae be silly, lass. 'Tis just a manner o' speaking. Brownies never eat fish."

"Oh." He released her hair, then taking her chin in his hand, tilted her face up to the light.

"Ye've the look of one bespelled," he said.

"Is that so surprising?" she asked, staring into his beautiful eyes. This morning they were a shade of sterling green and reflected the swaying leaves of the tressy yew that overhung the stream's far side. A part of her wanted to fall into their depths and drown.

"Ye've never felt the still-ones, have ye, Taffy lass? Never sensed them in the forests about ye, or watching from the rocks."

"Never."

"The blood has thinned then o'er time. Mayhap this is why they've brought ye here," he said absently.

"To learn about them?" she asked, feeling completely unable to move away from Malcolm, though they were standing so close that she could not draw breath without touching him. She was intensely aware of her nakedness beneath her clothes. Her supposed chainmail was utterly useless as a barrier to his heat.

"Nay. Tae teach *me* tae *travel* more like."

"Travel?" She dimly sensed the word had some greater meaning than her previous experience assigned to it.

135

Melanie Jackson

"I think I must leave this place soon. One way or another." He smiled oddly.

"Oh. Of course you must. We both must. As soon as the Campbells depart." She cleared her throat and made an effort to answer intelligently. It was difficult as her lips seemed more inclined to kisses than speech, her body to lean against the wall of muscle that was his chest than to pull away.

"They'll never depart. But let us not spoil the day wi' unpleasant things. Have ye no hunger left?"

"Actually, I am hungry." Taffy wondered if she could step back if she made the effort. But before she could decide if she should try, Malcolm's arm was quickly around her, pulling her scantily clad body close. The heat from his body was so great that her shift might not have been between them. Desire welled inside of her, unfurling like the rose in summer sun. It was delicious. Irresistible.

"So am I, and I would have my breakfast now." He lowered his head and brushed his lips over hers. His touch was gentle, but she sensed that it was kept that way only by great effort.

Taffy's eyes rounded, but she did not resist the sensation blossoming inside her. Too much of her own inclination was to return the caress, to breathe deeply, to pull his scent into her lungs.

"Bonnie and sweet," he pronounced with a smile, dropping his arm from her waist and stepping away. Cold air rushed between them, making her shiver where it slapped at her sensitized skin. The gray-green eyes under Malcolm's arching brows were brilliant, the pupils beginning to dilate. "Yet, I still hunger."

"Then I'll share my trout," Taffy answered, feeling the pink that tinted her cheeks, but refusing to give any other acknowledgment of this second kiss. What was she thinking to be so forward and allow this intimacy between them? Her body and mind were in some form of shock.

"Trout. I doubt of it being enough, but we shall see," Malcolm answered, taking her hand and pulling her up the gentle slope. The blisters on his fingers were healed and gone.

Taffy didn't answer him. She suspected that this morning's kisses were not idle flirtation, but rather a completely serious statement of his future intent.

The disturbing words written on the rock certainly implied as much as well, and she was of mixed feeling about that. Her whole mind was turmoiled and did not seem entirely her own. Her body, too, did not seem to know itself. Even now, her breasts ached where they had pressed tight against him.

The carpet of heather soon gave way to springy moss. Taffy was grateful for the soft vegetation as her boots had disappeared along with her dress and she was forced to walk with bare feet.

137

"I wonder where they took it," she muttered, not looking at the man beside her, but rather paying attention to the ground and the way her silver skirts swayed as she walked, closing and parting like a curtain of veiling. It made her more vulnerable than any nightdress she owned.

"To sew it up," Malcolm told her, guessing her thoughts with an accuracy that she was coming to expect. "Careful of the bent, lass. 'Tis coarse for walking barefoot upon."

"Why *my* dress? They've left your plaid alone and it has a hole in it," she pointed out, shivering a little as she remembered how the hole had gotten there.

"Aye, but then I've either been in it or on it since we came. They'll take it soon enough—can ye part me from it for any time."

The smell of roasting trout reached her then, and Taffy's mouth began to water. Though she was not particularly fond of fish, at that moment no other food she had ever eaten seemed as ambrosial.

Malcolm smiled wryly and said: "It's as I thought. One hunger at a time, then. We must quench the ache o' the belly first. My apologies, lass, but there is no salt tae be had here, such not being allowed on hallowed ground. But I think ye'll find that ye donnae crave it overmuch any more."

"It doesn't matter," Taffy assured him, hurrying to the small fire in the stone pit where a pair of trout hung, spitted between roasted berries. "This looks marvelous. I can't recall ever being so hungry."

"Aye. I warrant it does look like a feast, fasting as ye did the night just past." He plucked a spear from the fire and shook the fish into a waiting leaf, which served as a plate. It was a broad thing, glossy and thick, and of a type Taffy had never seen before. "Eat your fill, lass. It will make ye strong."

"Good. I need it."

Taffy, reaching eagerly for the fish, barely saw Malcolm nod his head in agreement.

Chapter Six

"I'm glad ye cannae kiss back the sunlight that kisses ye so boldly," Malcolm said into the hush that had followed their meal. "I would be a jealous man."

Feeling languid, Taffy turned her head toward him, not bothering to open her eyes or stir off the warm stone table where she lay, letting her hair dry spread out in the summer sun.

"Sing another song for me, Malcolm. Something beautiful and romantic."

Nodding, he stared for a moment at her lustrous tresses, which were a dazzlement to the eye, and then allowed his gaze to sweep down her body. It was more revealed than usual in this new garment.

"Are you thinking of a song?" she asked.

"I am thinking that a man should have a caution when making wishes," he muttered. Then more loudly: "I have a musical poem for ye in the Sassenach style."

> *I swear by fin and feather,*
> *By the fish out in the sea,*
> *By the birds in the heaven,*
> *By the grand and the wee,*
> *By the holy sprigs of mistletoe,*
> *That grow in holy oaken trees,*
> *That this day, mistress,*
> *Yer lover I will be.*

Taffy opened her eyes and then made one slow blink as she saw the hectic flush upon his cheekbones, the shadows stirring again in his dilated eyes.

"Have ye nothing tae say?" he demanded, his accent growing more pronounced.

"You have good lungs," she offered, at something of a loss to know whether she was supposed to take the verse seriously, and fearing that she was intended to do just that.

Her blood grew lighter, her pulse more rapid, her head dizzy as she considered all the things that might happen between them. Such immoral, yet wonderful thoughts she was having.

"Aye, he that's short o' breath shouldnae meddle wi' a chanter." He rolled to his feet and approached her stony bed. "Or a woman."

With him standing over her, Taffy was suddenly self-conscious about her mode of dress. The wantonness of her own attire—her very behavior, even—rushed into her mind, and awareness stained her cheeks until their color matched Malcolm's own. Still, she did not move to cover herself.

"How easily ye blush," he said, touching her fevered cheek. Then he shook his head. "Yer innocence is a bane, lass. I dree for it."

"I suffer, too," said some bold stranger with Taffy's tongue, causing her to color more.

"Do ye? Yet only yer actions can free us now."

"My actions?" she asked, thrilled, alarmed, and puzzled.

"Aye. Do ye not ken what all this signifies?" He gestured to her gown and then to the glen as a whole.

"No," she whispered. "I don't."

But she was beginning to. The still-folk had brought her here for a reason. She had thought it was to rescue Malcolm from the Campbells, but there had to be more to their plan, or they would have left the glen as soon as the Campbells tired of their search. Or they might even have guided her directly to the path back home.

" 'Tis you that must decide when we leave this place. I would sooner be dead and buried in the clay than have ye in my bed against yer will. But we may be here in this bower many a long year, lass, if ye do not decide in my favor. And though 'tis a bonnie enough spot, it is still a prison for us, and becoming more so wi' every passing hour." He dropped his hand and turned away. "I'm going down tae the river for a spell an' see if they will let me cross. Best we find the limits of our travel."

"Wait!" Taffy sat up and reached for his hand. When he turned back to her she could see the shadows were again moving in his eyes. His long, hard fingers closed about her wrist. The flesh was hot, nearly scorching where it lay against her skin.

"*That*'s what they want, isn't it?" she whispered. "For me to . . ."

"Save them. Through me."

Save them?

Sacrifice.

"Mayhap I'm the last wi' the sight," he answered, knowing her unspoken question. "The last *clanna* wi' enough faerie blood tae see the old ones. Whatever the cause, we cannae be leaving this place until there is some hope for the future."

"Hope? A child, do you mean?" She looked at the hand about her wrist and smiled. The dark of his skin looked right against her paler flesh.

"Ultimately." He shrugged. "No plan of the

still-folk's making is ever so simple to under-stand. But they want ye tae be mine. They would have me take you now, but I shall no' be doing anything against yer will. So ye must decide, lass."

"No one has ever left the important decisions to me," she confessed, still looking down at the strong hand that encircled her wrist. She was un-able to think reasonably. It was as though some-thing had peeled all of society's morality back from her brain leaving only selfish honesty. This new voice told her that this was a moment when the winds of change would either snuff out the spark that glowed between them, or else fan it to a blaze.

"Nay?" A tiny smile had crept into his low voice. "It seems to me that yer full o' a deal of decision regardless."

"I've been practicing."

This was her decision.

"Well then, lass? Ye should be prepared for this moment. What is it tae be? Aye, or nay? Be cer-tain o' yer choice now, though. There'll be no go-ing back once 'tis done." His beautiful voice was very nearly harsh now, as though he were an-gered by something.

"I know 'tis madness," Taffy whispered, staring up into his face. "Complete wanton wickedness to want you in this way."

"So the priests tell us. But, lass, life is short.

And happiness is rare." His thumb rubbed gently over the thrumming veins in her wrist. If it was meant to calm her, the gesture failed in its intent. "An we died on the morrow, would ye regret having passed this moment by? Never having a man tae yer bed?"

"I would," she answered, in barely a whisper, her mind finding the peace that came with decision, or at the heart of intense prayer. Her lonely soul was not meant to be confined to one body, one heart, but should venture forth and find its mate.

"Then so be it." He lifted his gaze from her face and directed it around the silent glen as though warning someone away.

"Are *they* here?" Taffy asked uneasily, pulling her hair about her shoulders in a curtain.

"Nay. We are alone, lass." Malcolm smiled suddenly, a grin as bright as the hot sun of summer. He repeated: "We are alone."

Around them, the trees lost their rigid posture and seemed to fold inward, weaving together their tressy arms into a bower. The tender leaves swallowed up the sunbeams from above, which gave a soft green twilight to the glen.

The moment narrowed until it seemed that mortal time shifted to one side and left them stranded in some unearthly place—like those stories of bespelled into a night of faerie revels who awoke only to find that one hundred years had passed, Taffy thought dimly. This was just such a place.

There was no breath of passing breezes, no sound of ripples from the nearby waters. The whole world, other than her and Malcolm, faded away behind the veil of emerald twilight.

Taffy sensed, as she lay back on the stone, that she was joining now in a long chain of magical events. She was at last taking her place in some vast design, spanning a gap between events and clasping the lives of those who had come before her, and yet also those who would follow.

Words would not shape themselves on her thickened tongue, but she stared with her eyes wide, two flawless blue pools in which Malcolm might see all that she could not speak. She wanted to abandon herself to this desire she felt to throw herself into his passion and be consumed there. It was her destiny.

Malcolm's eyes were a turmoil of color and emotion as he cast aside his plaid and sark and joined her on the altar. Taffy's silvered gown slithered away, the ties unfastening and slipping off her breasts before his fingers were even there to touch them.

As though she had been given a window into Malcolm's mind, Taffy could see and even feel what he wanted of her. He wanted to cleave into her, to become part of her very bones and flesh, to pour himself into her dew-damp body, to lose himself in the awed regard that shone in her fathomless, ocean deep eyes.

His thoughts moved her even as they terrified her with their intensity.

He glanced down once as he brushed aside the silken tassel shielding her maidenhead and folded back the tender flesh.

Her modesty protested being seen thus by him, but no protest could force itself past her mute lips.

He paused for a moment, returning his gaze to her eyes. She knew that he worried about hurting her, but she knew there would be some pain. This ceremony was both communion and sacrifice, and had to be sealed in the blood of innocence.

Her breath caught as he entered her, and the passion in her dimmed. He dipped many times into her body, fighting his own pleasure that she might know joy, too. But it was futile. Conduits of new thoughts had been forced open in her brain. A confusion of foreign emotions raced unchecked through her mind and body, and they overwhelmed her. Malcolm was asking her to fly with him, but though she wanted desperately to please him, she could not do what he desired. In the end, her own timidity was defeating her. Malcolm had to go on alone; she could not let go of the modesty and restraint that were the only familiar landmarks she had to guide her through this strange land of alien sensation and passion.

Yet though she had not allowed her body to be entirely swept away by Malcolm, in every other way Taffy felt herself give over to him. She poured out her feelings until there was nothing else to relinquish: He had her thoughts, her heart, even—for a moment—her soul, which flew with him where her body could not.

"Malcolm," she whispered, her lips finally unsealed. She closed her eyes when he stilled upon her.

Amidst all the strange notions cluttering her head there was, hovering at the back of her mind, the first small shadow of grief. Something said to her that though she had somehow failed herself—and Malcolm, too—she had given the stillfolk what they wanted. It was time for them to leave this holy glen.

"Have a care with yer thoughts now, lass," Malcolm warned gently as he rolled aside. "The old ones may take yer part and give ye yer sadthought destiny, an ye wish on it often enough."

"They can do that?" she asked, suddenly growing alarmed as her senses returned. Flushing, Taffy started searching for her gown, feeling more naked than she ever had in her life, but the meager protection of silver shift had disappeared just like all her other clothes.

"Here? Aye, they can."

"Wonderful. And what now—since we've fulfilled our destiny?" she asked, watching uneasily as the leaves overhead thinned and revealed a sky painted bright with stars and a full moon.

Only the night before it had been a crescent, she thought, the hair rising upon her arms. How much time *had* passed since they entered the glen?

"Now we dress—an' I can find my plaid. *Ah!*" Malcolm went quickly to a nearby gorse bush and plucked up the garment. The moon was bright enough to show that the tattered woolens had been mended. It also revealed Taffy's dress of jean laying neatly on a nearby shrub.

Feeling painfully naked and tender-skinned sitting on the cold, bare rock, Taffy hurried for the protection of her heavy clothing. She was fastening her blouse when she felt Malcolm's hands gently lifting her tangled hair from off of her neck.

"Little though it pleases me, lass," he said in his beautiful, calm voice, "I think we must bind these locks up so we may travel wi' stealth. The flora shall not be so cooperative once we are gone from the glen."

Taffy stood still as he secured her hair with a piece of wiry vine.

"Where will we go?"

"Where we must."

"But where is the door?" she asked, turning to face him.

"The door?"

"The way back. You said they would show me the door when I had given them what they wanted."

"Do ye still seek death then?" he asked sadly, his expression growing slightly aloof.

"Death! Of course not. What are you talking about?"

"The road ye traveled was the way of the dead, lass. The low road."

"No. It couldn't be. How could I have survived?" But she lacked conviction. The road certainly hadn't been anything of this world. Malcolm seemed so definite that way was dangerous, and if anyone should know about such things, it was he. Had she really traveled through the land of the dead to come here? And what would the return trip mean for her?

Too, though she knew she should rush back to reassure her father of her well-being, she found herself in no haste to leave Malcolm. Not even if it meant facing the wrath of all the Campbells without a single change of clothing.

Some strong emotions were teeming in her breast and she did not know what to do with them. They had appeared so quickly, with no time for conventional preparation. She now had a lover—yet there'd been no courting, no flowers, no mention of any future. Her whole world and all her assumptions about her relations with the male half of it had been turned on end.

She needed time to adjust to what had happened. To think about what she should do.

Malcolm saw her indecision. "Aye, it was the low road. Well, an it is the still-folk's wish, ye'll travel the spirit road again, ye may be sure of it. For the present, I think we'll content ourselves wi' departing from Duntrune. The Campbells are apt tae be in evil humor, what wi' me escaping and ye shooting so many o' their men. We'll head Kilmartin way."

"Thanks for reminding me about the Campbells. It had nearly slipped my mind," she grumbled, smoothing her skirt with a nervous hand. The ugly jean should serve her against Malcolm's lust as well as any armor had ever protected a knight in battle, especially now that it had been restored to wholeness.

The piper laughed softly as he pulled Taffy close. His body was hot, pulsing with life and energy, which made her own heart join the unwilling thrum of renewing desire.

"Aye. I'd no' Campbells in my head, either. All the same, best we recall them now or there'll be no more chances for sweet forgetfulness. Fetch yer gear, Taffy lass. We'd best be away while we may."

"All right." Reluctantly, she stepped away from

the shelter of Malcolm's arms. She didn't share his sense of urgency about being away from the protected glen and back among the hostile people of his world. Even with its strangeness, this all seemed preferable to the danger they had left at Duntrune.

"Take only what ye need."

"I need it all," she said firmly, donning her belts and checking her rifle to see that it was loaded. "I wish that there had been time to photograph the glen."

"Photograph?"

"Make a picture." Taffy gestured at her camera.

"A picture? Wi' that small box? The one ye carry about all the time?"

"It's called a *camera*. It captures images and puts them onto plates. Wait! I have a picture of you in here." Taffy hurried to one of the haversacks and began searching for the photograph she had taken at Duntrune. She was not aware that her sight had improved to the point that she could see nearly as well in the halflight as she did in the daylight.

"Here it is," she said, opening the thin boards and removing her most precious print for his inspection.

Malcolm stared in amazement.

"Are these my bones?" he demanded.

"They were," she corrected happily. "But they

won't be there now, will they? You didn't die after all."

"Nay, I didnae." His sudden smile was fierce. "Well, lass, I suppose we must bring yer magic picture-maker. But I'll carry it for ye. Ye'll have yer hands full wi' the Sassenach weapon."

"It isn't Sassenach. It's American," she said releasing her camera into his hands with only the smallest twinge of anxiety.

"Is it now?" he asked, eyeing her rifle with sudden interest.

"It is. It is called a *Winchester repeating rifle,* and it carries ten bullets in one load."

"Ten! So that is how ye shot so many o' those bloody Campbells. The MacColla would be a happy man an he had a brace o' those."

"No doubt. And I wish I could have brought him some," Taffy said, feeling a surge of belated anger at the woman who had tried to harm Malcolm. "I just wish I had shot that awful woman too."

"Aye, 'twould have been a grand thing, but ye must no' dwell on what might have been. Ye've taken a large revenge on the bloody Campbells." It was unbelievable to Taffy that there was no chastisement in his voice. No disapproval of her unladylike actions.

"I have, haven't I?" she contemplated thoughtfully, shouldering one of the packs. It was awkward with the criss-crossing ammunition belts. "Like a soldier."

"Aye, like a soldier. Give me yer bags, lass. We've a bittock distance tae travel and I don't want ye tae be laggard of foot an' we need tae run. I don't know how ye managed tae get here in the first place with so much luggage."

"Slowly," she muttered at Malcolm's back as he started away from her with a long, limber-hipped stride. It was a reminder of her own deficiency of leg on the last occasion when she had followed her long-shanked Gael into a hostile wood.

She knew immediately when the edge of the faeries' lands had been reached. Beyond a last ring of rugged stones on the hillcrest, there lay a thick brooding mist that covered over the suddenly sullen moon. The air felt charged and heavy with the heat and damp that always preceded a violent summer storm.

The gay stream they had bathed and fished in had dried to a trickle where the stumps of dead bushes rotted in shallow pools of still, stagnant water. Nothing swam within its thinning puddles.

"It's ugly," Taffy breathed, wrinkling her nose at the smell of decay.

"Aye." Malcolm's voice was equally soft. "Too ill a place for attracting men or beasts. Go softly now, lass. It may be that Campbells are nearby."

As if to prove his words, below their perch torches came into view—dozens of them, swarming like sinister fireflies though the woods and advancing upon them as surely as an ocean's tide reclaimed its beaches under the pull of a full moon. It seemed impossible, but Taffy was certain that she could hear their agitated snuffling as the men quartered the ground, searching for them.

Malcolm jerked his head once as a sign to follow and faded back into the woods. They could not escape from the glen that way. Taffy walked carefully, trying to still her burgeoning alarm.

He led her down a narrow path where sharp stones pierced the valley floor. There was a heaviness in the air that made the moon hazy and red. Presently, even its dim light was covered over with swollen black clouds that left a black shadow upon the land. The air around Malcolm and Taffy brooded, and every once in a while, the unpleasant smell of a lighted flambeaux was carried to them.

Malcolm moved swiftly through the ravine, seeking the woods on the other side. Such seemingly barren places could suddenly become riverways where streams churned with angry waters released by a storm. Already, there was an approaching rill from the spring and the faint sound of trickling water from the top of the gorge.

He did not curse the weather, though it would leave them cold and wet should it break before they found shelter. Pounding rains would discourage even the most ardent hunters, and it would confuse the hounds that were set upon their trail.

The first of the heavy rain did not come until they were sheltered within a copse of mountain ash, but the wind that came rushing upon them was a fearsome thing. Driven by some unknown purpose, it raced through the trees and shrubs with careless, tearing claws that propelled the dust and summer chaff like leaves before a hurricane. The short wall of heather that ringed the copse wailed for mercy from the torrent's lash. The tiny purple blossom's bells were frayed and torn before they were sent spinning into the darkening air.

Taffy could barely think; the storm filled her head, clotting her thoughts with noise that rivaled a raging river or a locomotive in a tunnel. It seemed for a moment that the wind would actually unseal her lips and rush down to bruise her lungs with its stinging particles before it dragged her up into the sky. But at the moment when she feared she should be lost, Malcolm's arms found her and anchored her to the earth. He dragged her swiftly into the shelter of the wood where the storm winds declined to follow.

"There was a croft," Malcolm began, but

ceased speaking as the dim light showed them that there was no longer a cottage in the glen, but only a tumble of stone blackened by fire. The sickening smell of recent burning permeated the air.

"I see that Black Bitch has been tae call." The words were soft, but Taffy felt the bitter anger behind them.

"Why did she do it?" Taffy whispered. The cruel destruction demanded a lowered voice.

"Because she could."

"But these are her own lands, aren't they?"

"Aye, her husband's, but not everyone is pleased with their laird's choice o' brides."

"But the destruction of their home would leave these people beggared—a costly charge upon Lord Dunstaffnager," she pointed out, baffled and dismayed by the woman's illogical heartlessness.

"Better a beggared body than a beggared spirit. Anyhow, if the inhabitants of this cot spoke out against the lady, they'll be beyond all human cares now."

There was a sudden soft whine from under a pile of stones, barely audible over the rain splattering above their heads. Taffy shuddered at the pitiful sound and moved swiftly to see what was trapped within the rubble. As they knelt on the ground by the largest gap in the tumbled stones, a giant furry head thrust itself out from under the tumbled wall and whined again. Inside, a long tail was flailing against the sooty stones.

"Poor baby!" Taffy cooed. "Don't worry. We'll get you out."

Malcolm didn't bother with words. Setting her bags and camera aside, he began to carefully dismantle the blackened cairn that had the hound trapped. Before the job was even half done, the poor beast was thrusting his way out of the stone prison, careless of any fur and skin he might leave behind.

He was obviously distressed from his time in captivity, Taffy could see, but though thin, he was not grievously damaged or even burned like the ruined building which had held him.

"There now," Taffy said, gently running her hands over the animal's singed coat. "You're safe. Good doggie."

Malcolm grunted as he rubbed his dirtied hands over his plaid and then came to kneel beside her.

"He's one of the Campbell's hounds, a *mial-choin*," he said. But obviously that didn't weigh with him for he, too, reached out a helping hand to the abused beast. "And how are ye, *cu*? No' so badly all things considered."

The hound wagged a hesitant tail.

"He must be thirsty," Taffy said.

"Well, we've water aplenty," Malcolm pointed out as the rain had finally begun to penetrate the leaves above them and was sprinkling its cold tears upon their bare heads. "This storm willnae dwine 'til the morrow, I think. Best we be finding some shelter away from here before the water overflows the burn."

"Is there shelter?" Taffy asked hopefully.

"Aye. There's a cave a distance on. I would have preferred tae stay here in the glen, but we've no choice now. Come along, *cu*," he said to the hound as he helped Taffy to her feet and again took up his burden. "I doubt your poor life would be worth even a copper coin an ye return to yer bloody mistress now."

"It's getting warm again," Taffy commented as they pushed deeper into the wood. The rescued hound paced silently at her side, seeming to prefer her company to Malcolm's. Or perhaps he simply liked the comforting hand she rested upon his singed head.

"Aye, it'll be smooring warm once the sun is out."

"But," she began, only to notice that the dawn was indeed beginning to force itself into the storm clouds. "Is it morning already? How can that be? Surely we didn't walk all night."

Malcolm stopped by a low, flat stone that had a convenient depression filled with water where the hound could drink.

"Aye, we did."

"But," she objected again, blinking at the rain

that ran into her eyes. "We couldn't have walked all night. I'm not at all tired."

"Lass, ye've been touched wi' the still-folk's magic now. Yer—" he searched for a word. "Yer filled with magic. It was in the water ye drank and the food ye ate and—"

"And what happened on the altar," she finished, feeling her face stain as she mentioned her fall from grace.

Malcolm nodded.

"That too," he said matter-of-factly. "Now ye can see at night. Find yer way in the woods. Avoid the worst of the storm's rain and wind. Go long periods without eating of human food. And ye may e'en befriend some o' the savage beasties in the forest."

"Savage beasties?" Taffy looked down at the hound as he lapped up the last drops of precious water. He was, she had to admit, rather large and possessed a commanding pair of jaws.

"Aye. Anyone else who tried to pat the beastie there would likely have been dead by now. Campbells donnae keep lap-dogs, Taffy lass. These hounds are for hunting wolves and deer, but people mostly."

"Dear Heaven." In spite of the rising temperature, Taffy shivered. "I knew that, of course. Had read it, but I just didn't believe it. Not in my heart. Such cruelty doesn't seem possible."

"We must away now, Taffy lass," Malcolm said

GET TWO FREE* BOOKS!

SIGN UP FOR THE LOVE SPELL ROMANCE BOOK CLUB TODAY.

LOWEST PRICES EVER!

Every month, you will receive two of the newest Love Spell titles for the low price of $8.50,* **a $4.50 savings!**

As a book club member, not only do you save **35% off the retail price**, you will receive the following special benefits:

- **30% off** all orders through our website and telecenter (plus, you still get 1 book FREE for every 5 books you buy!)

- Exclusive access to dollar sales, special discounts, and offers you won't be able to find anywhere else.

- Information about contests, author signings, and more!

- Convenient home delivery of your favorite books every month.

- A 10-day examination period. If you aren't satisfied, just return any books you don't want to keep.

There is no minimum number of books to buy, and you may cancel membership at any time.

* Please include $2.00 for shipping and handling.

NAME: _____

ADDRESS: _____

_____

_____

TELEPHONE: _____

E-MAIL: _____

_____ I want to pay by credit card.

__ Visa   __ MasterCard   __ Discover

Account Number: _____

Expiration date: _____

SIGNATURE: _____

Send this form, along with $2.00 shipping and handling for your FREE books, to:

Love Spell Romance Book Club
20 Academy Street
Norwalk, CT 06850-4032

Or fax (must include credit card information!) to: 610.995.9274.
You can also sign up on the Web at www.dorchesterpub.com.

Offer open to residents of the U.S. and Canada only. Canadian residents, please call 1.800.481.9191 for pricing information.

If under 18, a parent or guardian must sign. Terms, prices and conditions subject to change. Subscription subject to acceptance. Dorchester Publishing reserves the right to reject any order or cancel any subscription.

kindly, unable to offer her any comfort about the horror they faced, and choosing not to lie to her lest she be lulled into a false belief of their safety. "We dare no' tarry here wi' the sun on the rise."

"But where are we going—ultimately? Kilmartin? But what is there? Is it safe? Is anywhere safe?" she asked, growing frustrated and a little frightened.

"I shall keep ye safe, lass. Never doubt it," he said sternly.

With that, Malcolm turned from her and resumed his walk down the path—a path, Taffy suspected, that would not be readily visible to anyone who had not had a brush with faerie magic.

"We go tae *Caislean na Nor*," he said softly. "I cannae think where else tae take ye. We shall seek Thomas Rimer and ask him for advice."

161

Chapter Seven

Taffy spoke to Malcolm and the hound in an undertone while they pushed on through the rain. As the sun crept closer to the eastern horizon shading the night from black to gray, she told a fascinated Malcolm about her velocipede, life in London, her stay in America, and her aspirations to become a renowned photographer.

Though Malcolm asked many questions of her, he did not reciprocate with any like confidences about his plans for the future or reminiscences of his past. An increasingly frustrated Taffy couldn't decide if it was just a natural reserve on his part or if he did not, in fact, have any plans beyond living for another day. He had only once mentioned a desire to go to America, but she would have thought that simple politeness, except that his many questions regarding the people certainly suggested curiosity about her impressions of it.

She wondered, uneasily, would he emigrate when the opportunity arose?

The thought laid another worry over her heart. The American colonies in the early seventeenth century were barely civilized. So many died of disease and in conflicts with the natives. What might happen to Malcolm if he went there? It was not a pleasant notion for the faint of heart to contemplate—and lately, her heart had been fainter than most. The smallest of things seemed to disturb it!

Still, Malcolm was undeniably special, gifted with some form of *glamourie*. That would likely protect him. Hadn't the still-folk intervened once to save him? They wouldn't let anything happen to him now. Not in America. Not in Scotland. Anywhere he went, Malcolm would be safe.

She inwardly repeated that thought several more times, finding that the mental incantation helped her to remain calm, even though deep down inside she had doubts about the faeries' ability to protect the piper once he passed beyond their realm and they were divided by a sea.

A league on, they came to another black stream where the water glinted darkly beneath a thick growth of stunted shrubs. The ancient, knotted plants stooped in the stony soil, dropping their long, mossy beards into the murky swirling waters, which waved them to and fro.

Though it left them exposed to the heavens and any eyes that might be watching, Taffy and Malcolm patiently waited at the stream's side as the dog drank his fill. The hound lapped with a sort of noisy enthusiasm, snapping his jaws together after each swallow with a force that would have shattered human teeth.

Neither Taffy nor Malcolm had a thirst for the black stream, but Taffy was pleased to rest on a nearby hummock while the hound partook. She was not exhausted but glad to give her feet a moment of weightlessness. Her hiking boots were sensible, but did not allow for a great deal of comfort.

"Poor beast," Taffy said softly, no longer bothered by the rain that fell upon them. She had reached a level of dampness where no further moisture mattered. "We'll have to feed it soon."

Malcolm snorted. "The poor *beastie* is a ferocious hunter. He can feed himself an he wishes."

"But he's tired and hurt."

"And we are not?"

Taffy stared at Malcolm in the hazy light of newest day. He didn't look tired. In fact, his body radiated with vitality that infected her spirits. She wondered idly if such strength was inherited, or if it had been acquired during their stay in the glen.

Experience told her that she should be collapsed from exhaustion. Ladies did not hike through the night in raging storms and still feel like they could march a dozen leagues more.

Still, she had always been strong of body. A characteristic she inherited from both father and mother. And there had never been any reason for her to test the limits of her endurance before this day, so perhaps her seemingly endless strength was not truly out of the ordinary for someone like herself.

Malcolm turned from his close inspection of the unstable causeway where they had to cross the stream and smiled gently at her.

"Ye needn't worry so. The cave is but a wee bit on. I doubt it's been found by the Campbells or any other. Ye'll be safe enough there," he said encouragingly.

"*I'll* be safe enough?"

"Aye. As ye pointed out, we'll need food soon. I'll do a bit of hunting before the sun is too high up."

"Is that safe?" Taffy asked, searching Malcolm's eyes for the truth.

He shrugged.

"As safe as anything in this world, Taffy lass. Just remember that though we are no' longer in the glen, still a certain magic creeps through these woods and forgotten dreams and power reside here. So guard yer thoughts and words whilst here. I shall be back afore too long."

Taffy looked about uneasily at the shadows weaving in the wind, casting the shade of fresh phantom worries over the wet ground. So keen was her new sight that even with darkness still clinging to the edges of the forest, she could discern shapes in the pale light as they passed along.

"At least the rain is slowing. We'll be dry soon," she offered with forced cheer, though rather dismayed at the state of her muddied jean skirts.

Malcolm chuckled as he reached down to help her to her feet. As ever, his hands were immediate givers of warmth and comfort.

"Yer no' so neat and tidy now, lass," he teased. "Ye'd do better to wear yer skirts endwise like a Scotsman would and keep them out of the dirt and water. Still, yer a grand enough dower in yerself. I suppose I shall keep ye in spite o' yer muddied clothes."

"Actually," she said, feeling just a touch breathless at the teasing words, "I have quite a grand dowry. It was left to me by a maiden aunt. She was sister to my grandmother, and had an income derived from shipping."

"Do ye then? Well, 'tis a fortunate man I am," he said lightly, handing her the rifle and then taking her other hand.

"You are?" she asked, suddenly very short of

breath as Malcolm leaned over her to grab a pack. Her grip on the rifle was unnecessarily tight and didn't lessen as he turned away.

"Aye. It's not every man who flees for his life wi' a bonnie lass who has a fearsome weapon and silver in her pockets." The careless answer didn't stop the pounding of her heart.

Feeling the sudden racing of her pulse beneath his fingers, Malcolm turned back around for a quick peek at her face. Unable to stop herself, Taffy colored and looked away.

"I think I'd best be getting ye into that cave and finding some breakfast for ye. We can risk a fire an we are quick about it."

"That would be wonderful," she answered, looking back at their hound with exaggerated concern so she wouldn't have to face Malcolm with hope shining in her eyes. The thought of marrying this man from another time, perhaps having a future with him . . . it was too much. "You know, I can't go on calling him *dog*. He needs a proper name. Something appropriate."

"Watch yer step now, lass, or ye'll be getting a cold bath," Malcolm cautioned as they crossed the stream, stepping carefully from broken stone to even worse broken stone. "And what sort of name would ye be giving the beastie? Beelzebub, perhaps?"

"I think I'll call him Smokey." Taffy found herself sure-footed, even on the slippery, submerged rocks. Which was good, as the stones were barely visible with the stream swollen as it was.

"Aye? Well, he'll like that, no doubt." Malcolm sounded amused. " 'Tis a fine dignified name for a fierce hunter after all. And he'll be pleased tae be reminded of his time in the smokehouse where the kindly Campbells left him tae die."

"Well, he isn't very fierce," Taffy defended. "Though he is quite dignified, I must say. Even if he smells like a chimney."

Malcolm snorted. It was an uneuphonious sound, but Taffy was growing extremely fond of the expression of mirth. Doubtless, Malcolm could make gargling sound like the sweetest music, so wonderful was his voice.

"Come along, Smokey. The water isn't deep," Taffy urged, patting her leg.

As if to make Malcolm's point about his abilities, Smokey leaped the stream in a single bound and took up what was becoming his accustomed place beside Taffy. The corner of the hound's wide mouth turned up and he seemed to be grinning with pride at his prowess.

"I pray ye never have cause to think otherwise o' him, lass. Ah!" Malcolm shouldered his way through a shrub wall and stepped into a thicket on the far side of the stream. When Taffy hesitated, he reached out and pulled her in after him.

Even with her newly empowered sight, the way seemed tangled and obscure, but a few paces on a narrow opening, similar to the mouth of the underground tombs at Kilmartin, presented itself to them. Taffy eyed the trysting stones that flanked the entrance. It was just barely possible that they were naturally placed thus, but she didn't think so. She felt sure that these were the work of human—or some sentient being's—will.

"In wi' ye, lass" Malcolm said.

Taffy eyed the opening in the strengthening light, checking it for cobwebs or objectionable droppings. It seemed blessedly free of spiders and other inhabitants, but even had it been filthy with chitin she would have entered, for suddenly she was overcome with a wave of exhaustion that began behind her eyes and passed down her body like a spill of ocean water.

"There's tinder inside. Build a small fire near the rear o' the cave," Malcolm instructed, standing back so that the dog might precede them into the cavern. "I'll be back afore ye may twice blink yer blue eyes, and then we'll have some food and a long rest."

"All right," she answered, refusing to again express her concern for Malcolm's safety. They had to have food. If he could face the risks unflinching, she would not show him a pallid countenance as he left.

"Good lass," Malcolm ducked his head and bussed her quickly, his lips warm on her chilled skin. He spoke softly into her hair: "Dry yer clothes. We'll want them for a pallet."

Then he disappeared into the silent gray-green of the new morning.

Smokey took up a sentry watch at the mouth of the small cave, his heavy head resting on forepaws as he faced out into the wind and dying rain.

Taffy found the dried grass and wood stored at the back of the cavern. The scorch marks on the floor and walls showed her where previous fires had been built. Obviously, there was some form of natural chimney at the back of the cavern, for there was little griming on the smooth, vaulted roof just overhead.

Suddenly aware of being very damp and cold, Taffy opened the pack that Malcolm had left and extracted her lantern. Once the lantern was lit, she was able to light grass twists and steadily feed the twig fire until it was blazing on its own.

The same pack revealed her borrowed flask, which still had a generous measure of whisky. Taffy was tempted, but decided to save the liquor for a true emergency. Instead, she drank a little of the water that Malcolm had brought from the glen in his sheepskin bag. It tasted peculiar but was still refreshing, and it killed the thirst that parched her tongue as no whisky could do.

Not feeling inclined to sit about naked while she waited for Malcolm's return, Taffy nevertheless did her best to spread her skirts where she sat at the edge of the fire so that they might dry as Malcolm had instructed.

Though not particularly uneasy of mind, Taffy also kept her rifle close at hand as she rested her head upon her drawn-up knees and considered the events that had overtaken her. She was too weary to fully relive the fear, delight, and passion of the last days, but they were remembered. Her gun was close, her heart—foolish thing!—was somehow quite happy, and the rest of her . . . Taffy shivered and moved closer to the fire. The rest of her was still very aware of where Malcolm had bestowed her with kisses and caresses and laid his weight upon her.

For a long while, there was no sound in the cavern to distract her, except the snapping of twigs consumed in the flames and the soft fall of slowing rain, but presently Smokey dropped into a noisy sleep, which had him whining as his paws twitched and small shivers worked their way down his spine.

Did the dog weep for his sins under the mastery of the Campbells? she wondered. Or was he lonely and dreaming of a familiar hearth or stable where his canine friends waited?

It didn't matter, she decided. The high sound was troubling and likely to give them away to any passersby in the wood.

"Smokey—*cu*," she called softly, using Malcolm's name for the dog.

The hound's ears pricked at once and he turned to look at her with intelligent brown eyes. "Come here, boy." Taffy patted the ground beside her in invitation. The hound turned for a last look at the dripping green outside the cave, sniffed deeply of the wet air, and then came to join her by the fire. Once laid down with her hand upon his brow, Smokey gave a heavy sigh and returned to his sleep. This time it was an easy slumber, unbroken by shivers or lonely sighs.

Unable to resist the pull of bone-deep exhaustion, Taffy slumped over against the hound and slept, too. She dreamt uneasily of being chased by a giant-tusked boar.

Malcolm returned only a while later, bearing a skinned hare. Though weary to the bone, he still had to smile at the picture that greeted him inside the cave. His golden lass was a right mess—mud-spattered and bedraggled—but she was still pretty as the innocent dawn, curled up asleep with her American firearm and her adopted Campbell hell-hound.

She had done a good job of building a smokeless fire, too. The few curls that headed for the roof's vent were nearly invisible and it burned with even brightness.

Wasting no time, Malcolm spitted the rabbit carcass, and arranging some stones, set the meat to cooking. His sodden plaid was quickly doffed and spread out on the floor to dry. He did not grease his woolen as some crofters did and therefore it easily took on the dampness from outdoors.

The pleasant smell of roasting meat soon had Taffy stirring. A rumble deep in her belly was loud enough to wake her and she opened her eyes upon the pleasant sight of a half-naked Malcolm, turning their breakfast so it wouldn't singe in the fire.

"Hello," she said groggily, pushing herself erect. "I hadn't meant to fall asleep. I guess Smokey and I were both tired."

Malcolm smiled gently as he tested the meat. "I'd have been muckle surprised an ye had been awake, lass. It has been a brutal time for ye, being raised as ye were in gentler climes and kinder days."

"It hasn't been all bad here," Taffy answered, rearranging her skirts so that new folds were turned out to the fire. The activity also kept her from staring too long at Malcolm's bared legs.

"No? I am glad tae hear it."

Her eyes flicked up and then back down. Her fidgeting was ridiculous, considering what had passed between them, but she was feeling shy and tongue-tied now that the time to sleep had come again.

"Come have a bite tae eat. Then we'll grab a bit

173

o' shut-eye. I doubt the Campbells will be out this morn. 'Twould be a hard task to follow even a bleatin' sheep through this godless storm."

Taffy eagerly accepted the haunch Malcolm pulled from the carcass and began eating with dainty greed. Malcolm pulled off a hank for his own consumption, but seeing the hound's plaintive eyes fixed on his face, tossed the bit of meat his way.

"Eat then, ye poor beast," he said to the grateful hound. "Living wi' that heartless woman cannae have been a life full wi' pleasure and mirth."

Malcolm took his knife and quartered the remainder of the rabbits, and the three of them set about a companionable but silent meal.

Taffy rose when she was done, murmuring an excuse to step outdoors alone. Malcolm stirred as though intending to accompany her, but a quelling look kept him seated by the fire.

"Take the hound with ye and keep a weathered eye out," he said instead, jerking his head at Smokey, who rose immediately to follow his new mistress out into the cold.

Taffy was relieved that the rain had finally ceased, but found the thick mist boiling up from the stream to be slightly disorienting. The sound of the water battering against stone guided her to the stream's edge where she was able to wash her hands and face in the punishingly cold spray. The liquid penance that was highland water left her face stinging, but she was slightly more alert.

"You keep watch," she told the dog, while slipping back into the privacy of a gorse bush to attend to her other needs. "I don't want to be surprised by Campbells or any wild creatures."

The dog sighed, but sat obediently at the side of the stream, scanning its lonesome banks with careful attention. Taffy, amazed at his comprehension and obedience, began to wonder how—if Malcolm didn't want him—she would manage to take this clever dog home with her. *When* she went home, which likely wouldn't be for a long while, she assured herself.

The two of them returned to the cave to find Malcolm waiting impatiently.

"You needn't have stayed up," Taffy told him.

"Aye, I did. Ye took our pallet wi' ye."

"Our pallet?" Taffy willed herself not to color.

"The floor is hard, lass. Ye'll be bruised an ye sleep on it wi' out a bit o' padding. Shuck yer skirts," he directed, picking up his plaid, testing it for dryness. He showed no concern for performing tasks while clad only in his long sark.

"Of course." Knowing that she was flushed crimson, Taffy nevertheless undid her skirts and arranged them on the floor. Never had she so regretted the loss of her shift or her disinclination to wear multiple petticoats.

Malcolm was quick to wrap his dried plaid

around her bared legs, but she sensed his amusement at her rediscovered modesty.

It was silly, of course. She realized that. But somehow this was different from what had happened back in the glen. That had been—well—an act of necessity. Anything further was—this was embarrassing. Wanton. Her outraged father would say *disgraceful*. If anyone heard of her behavior, she would be ruined both for marriage and for polite society—and that was simply for the sin of sharing a cave with Malcolm, not . . . not . . . What else they had done.

"Relax, lass," Malcolm told her gently. "We need the healing sleep. I'll not be ravishing ye again for a while yet."

With the ease of experience, he rolled them into the plaid and turned her so she faced the dwindling fire, her back fitted to his front as if they were spoons in a chest. His larger body blocked the worst of the draft creeping in from the mouth of the cavern.

"Ye're redder than a rose, Taffy lass."

"I hate blushing," she grumbled. "I wish I could stop."

Behind her, she felt Malcolm chuckle.

"Ye do give yerself away a mite. Still, a maiden's blush is a bonnie thing. I'd not be wishin' it away. Sleep now, lass. We've another long night ahead of us. Goodnight, *a leannain.*"

Goodnight, sweetheart. But those words didn't

necessarily mean anything, did they?

Goodnight, *a ghaoil*, she thought. Then, Taffy wondered in the last moments of wakefulness, if she had actually spoken the lover's endearment aloud.

She didn't stir until the sun was well over in the western sky and night was again settling its shadow over the land. The air carried with it a new scent, a blend of the wild flowers on the sunny stone machair, sea spume and the smell of burning pine trees. The wind was still aswirl with agitation in the topmost branches of the thick wood, but the hard rains of the previous night had ceased and the thick fog was gone.

There was another scent, too, this one particularly appealing in her half-conscious state. Looking down with sleepy eyes, Taffy could see that Malcolm's darker locks had mingled with her own and rested on her breast. Their limbs, too, were intertwined in a confusing tangle.

Malcolm's body was possessed of the male hardness that came with exercise, but the particular stretch of flesh pressed against her buttocks was not the result of hiking through the braes.

"Are you awake?" she whispered.

"Nay, that I am not. Are ye?" he whispered back.

"No."

"Well, good. This way neither of us need ever

ken what happens." Malcolm gently shifted her onto her back.

"We needn't?"

"Yer peekin', lass," he scolded gently when he saw her slitted gaze.

Taffy promptly closed her eyes.

The buttons of her blouse presented Malcolm with little challenge and soon the cool breath of evening air was mingling with the piper's own exhalations and touching of her naked breasts. She made a soft, surprised sound. Feeling the now familiar stain mount her cheeks, Taffy decided that no power on earth could force her eyelids open.

The sensation of Malcolm's legs shifting against her own made her poor heart lurch clumsily before stumbling to a gallop. The sight of his nudity would, she was certain, cause it to burst.

A hand molded over her left breast, cupping in the heat of a calloused palm. A hardened thumb rubbed lightly over the nipple. The taint of color traveled south, making the flushed flesh burn from within as well as from without. Taffy knotted her fists into their jean bed and pressed her lips together to prevent any unplanned words from escaping her lips. She was unprepared for the hunger that marched through her, leaving a wake of sensitized skin that longed for more of his touch.

"Such dreams we are having, Taffy lass," Malcolm commented softly.

Taffy shivered as his warm hand traveled slowly down her ribs and over the valley of her waist to settle at the flair of hips. A blunt fingertip brushed lightly at the junction of her thighs and then was withdrawn.

"It must be something most wicked tae have ye chittering so hard," he whispered. "Will ye no' speak of yer dreams that brought ye here, Taffy lass?"

Taffy shook her head in refusal. *Speak? Never! She couldn't.*

"I wonder what might unseal those lips and let them make their confession." A finger touched softly on the bow of mouth.

Taffy's muscles clenched painfully and she had to bite down on her lip to keep from answering.

"Stop that now!" Malcolm scolded. "Ye'll bruise that bonnie mouth and make it too sore for kissing."

She risked opening one eye long enough to see Malcolm's bewitching gaze glittering down at her, then hastily closed it again.

"Um . . . Malcolm?" she whispered, squirming involuntarily as the heat traveled down from her breast and flooded her loins.

"Hush." Soft as snow his lips brushed over her own. "Go back tae yer dreams, lass. Pay me no mind. 'Tis naught but a phantasm yer feeling

179

now. A wee bit o' the fever dream lingering in yer mind."

Taffy shuddered and let go of her death grip on her skirts. Her freed hands came to rest on the plane of his chest, which was still half covered by his shirt. Distracted by the feel of flesh beneath her hands, she allowed him to take the kiss where he willed.

He was contented at first with a feathery touch, but soon the kiss was turned to one gleeful plunder that stopped just short of cannibalism.

Deprived of sight, Taffy's other senses raced happily to their zenith, and at the fore was the hundred different touches that brushed at her skin: the rough wool, the smooth jean, the crisp hair on Malcolm's legs as they pressed against her own restless limbs. His skin at the open neck of his linen shirt was smooth as finest kid and warmer than sunshine on a summer's day.

Taste, too, was overwhelming, the mingling of breath and mouth with another. It was timeless oceans and soft peat smoke and the very essence of life that passed over her trembling lips.

Feeling a little bolder, Taffy allowed her hands to move around to Malcolm's broad back and then rove down to the smooth skin of his flank. Her sensitive finger pads discovered the mark of hard living that marred his lightly scarred flesh. Bullets, knives, accident, or deliberate malice? Something had marked him. Her hands followed the line of his vertebrae until the cloth of his back interfered, and then she allowed her fingers to be redirected around his hips to his lightly furred belly.

She hardly noticed when Malcolm's own hands stilled upon her torso, or when his breath was drawn in deep as a bellows and then failed to expel at the expected interval.

But Malcolm was aware. His head swam with dizziness. His frozen, unbreathing pose was broken only when she brought her right hand back around to the front of his body and began a sneaky catwalk past his rucked-up sark and down through the trail of curling hair to where his maleness assaulted her pale thighs. The exhalation that followed their meeting was a hurricane gust.

Taffy's eyes might have remained firmly shut but Malcolm's were wide open. He watched, somewhere between anticipation and agony, as Taffy's pale fingers finally settled against the end of his aroused flesh. Torn between a groan and a howl, he shifted his weight back far enough then that she might explore further, if it was her will to do so.

It was her will—but with a touch so light and tentative he thought he would go mad. Slowly, deliberately, and delicately, she pushed back the skin there. He felt himself tighten. Her fingers as they went lower cupped him for a moment in a

Melanie Jackson

gentle grasp, had his body pulling up tight.

"Cruel, teasing woman," he whispered, dragging his gaze up to the face of his tormenter. Her soft lips were curved in a dreamy half-smile. Her eyebrows, a softer, paler version of his own, were drawn slightly together in a passion of concentration.

Unable to endure any more teasing, Malcolm snared her hand and brought it to his lips to kiss. But another impulse overcame him and he found himself nipping gently at her smooth palm and biting at her fingers.

Recalling where he had been before Taffy's unexpected diversion, Malcolm dropped his head onto her breast and laved the tiny nipple, which was no larger than the smallest coin.

So bonnie! And they were just the beginning of her feminine bounty. She lay before him as the promise of Spring after the dark of February winter.

Her busy hands, deprived of the front of his body, had found their way into his hair where they were burrowing for purchase among his tangled locks with nervous, tell-tale flexes.

There was no resistance in her limbs when his hands went on to explore her. Taffy's legs shifted willingly at his stronger touch, allowing him to roam at will. It delighted him that she was already slick with desire, and he returned her earlier caresses with like gentleness.

Feeling a selfish cad, but knowing that a plateau had been reached and that he could delay no more, he shifted to his knees and pressed himself against her. He stroked his way inside, groaning happily at the smooth tightness that closed around him.

He rolled his hips against her in heavy surges, willing her to join him at the crest that was rapidly overtaking him. She was pure heat, pure sensation that blinded him to everything except their approaching ecstasy. She stopped his breath, consumed his thoughts.

And then she was gone from him. Physically she was there, but he could feel the moment when she retreated from the fire that burned between then.

"Taffy!" he pleaded, pulling back to look at her face. But her eyes were still closed, her head turned aside. He whispered: "Why do ye no' want me now? Wha' has happened tae ye?"

"I *do* want you," she answered, wrapping arms about him. She said desperately: "Don't leave."

Malcolm fought with himself, to find the will to retreat long enough to catch Taffy back up again and bring her with him to ecstasy. But the tide of his passion had him locked into an unalterable course. Frustrated, but plunging toward the inevitable end, he was washed away by waters of rapture which were deeper than he had known existed or suspected could exist. He poured himself into her and became one with that sea.

Taffy stirred reluctantly. Embarrassment and frustration were vying for her attention. She did not know what to say to Malcolm—how to explain what had happened. She had been caught up in the moment, following instincts, and then of a sudden there had been a feeling that someone was there with them, watching. The thought had recalled her to her senses and made her feel ashamed.

Taffy curled her fingers into Malcolm's hair and sighed wistfully. Physical awareness was returning to her as well, and the most intrusive of life's sensations was the hard stone of the cavern floor pressing into her back. The second bit of unpleasantness was the heavy scent of canine breath puffing over her flushed cheeks in friendly, but pungent pants.

"Oh, go away do!" she pleaded, causing Malcolm to stiffen and then rise above her. His eyebrows swooped upward in a comical manner and his lips twitched.

"Well, and a good evening tae ye, mistress. Ugh!" Malcolm turned his face in disgust as Smokey shared his eventide greeting. The hound had obviously been out hunting and found some carrion.

Smokey retreated with a disgruntled look and

plopped down by the cavern's entrance with a melodramatic blast from his lungs that expressed his opinion of their continuing laziness.

Unable to help herself, Taffy began to giggle. The more she did so, the more she became aware of Malcolm still resting inside her. This led to even more giggling until finally, tears were leaking from her eyes.

Malcolm watched her worriedly, even as his flesh responded to her muscles' soft contractions.

"I'm not over fond of yer laughter just now," he told her. "But I'm right craven about seeing ye in tears. Yer no' hurt are ye, lass?"

"No." Taffy made an effort to rein in her near hysteria. She said practically: "But this ground is awfully hard with you atop me."

"So it is," he said remorsefully, reluctantly pulling away from her and rolling to his feet. His long sark quickly returned him to a nearly modest state.

Taffy pulled the fullness of her skirts over her bare legs and glared at Smokey. It was easier than looking at Malcolm.

"This isn't my dream of true love," she told the panting dog. "At no time did I think to sleep on a stone floor and share my bed with a mangy mutt."

"It has no' been a usual reiteach," Malcolm agreed, either oblivious to her embarrassment, or kind enough to pretend to be. He reached

185

down and pulled her out of her protective nest. "We'll away tae the stream for a swim. That'll help yer back."

Smokey, who apparently knew himself to be very well bred, simply ignored her complaints.

"Will it?" Although it was impossible to imagine, more heat surged into her cheeks until Taffy felt as red as a radish. Her naked state and the feeling of dampness between her legs so overtook her mind that she didn't notice Malcolm's casual mention of the *reiteach*, the traditional Scottish festivities that preceded a wedding.

"Aye, it's nice and refreshing. *Cu*, make yerself useful and go down tae the stream and chase any bloody Campbells away. Yer breath alone should do the trick."

The comment brought Taffy unintentional alarm, momentarily pushing away embarrassment or thought to the discomfort of bathing in a frigid stream.

"Campbells?" She pulled on her skirts with new haste and reached for her stockings and boots.

"Aye. I fear they are nearby." Malcolm anchored his plaid securely and then pulled on his own brogues.

Taffy looked out the cavern's narrow door as she tightened her laces. Night had fallen, but there was an ugly orange glow far in the distance and the smell of burning had grown stronger. It was now an acrid stench that crept into even the nose and mouth and coated the membranes with ash.

As she looked into the night, she thought she saw a shadow of something moving low to the ground. She started to draw Malcolm's attention to it, but hesitated. Smokey was not making any alarm and she did want to appear overly timorous.

"And we're going for a swim out there?"

"Aye." Malcolm stooped and inserted his razor-sharp *sgian dubh* into his sock and then checked the dirk hanging at his side. The fact that he was dressing as though expecting to give battle or flee when they were supposed to be going for a swim was suggestive of the danger that surrounded them. "We've need o' it after yesterday's wallow through the mud. An I donnae want ye tae be so stiff ye cannae run if we have a need to."

"But if the Campbells are out ransacking the neighborhood shouldn't we try and help—"

"It mayn't be Campbells."

"But—"

" 'Tis either Campbells burning or being burned, and either way it'll bring more o' Dunstaffnage's men tae call—and soon. But we should have a few hours yet before they are near." He frowned at her disturbed expression. "There's nought we can do to aid the poor bug-

187

gers, lass, whomever they be. 'Tis war after all."

"Someone else might be burning the Campbells' homes?" she asked again, baffled and alarmed at the introduction of a new source of brutality. "Who could it be?"

Malcolm handed her the rifle and the gun belts.

"The MacColla's men, most likely. But it could be others, Gallowglas or covenanters. It matters naught for I'll no' be taking ye near them, love." And with that, Malcolm scooped up their packs and strode out into the night on his long, powerful legs. "Bestir yerself, Taffy lass, an ye want that bath."

"Is that it? Not even a kiss? Or a word of thanks before you walk away? Oh, you're welcome, Mister MacLeod," she muttered at his rapidly retreating back, refusing to admire the sway of his plaid. "Don't give your lover a moment's thought. I am ever so glad that you found the time to enjoy yourself with me this evening. Do come visit me again some time."

A throbbing of her loins was her only reply.

"What if I said that I love you—you exasperating, unromantic Scotsman? Would that give you pause?"

But she wouldn't say that. Not ever, she vowed, unless he opened that door himself. It was too much to hope for.

"Are ye coming? Hie ye, Taffy lass," Malcolm

called back softly. "This is no' time for feminine dawdling. Fuss wi' yer hair later."

For one moment, the urge to hurl something at him was overpowering. Unfortunately, she had nothing to throw except her rifle, and that was too extreme a sacrifice. She might need it later and couldn't chance bending it on the piper's hard head.

Chapter Eight

The silence about them was complete as in a church before mass and demanded contemplation of one's life course. Temporarily undisturbed by dangerous—or even lustful—distractions, Malcolm allowed his mind some time to consider his course of action.

First and foremost of the questions in his mind was what were the still-folk up to? Did they intend that he die after he had seen Taffy to *Casilean na Nor?* Was that why he continually sensed that the low road neared him, why he dreamt of endless darkness and the smell of ancient earth around him?

But why wait for their arrival? It made no sense! The still-folk could show her the way back to her home anytime. They had no need for him to escort her to their golden castle. Or anywhere.

Indeed, the delay of her return was a seemingly irrational act, for every day they left her here, the risk to her safety—and that of the bairn they so wanted—grew stronger.

As he and Taffy walked in wary silence through air so full with smoke that it made the bloated moon glow like harvest time, Malcolm considered the possibility that she had not yet conceived a child. But that was highly unlikely. They would not have been able to leave the glen's sheltering prison were the still ones not certain that she was with child.

A *bairn*. The notion was stunning. No child had he ever fathered. He had thought himself incapable, and had been just as glad that it was so. Or so he had told himself. But now?

His feelings had altered. He wondered what was this babe like? Was it a lad after himself, or a sweet bud like his golden lass? Was it healthy and contented?

He could know these things. If he wanted.

Aye, he could. If he wanted to know enough to use his new *sight*.

But did he want to accept this new gift? Knowledge could be a blessing, but as often was a curse.

Malcolm thought on it for a while. Reaching a decision, he took a deep breath and then cracked open the door inside his mind. He hesitated for a moment on the threshold, sensing that there would be some steep price for this knowledge. But curiosity was very strong, and his time upon earth was drawing to a close. He allowed himself a brief look inside.

Aye, there was a bairn! A female. She smiled at him with a happy, toothless grin and waved tiny, but already graceful arms.

He allowed himself one small smile in return and then quickly eased the door shut again, not wanting to see too much of what might be waiting there in the place of knowledge.

He took a deep breath and then released it slowly. There was no denying now that the sight had truly come to him just as his mother had predicted.

Malcolm looked back at Taffy, wondering what he should say to her about the daughter she carried, but was distracted from his purpose by the sight of her bathed in moonlight.

So bonnie was she!

There had been other lasses who had caught his eye and even his imagination, but never one who had stolen his heart. That part of him went with her now, and with their bairn, though Taffy did not know it.

He watched as her graceful walk covered the cluttered ground beneath them in total silence. She moved with the deceptive ease of the gifted MacLeods who came from the faerie line. Every day that passed brought her greater strength of mind and body, and beauty of face as more of her magical gifts awakened.

So, he was not the only one who had altered in recent days, grown more adept at finding his way by dark—at sensing and seeing invisible things. He felt pride in her bearing. She had done well with all the violence thrust upon her.

The only aspect of the alteration that disturbed him was the thought that it was not a voluntary change, but one forced upon her by grave circumstance.

Had she the choice, would she refuse these arcane gifts? And should he add to the burden she carried by sharing his foreknowledge about their child—and that he would likely be parted from her?

It would aid his decision if he knew better what was in her mind. What was his beautiful, silent companion thinking as she stared so hard at the rusty moon? Did she ken what had happened in the sacred glen? Was she embarrassed by the fact that the still-folk were aware of what she and Malcolm had done? Would it always bother her when she reflected on the circumstance of their first union?

Worse still, would she someday see their daughter as a bastard—as something unholy?

Nay! She could not.

Still, it gnawed at him that they were unable

to seek out a priest and have the Church's formal words spoken over them. His father's teachings meant little to him anymore, but they likely did to Taffy, and perhaps it would permit her to put aside her modesty and accept the rightness of sharing pleasure with him. And perhaps it would rid him of this lingering sensation of some task left undone if he undertook the ceremony before she departed. It might even afford her some protection in mind, if not in body.

Malcolm frowned, not caring for the trend of his thoughts.

Why would she need protection? He was there to see after her. He would protect her with his life; it was his purpose. And in her own time, she had a father to look after her. And surely the still-ones meant her no harm! He was starting at shadows.

Her own time. . . . That bore some thinking on.

What he would do once she was taken from him, he did not know. A few days before, he had been resigned to death, but now hope and life had been reawakened in his breast.

He had thought at one time to go to the colonies, but now? The thought brought no joy, even should his life be spared so that he might go there to his family.

If only there was a way he might go with her to see her world! How he would love to have a glimpse of her wheeled horse and visit the America that she described. And, of course, to have her with him always and watch their child grow! That was what he truly desired. The where and what-have-you didn't really matter, he said fiercely in the corner of his mind where he spoke to the still-folk. Surely there was some way that he could be with her forever. Someplace that they could live out their lives, even if it had to be among faerie kind.

But there, as it had been for many days, was only more unanswerable silence. He waited a moment longer in the shadowy place, but there was no reply. No sign of a new path. No reason for hope.

Very well, then. It was pointless to think on this chance—and crueler still to speak of it and put the thought into her mind. Every tale he had ever heard told of mortals who were returned to the world from a stay in faerie land had ended with them crumbling to dust when struck by the light of new day. Taffy came from the future; the passage of time in the past would not affect her. But for him? That was another matter. He had never dwelled within the *shians* and *tomhans* of faerie kind, but he had walked their ways, dined on their unsubstantial food, and played their be-spelling music upon his pipes. He even shared a small measure of their blood.

But he was not truly one of them, and their powers, longevity, and weather magic were denied him. Sometimes, even the simple understanding of their purpose was refused him.

Such was the case now. And on this occasion it angered him, for it was not simply his own life that was endangered and altered by their tricks. Again, he tried to apply reason to their actions, to guess their motives and foresee their actions.

He knew that the still-folk were much in the habit of stealing mortal women and babes for the pleasure of their own kind. Such thefts meant nothing to them. If aught pleased them from the world of men, they took it with little or no thought for the unhappiness they caused.

Perhaps they had sensed his longing for her apparition and since she was of his kind, they had carelessly fetched her to him as a gift. Perhaps any female would have suited their purpose as well and her being with him was all his own doing, he thought with a frown.

It would certainly seem to an observer that they cared nothing for her welfare. Had they not given her horrible visions of war and death, forced her to travel alone the low road, which often made men and women insane? And now they had left her—with a bairn—in a forest full of murderous men of every ilk.

And if they had done this, who would wonder at it? After all, what would one mortal woman's happiness, dreams, and ambitions mean to them? Her poor, short life would be lived and over in the space of one night in their kingdom.

Even if they observed her, they would not understand the value of the free gift of her grace to a rootless soul such as he. They did not appreciate that it was hope—cruel and beautiful—she gave with every smile when she welcomed him into her body, something she did willingly even though there was as of yet very little pleasure for her in the act.

Hope. Perhaps that was it.

But he did not understand their methods in this instance. The root of their many branched plan was still buried from his sight. But he had come in recent times to sense their habits and feelings. Whatever their final intent, they were certainly in some way taken with Taffy, and they shared his pleasure that she was with child.

Something about the woman—about their union—was of special importance to them. Given this as fact, then it followed that they would not risk her to the human battle waged about them without some good purpose.

"Come away, *cu*," he instructed softly, noticing that the hound was scenting some other, human trail. He abandoned his speculations to concentrate on the dangerous matters nearer at hand.

Forewarned by the canine's sensitive nose, Malcolm used more than routine caution as they slowed their pace at the crest of a small, bald-crowned hill and looked about carefully before beginning their descent into the wooded vale below.

Taffy did not need a warning to move deeper into the shadows and become as a ghost drifting over the ground. She, too, sensed something in the air.

Smoke from the fires begun earlier in the day still curled in ghostly billows out of the red embers and joined the pall in the sky. He could see no evidence of dead about and concluded that this had been a raid by the Irish mercenaries of Colkitto's Gallowglas. It was their character to destroy property, but not slaughter the women and babes of the crofters unless specifically ordered.

Just as they reached the foot of the hill, their hound began whining softly. It was not alarm, but curiosity that colored the beast's voice.

Malcolm hesitated for only an instant while he, too, scented the darkened air. Then, sensing no danger, he gave the Campbell beast a signal to move on.

"Smokey?" Taffy whispered, her voice softer than wind through grass. "What are you doing?"

The hound didn't answer. He was happily following his nose and loping off toward an unscorched stand of trees at the base of a hillock with thickly bush-clad slopes.

"Let us see what the beastie has found," Malcolm answered softly, turning to follow the hound. The ground, being uneven and full of loose scree, had to be taken at a slow pace and he was careful to remain close to Taffy in case she slipped.

Smokey had been trained not to howl, so he contented himself with doing a quivering dance beneath the tree where one of his favorite scents was emanating. It took his master and mistress a while to arrive, but he was patient because he knew that he couldn't fetch down the lovely ball of orange fluff that was lying about up in the branches taunting him.

"What is it, boy?" Taffy asked, peering up into the leafy bower.

"A cat," Malcolm answered. He didn't add that it might be a very particular kind of cat.

"Where—oh! I see him. Hello, puss. Would you like to come down?" Taffy asked politely, keeping her voice soft. "Hush, Smokey! You'll scare the kitty."

Unhappy, but compliant with the order, Smokey ceased whining.

The cat looked down at Taffy with unblinking eyes. He was a pleasant beast, large, cheerful of face and, excepting only his darker orange color, resembled nothing so much as a shaggy dandelion growing out of the tree's wide-spreading limbs.

" 'Tis fortunate that this moggie is not black, for they would have burned him for a demon an

199

they had to set the entire hill afire tae kill him." Malcolm spoke to her, but was staring pointedly at the lofty feline. There was no humor in his voice, no twinkle in his eye to suggest that he jested about the animal's fate.

"A demon!" Taffy looked at the cat again.

It grinned at her, amusement showing plainly in its gray, nearly human eyes. Its ears were exaggerated in length, she saw. Rather like a lynx, in fact.

"Well, I'll admit that cats can seem rather canny at times, but it's ridiculous to suppose that they are anything but animals."

The moggie yawned at her comment and examined his paw, alternately ejecting and then retracting his black claws. The sight of those dark talons gave her another moment's pause. She had never seen such weapons on any animal. They looked like hooked obsidian knives.

"Malcolm? I don't believe in demons, of course, but there is something very odd about this cat."

"Aye. He is a messenger. Well, puss, what wish yer folk wi' us?"

As an answer, the cat sat up and began clawing at something in the fork of the tree. Two small silver objects tumbled to the weedy ground below him. One fell more heavily than the other and gave a low but musical ring when it struck a stone.

"My knuckles!" Taffy exclaimed, picking up the knuckle-duster, which had been missing when her clothes disappeared. She stared in amazement at the carvings that had been added to the silver. She was sure they had some meaning that she would be able to discover if she just studied them long enough. They were runes or letters, or some sort of powerful symbol. It was hard to make out, for the lines seemed to shimmer and shift when she stared at them.

Malcolm retrieved the other offering, and was pleased to discover that it was his lyart reed. It was entirely possible that his pipes had been pierced with arrows or even burned by an enraged Lady Dunstaffnage, but his precious reed had been saved. That it had been returned to him was a sign of continuing grace.

Smokey whined sharply, alerting them even before they heard the slight rustling overhead, that the cat was departing. Though they peered closely, no sign of the feline was to be had anywhere in the leafy branches that shivered overhead. There came a tiny shower of silvery sparks and then there was only calm.

"He's gone. Just disappeared," Taffy marveled.

"Aye. 'Tis their way."

Dejected at being deprived of his toy, Smokey wandered off to nose a stand of gorse.

"What is that you have there?" Taffy asked, looking away from the empty bower and noticing the reverence with which Malcolm handled a sliver of moon-bright silver.

" 'Tis my reed," he answered cheerfully, opening his sporran and dropping the needle inside the pouch. "It means I shall play the pipes again. And what is that bit o' fancy mongery there?"

"These are brass knuckles. They're for fighting," she said, slipping them over her fingers in demonstration. She mimed a blow at Malcolm's chin.

His elevated brows arched higher.

"Ye'll break ye hand hitting out like that. Donnae be bending yer wrists so. And, Taffy lass, ye need tae be learning yer metals. This isnae brass. 'Tis very pure silver."

"Well, no. These knuckles are sterling silver, but most are brass or lead. But look! Something has been added. These symbols here. They look like writing. Do you know what they mean?"

Malcolm leaned closer and then laughed softly.

"Aye. They mean *trickery*. I think the still-folk approve of yer weapon."

"This is faerie writing?" she asked, awed. "They actually write things down?"

"Aye, nobody has a flawless memory and they do live a long while. Now come, we'd best away whilst we have the dark and solitude tae travel in. These burned out Campbells will be back soon enough, and have the black-bitch's men wi' them."

"Malcolm, will we ever see the faeries, do you think?" she asked, carefully stowing her decorated weapon deep in her pocket.

"I pray not."

"Why?" she demanded, rather startled at his vehemence. "Aren't they fair and handsome? And they've been friends to us, haven't they?"

"Well, lass, they have been friends after their own fashion."

"But . . . Malcolm, I don't understand. What do you mean? Are they not like in the stories? Beautiful and slender and tall?"

"Aye, that they are. Just like the stories as tae their appearance. Only they are not fair like Sassenach folk. They are tall, and dark, and favor green clothing. They have pointed ears, too," he said, tapping the side of his head before taking her hand to lead her away from the copsewood. "But the still-folk who dwell in this part of the hielands are something o' a mixed blessing tae us just now. They've kept us safe from the Campbells and offered us their own food—all that ye might have the *sight*."

"The *sight*? Like visions?"

"Nay. Eyes! The ability tae find their paths through the woods in the darkness." Malcolm waved his hand overhead, reminding Taffy that they were conversing beneath a night sky.

203

"*But?* That isn't bad though. I needed to be able to see. So what else have they done that makes you uneasy? There's something more, isn't there? Something that has troubled you since we left the cave. I wish that you would speak plainly about it, for I can sense you fretting, more and more with every hour that passes." She laid a soft hand upon his arm.

Such powerful persuasion she carried in one small hand. Malcolm studied her calm but determined face for a moment and then nodded.

"I'll tell ye then, for mayhap it is better that ye know. I donnae understand all their thinking, but the still ones didnae help us get away from the Campbells out o' Christian charity. They never die, lass. Remember always that they have no reason to love mortals. Of a rare occasion they may be taken wi' one of our kind, but man has been their enemy since first we met, and the first spear of iron spilled faerie blood."

"I see." Taffy looked down at her boots, contemplating them for a moment before reluctantly asking: "Then they might betray us later on?"

"Nay!" Malcolm sighed and looked up at the sky, the moon had passed its zenith and was setting. He tried to find a way to explain the nebulous doubts that troubled his mind. "I believe that our circumstance is something like this old tale of the midwife."

"A parable?"

He nodded.

"Aye, a parable. Once, there was a midwife fetched tae aid in the birth o' a fairy lady at the hinder end o' the harvest time. It was the *oidhche shamhna*—All Hallow's Eve—a time o' great magic. She saved the mother and bairn a deal o' pain and as it was a night of special power, she was offered a reward by the grateful husband. Kenning that they were of the still-folk of *Tomhn-afurach*, she shrewdly asked that her gift be the ability tae always bring babes live intae the world, and that the gift pass tae her children when she was gone."

"That seems a fairly selfless ambition. Can the faeries really do that?" Taffy asked, her voice half hopeful and half afraid.

"Aye, they could on the *oidhche shamhna*. But they didnae wish tae grant this tae the woman, so they did a humbuggit. The woman thought tae one day have a daughter tae be a midwife. But though she had only sisters, and the sisters had only female babes, yet she herself had only sons. And as they didnae become midwives she was eventually in despair o' having wasted a wish."

"And it was the faeries' fault that she had no daughter? They did this so that they wouldn't have to keep their word to the woman?" Taffy demanded, with a growing mixture of unease and disapproval.

"Aye, they spelled her that she would have no

Melanie Jackson

daughters tae become midwives, for they wanted no more people born near *Tomhnafurach*. But they didnae fail tae keep their word." Malcolm half-smiled, his tone laced with irony. "The sons always birthed living sheep and cattle."

"Well, I—" Taffy froze in place, suddenly aware that something was missing.

"Malcolm, where is my camera?"

They looked about swiftly on the shadowed ground, under the shrubs and even up in the trees, but Taffy's camera and tripod were nowhere to be found. The only thing they discovered was Smokey, who had fallen into a deep, unnatural sleep and was hard to rouse from it.

"Oh, Malcolm!" she cried, truly distressed at the loss of her camera and Smokey's groggy state. "They'll bring it back, won't they? They are just curious about it? Wake up, boy, come on now. There's a good dog! They didn't hurt you, did they?"

"Sure they will, lass. They brought back everything else. No doubt they were, as ye say, curious. Or perhaps wished tae decorate it for ye."

Malcolm kneeled down by the sleeping hound and laid a hand over his eyes. Muttering something under his breath, he pulled his hand up sharply. Smokey blinked once and then scrambled to his feet growling.

Taffy stared, too tired to be amazed.

"But, Malcolm, I meant to take photographs . . ." she trailed off, realizing that though she had had every opportunity, she had not thought once to use her camera. Why was that? Was she so distracted by what was happening to them that she had simply forgotten?

Or was this more faerie glamourie being practiced on a human because they did not want her, for some reason, to have a record of her time with Malcolm.

"Give me that pack," she instructed urgently, pulling the sack away from Malcolm and searching for her precious photograph of Duntrune.

The thin boards were easily found at the side of the pack, but not trusting that evidence alone, she opened them up to be certain the plate remained within.

It brought her immediate relief to see that Malcolm's ghostly image was still there and untouched by any added faerie art.

"Thank heavens!" Taffy closed the boards back up and returned them to the pack. "I thought that they might have taken this away, too."

Malcolm shook his head and reslung the pack.

"Ye worry o'er strange things, lass," he said, but his smile was kind. "Have ye not the very flesh o' me right tae hand?"

"Yes." It took an effort, but she returned his smile.

"Are ye prepared then tae depart?"

"Yes. I'm sorry about the delay. I just—well, it's the only picture I have of you. Perhaps the only one I shall ever have."

Her soft words penetrated Malcolm's amusement.

"Aye, so it is." It would be something for Taffy to show the bairn. Without thinking, he broke his own rule of silence about their uncertain future by adding: "I wish that I had such an image of ye tae keep."

"We'll make one," Taffy promised. "I think I can find everything I need to develop the plate here. Thank heavens I have an older, simpler kind of camera! Well, *had* an older camera."

Seeing her renewed frown, Malcolm answered lightly: "We'll speak o' the matter to the next moggie we see. Ye'll have your picture box back soon, Taffy lass. Meanwhile, we'd best be off."

Even as he finished speaking, a shadow passed over the land followed by a sudden chill. Looking into the sky, they could see a bank of dark clouds riding low beneath the yellow moon. In its train there came a sighing wind, which played some unpleasant auditory tricks with tree tops above them.

Taffy was beginning to recognize what elements made up an unnatural storm.

"I suppose this is a hint that we should be leaving," Taffy said, feeling more than a little annoyed at the further evidence of manipulation of their world by the unseen still-folk.

"The Campbells are coming," Malcolm answered, taking her arm and urging her to speed. "The rain will hide our scent from the hounds, but we must find shelter afore the first light."

Taffy looked up at the densely wooded slope they were climbing and found a dark thicket set with boulders that looked strikingly familiar.

"Another cave?" she asked with a sigh.

"Aye. I'm sorry, lass. There would have been a soft bed for ye this morn, but the damned Campbells have other plans for our day it seems."

But the cave, when they reached it, was found to be rather different from their previous lodging. It was not actually a cave at all, but proved to be the start of a long tunnel running due south, like an arrow pointing the way to Kilmartin.

The passage was narrow and somehow unpleasant, and Taffy hesitated outside the opening. It reminded her of the barrow where she had first encountered the faerie door and she knew it to be uncanny.

In the distance, she heard a mournful howling. Normally, such an alarming noise would have spurred her into the shadowy recesses without a thought, but Malcolm's rigid posture and Smokey's sudden whining made her assess the relative dangers with great care.

Lightning sheeted out of the sky, hitting

nearby boulders with a blow that shook the very stone beneath their feet. The acrid stink of burnt rock filled their nostrils.

"Damn yer twisty minds," she thought she heard Malcolm mutter as the thunder rolled over them.

He ducked inside and began forging through the blackness. With only an instant's delay, Taffy followed. Smokey continued to whine, but a second sheet of fire at the mouth of the cave, followed by a watery torrent violent enough to have been conceived at sea, convinced him to enter the tunnel, too.

None of them saw the enormous tusked boar that charged into the wood they had just vacated, but Smokey sensed him, and the beast's scent set him to growling.

A nameless foreboding grew in Taffy's breast as they went deeper and then still deeper into the mountain. This tunnel definitely reminded her of the barrow she had entered in order to reach Malcolm. There was that same feeling of blankness, a lack of earthly time and space. Smokey's continuing low growls from the blackness behind her did nothing to lighten her mood.

Ahead of her, came Malcolm's voice. "Lass, watch yer step now. There is a stair."

Taffy wasn't sorry to have Smokey's familiar head pushed beneath her chilly hand. The gloom about them was nearly complete, even for her new vision, and she was barely able to make out the steep, narrow treads of the stair hewn into the gray rock.

Whose feet, she wondered, had these steps been designed for? Why had anyone burrowed downward into the heart of the stone hillock?

"Nearly there, lass," Malcolm said comfortingly. "I see light ahead."

So did Taffy. *Daylight*. Full eastern sun.

"How can this be?" she whispered, the hair furring on her arms at this further display of magic.

Malcolm did not answer, but she sensed his perturbation as they left the tunnel behind.

It was very different on the other side of the hill. They stepped out into a fall day, crisp and sunny. They were surrounded by heather, but the blossoms had long since pulled in upon themselves and rained their faded cast-off petals upon the ground.

A tiny stream gushed from a gash in the rock face, its waters a pure, icy blue that sparkled in the morning sun. A few colorful seedheads, the remains of some summer wildflower, nodded cheerfully as stray waterdrops splashed over them. Tufts of gold lichen and green moss decorated the nearby stones and there was a patch of emerald grass where they might rest in comfort.

It was all very beautiful and peaceful, but Taffy

211

found herself shivering, her previously bound-less strength drained in an instant.

Immediately, Malcolm's arms were around her, holding her close until the worst of the chill left her quaking body. She knew from the faded sounds of his breathing that he had turned his head to the north, watching, waiting, listening for sounds of pursuit or any other danger.

"It was night," she whispered into his sark. "And it was raining."

"Aye, love, it was," he answered soothingly, looking down at last and laying a cheek against her wayward hair. "And it was a nasty shock for the still-folk tae send us. But bear up a wee bit longer, lass. 'Tis time tae eat and then we shall rest for a spell. Ye'll feel more yerself after sleeping."

"Shall I? Truly? Or will they just make me believe that this is so? Because the still-folk could do that, couldn't they?"

Malcolm was slow to answer.

"I cannae say."

"We should be at Kilmartin by now." She still spoke into the folds of his shirt, preferring the warmth of his body to that of the autumn sun, which seemed unnatural to her. She had grown accustomed to the night's gentler light. "Do you know where we are? Now. Here."

"Aye. We've not gone astray."

"Except in time." She sensed that much. Taffy

took a slow breath and strove for calm. After a moment, she asked: "Are we going to Kilmartin?"

"Somewhere near there." A warm hand caressed her back, trying to soothe her.

"It's just that nothing looks familiar to me," she excused herself, some of the dizziness at last leaving her. "Most of the trees are gone. In my time."

"Are they now?" His breath stirred her hair. As her disorientation left, Taffy's senses awakened to the pleasurable sensations that came from being held close to Malcolm's harder, larger body.

"I hate feeling lost and confused," she explained.

"Nobody cares tae be lost." Malcolm stirred reluctantly. "Let us see what the still-ones hae brought us tae dine on. Fish, coney, fatted calf? That would be fitting."

"It doesn't matter, does it?" Taffy pulled away but looked into his eyes. Her pale cheeks bore new lines of weariness, but her gaze was unflinching and a strong pulse beat in the side of her neck telling of a strong heart. She said clearly and calmly: "It doesn't matter because it is all the same. It isn't real food, and this isn't a real place."

"No, it's real enough," Malcolm answered. "It just isnae the food or abode o' men."

"What would happen if I ate that heather?" she asked, pointing at the gray-green shrub.

"Ye'd get a mouth full o' slivers," he said, beginning to smile.

"And if I drank the whisky in my flask, what would happen then?"

"Let's find out, lass." Malcolm's eyes were twinkling as he set their packs upon the ground and took the rifle from her. "Ye've earned a small nip."

"All right. I will drink it, too, because it's real." Taffy shrugged out of her gunbelts. "And then—"

"And then we eat."

Taffy shrugged impatiently.

"If we must, but after that—"

"We sleep."

"No," she contradicted. "After we eat, I am going to teach you how to use this rifle."

"Are ye?" He sounded doubtful.

"Yes, I am. And how to load it and clean it, too. And you are going to show me how to hit someone. As a man would," she said with determination.

Mobile eyebrows flew up at the command. But his answer was a meek: "Aye, lass."

"I don't like being taken advantage of, Malcolm. It makes me very angry. I am not some simple-minded child to be led about by the hand because someone thinks that this is the proper course for me."

"Nay, lass." His voice was even meeker. "I'm right sorry about that. I ken not wha' came o'er me taking advantage of ye that way."

"Don't be a—a dunce!" she scolded, stepping out of his arms. The small separation caused her body to protest. It had quickly developed a liking for its place by his side. "I didn't mean you. And anyway, you are only taking advantage of me because I let you."

"Is that the way of it? And here I thought ye too shy and modest tae speak o' such a thing."

"Modesty is not stupidity or cowardice. We are lovers because I wish it," she insisted.

Malcolm chuckled, enjoying the small flash of temper, which suggested that Taffy was regaining her spirits. Walking through a faerie door had been most disconcerting even for him. Many folks lost their senses along the way and never recovered them. They spent the rest of their lives in some mad twilight of ghosts and unreason. This brave lass had taken the faerie path twice and come out whole in mind and body.

"Ye've relieved my mind, mistress, that I'm tae be spared responsibility for yer bedding. I feared ye'd be draggin' me afore a priest and having the words read o'er us afore the day was through."

"Whyever for? A priest wouldn't be of the slightest use. He'd just say that we were damned or something equally idiotic."

The answer startled Malcolm into sobriety.

"And this is no bother tae ye? Truly?" he asked, slightly appalled.

"It doesn't matter if it is." Her voice was firm.

"But it could perhaps be put aright, an ye wished it tae be."

Taffy stared in consternation.

"How could *this* be put right?"

"We could be married," he pointed out. "It was my intent all along."

"Oh." Taffy flushed crimson and then shut her eyes. "I didn't realize . . ."

Malcolm studied her cheeks with interest.

"Ye were no' thinkin' about marriage then . . . Well." He tilted his head. "Then ye were thinkin' on being born a MacLeod and having the faerie blood inside ye. And this belief that we are damned for having relations wi' the faeries holds no terrors for ye?"

"Of course not." Taffy opened her eyes and glared at Malcolm.

"Why no fear of this?" he asked, truly puzzled and more than a little amazed. "Dae yer kirks no longer preach of Hell?"

"I have no fear because it's absolute codswallop," she told him, shocking Malcolm for a second time. Before he could think what to say, she was stepping around their packs and over to the small waterfall tumbling out of the hillock's bald face. "And we are not damned for being lovers. This was no sin of our making. In fact, I do not think it is a sin at all."

"*No sin?*" he repeated.

She tested the water with an imperious finger. It felt pleasant on her prickling skin. Not as pleasant as Malcolm's hands, but she wished to cleanse herself in the purifying waters before . . .

"It's warm and I am going to bathe." She turned and looked Malcolm directly in the eye. She took a breath and then smiled and asked boldly: "Would you care to join me in a bath?"

The sudden smile she sent him could be felt all the way down to his heart, and, in point of fact, even lower as the stirring beneath his plaid proved.

"Aye, I would." Bemused, he reached for his brooch and began to unwind his plaid. "Yer daft, Taffy lass, tae be sae fearless of the kirks' preachings, but it doesnae detract from yer charm."

"I fear that you are correct—about the daft part. But I wish you to know something," she added, looking down as she unbuttoned her blouse with slightly clumsy fingers. "It didn't occur to me to think of marriage in conjunction with our talk of a priest because I'm not Catholic. I was raised in the Protestant faith, you see."

She cleared her throat and peeped up at him, wondering how the news was being received. Encouraged by his fascinated expression, she went on: "I wouldn't mind getting married, Malcolm— in fact, I would like that very much—but I suspect that the Protestant ministers around here are just as superstitious and *unchristian* as the

Catholic ones. I don't think that we dare approach them. We shall have to settle for being lovers and know that we are married in our hearts."

The last sentence claimed her final reserves of boldness, and she demurely turned her back on her lover as she peeled off her smoke-grimed blouse.

After all, though she was not a child, and not regretful of what they had done—and would do again—it was still high noon and they weren't even undressing in the modest shadows of a cave or shady, tree-lined bower.

Chapter Nine

"Taffy lass." A flask appeared over her bare shoulder, which was sporting fine crop of goose-bumps. "This will keep out the cold."

"Thank you." Her voice was sincere. It wasn't cold that had her shivering, but the remedy would work for what ailed her. Taffy had screwed up her courage, prepared—as many women had no doubt been before her—to give her all for love. But a little liquid courage suddenly seemed like a sound notion. The suspicion that the role of forceful temptress was not going to be a natural one was rather strong in her mind, and some outside aid would probably not come amiss during this debut as a siren.

Of course, the situation was an unusual one.

Had she ever imagined taking a lover, a notion which had not previously presented itself as a realistic one, it would not have been in these less than romantic circumstances.

Instead of playing the idyllic roles of Marlowe's *"passionate shepherd to his love,"* where two well-dressed lovers lounged about sipping from the milk of paradise, it seemed to Taffy that she and Malcolm were more likely to end as *Tristam and Isolde.*

And she didn't want to be Isolde, she thought resentfully as she screwed the cap back on the flask and set it on a conveniently placed stone table. She began to change out of her dusty skirts.

It galled her to admit it, but her father was right about the level of unattractiveness of this mode of dress; the fabric was an absolute insult to all romantic thought. She sighed quietly as she put the skirt aside, wishing for just one silk chemise.

Malcolm made an excellent Tristam though, she had to admit. But she had never had much taste for the great Wagnerian tragedies. Not even in the original Gaelic. They had too rigid a code for their lovers' immorality. The hero and heroine always perished in some horrible manner— *You have drunk your death!* Wasn't that what Isolde's nurse said to the lovers?

Taffy sneaked a quick peek at Malcolm's gorgeous, tanned legs as he pulled off his brogues, and then seeing the plaid puddled on the ground behind them, she turned and reached for the flask, taking another swallow of burning Scotch.

Yes, those were definitely epic legs on that man, she thought hazily. Legs like that could run forever, climb the steepest mountains. And his chest! That was more than epic. It seemed nearly invulnerable, something to decorate a Viking's shield, or the prow of a ship. It provided her with inspiration.

And it was all hers for the taking, said something inside of her—if she could just muster the nerve to appropriate the moment. To be bold and lead the way. She needed to go to him.

Could she truly do that? Throw all feminine modesty aside and come to Malcolm as a full participator in love—a consort like—like—Cleopatra?

Or someone like Cleopatra who didn't die. At the moment, Taffy couldn't think of a single bold heroine who hadn't perished in the end . . . but there had to be some bold woman somewhere who survived.

Taffy stared into the distance and strove for the audacity to be that heroine.

The wicked voice urged her to do what she secretly wanted. To take charge and not be a pawn—to make love to Malcolm because she wanted to, not because she had convinced herself it was a necessity. And she was listening because she couldn't help but feel, though there was no proof, that if she completely possessed his body, she would finally possess his heart, too. Because she believed that by actively giving, she made herself worthy of receiving.

But there was a part of her that was still fearful. The notion of Malcolm's powerful body being at her call wasn't much consolation when facing the realization that if she was to return home, he would be parted from her forever more—dead and buried in some unknown grave long before she was even born.

Better not to think about such things, the wicked voice said. *Live in the moment. It is all that you can ever with certainty possess. It could as well be you, not Malcolm, lying dead on the morrow.*

Taffy took a last hefty pull on her flask and then bent to remove her boots. It was tiring and confusing to have her brain pulled in two opposite directions, to constantly hold two contradictory thoughts—and that only when she wasn't being harried and had time to think.

Naturally, she couldn't explain her war of emotions to Malcolm. Everything she felt was either depressing or depraved. She was better off not thinking of the future at all, at least for the moment, for she found that she was in another kind of mood altogether. A romantic one.

Actually, she was excited and frustrated, and all but crawling out of her tingling skin. She felt this way every time they brushed up against these faerie lands. It was as though their magic touched some chord inside of her body that started it resonating. The inner vibrations at first exhausted her and then made her feel reckless and irresponsible—free of moral constraint.

Or perhaps it was just intense hunger or a heat rash plaguing her, making her feel flushed and . . . whatever she was feeling. No matter what the case, Malcolm—she was certain—was the antidote to her woes. He was release, freedom—and most importantly, peace.

"Bloody laces," she muttered plaintively, sorting through the knots that held her boots together. "Cleopatra didn't get knots in her sandals. She didn't have to run away from Campbells through mud and thunderstorms and mess her hair up."

It was not helpful that her first attempt at leading a seduction would be somewhat overshadowed by war. Battle and its aftermath was not at all what she had been led to believe by the great poets. It wasn't glorious. It was wasteful and sad—and ugly beyond all measure she had ever applied to life.

But in this place, it was easy to forget the destruction they'd witnessed. Taffy paused in her tugging long enough to look around. The land-

scape that met her eyes was a study of artistic
hues, lavenders and greens against a perfect blue
sky. No trace of war or death ruined the scene.

And her wicked voice was right about one
thing. Now was all the time they had. Regardless
of other unfortunate circumstances, and the not
quite real feeling of this outdoor corrie, she was
certain that she wanted do this one wild, licentious thing.

Yes, she was certain. For Malcolm was the
most—well, gorgeous—man she had ever seen.
He would be her only lover. He deserved a
woman who was courageous and strong. She had
faced ghosts, living nightmares, and Campbells;
she could be brave about this. She could seize
the moment offered and bend it to her will. She
would no longer close her eyes against her lover.
All her life she had followed; it was time to be
audacious and lead.

Taffy reached again for the flask, deciding that
one more nip would restore her to a happy equi-
librium. She would be like the swaying wild
grass; she would bend her morals without
actually breaking her sense of integrity. Of
course, society would say that she had sinned
with Malcolm. And her father—

Suddenly, Malcolm was kneeling before her,
assisting her with her knotted laces, which would
not come undone. Golden sunlight glinted on his
powerful shoulders. All thoughts of her father

and society's displeasure left her mind, displaced by Malcolm's presence.

"Ye've badly tangled yer laces, lass. Let me sort them out."

"Thank you," she enunciated clearly, finding the *th* rather hard to produce with lips that had gone numb. She recapped the flask without drinking. "They seemed to be caught in a Gordian knot."

"I'll have ye free without cutting through them," Malcolm said as he looked up at her and then laughed. He pulled her boots off and tossed them aside. "Ye nearly look an Amazon, lass. All ye need is a bow and arrow."

Taffy forgot her own nearly naked state and stared in appreciation at the rare and adorable crinkles at the corners of his beautiful eyes. How she loved seeing him smile.

Malcolm stood in a dizzying rush, one instant at her feet, the next towering over her.

"Come, Taffy lass." He stepped backward toward the waterfall, and since he had taken a firm hold of her wrist, Taffy went, too.

"You don't mind that I'm not a Catholic, do you?" she asked. "I mean, you're not hide-bound about our religious differences," she blurted, tackling one of the few barriers that might remain between them.

Taffy made her eyes stay on Malcolm's face. Raging curiosity was no excuse for staring

225

rudely. To lower her eyes would be to commit the last act of immodesty. She stubbornly refused to give in to the impulse.

"Nay, Taffy lass. I am no' so set in my ways." The voice was faintly amused, though she could not imagine why. "Have a care, sweet. The ground is uneven and I fear that ye are a bit the worse for the drink."

Taffy walked slowly because the whisky was swishing around in her head and she didn't want to make any unladylike staggers.

"I am not inebriated," she told him, speaking very carefully, as the *uisge beatha* had drastically thickened her tongue. Perhaps it was the lingering faerie magic, but those few sips seemed to have affected her like pints. "I am simply tired from walking all night."

All the while that she was speaking, Malcolm was watching her with his alert, gray eyes. Eyes that were very like the ones on the cat they'd seen in the woods. Eyes that were inhumanly beautiful and wise.

"A good rinse in the cool water will make ye feel more awake. More lively. I shouldnae have given you the flask. I'd forgotten that such things will affect ye more now." Malcolm's other arm reached around her, his hard hands hot on her bare skin.

Yes, she thought, this was the anodyne she sought.

Cold water splashed playfully at her toes. Taffy paused.

She was naked but for the covering of her hair. With a man. Standing in the middle of a rock corrie where anyone might see her, including curious still-folk.

Suddenly, the notion of communal bathing seemed unbearably forward and wanton. All she wanted to do was hide—either in the bushes or in Malcolm's arms. She suppressed a groan at her cowardice and concentrated on the small cleft in Malcolm's chin.

"Am I so very fearful then? That ye needs must drink some courage afore inviting me tae yer bed?"

"I haven't invited you to bed. I've invited you to bathe," she answered, pleased with her ability to reason. She stepped to one side, half-turning from him and scanning the acreage about them. "And I invited you to join me before I tasted the whisky."

"So ye did. Then obviously ye have no fears." Malcolm glanced at the cascading water and then stepped completely into the stream.

Taffy's eyes slipped briefly downward as he disappeared under the falls and she caught a brief flash of tanned leg and *other things* before she hastily diverted her eyes.

"This is insane! I can't do this. Anyone could be watching us." She turned completely away, but before she could escape back to her clothing, Malcolm had her caught. A quick tug and she was pulled under the waterfall's cool rain.

"Malcolm!" she gasped, trying to elude the deluge that was sopping her hair with an ice bath that was suddenly much colder than it had seemed on her hand.

"I am sorry aboot the cold water, but I wish for ye tae be somewhat alert for what comes next," he said, subduing her thrashing arms.

Malcolm turned his suddenly shy temptress about and took a look into her eyes. Taffy was shocked and dazed—and a wee bit the worse for dipping so deep in the whisky—but not fearful or deeply ashamed.

"Go on now. Ye were doing fine. I'm willing tae be ravished," he teased, surprising himself with such brash words. "Even if ye are no' Catholic, and a Sassenach tae boot."

Taffy spluttered, but she had stopped twitching and her eyes began to gleam.

"Oh, *are* you? How noble of you to sacrifice yourself to the enemy."

"That I am. But yer no enemy of mine, lass."

Pleased that she didn't shy away, he gently captured her hands and slowly dragged them down the length of his body. Her fingers kneaded him slightly, nipping with gentle claws until they reached his manhood.

Strange, new emotions were raging through

him, making him surge hotly under her warm, delicate hands. The pace of his heart doubled and redoubled while all around him, the moment expanded until time itself all but stilled.

"Are ye awake now, lass? Mindful of what yer doing?" he asked softly, before pulling her close and allowing himself a taste of her lips. Every time he touched her, she grew more attractive to him. More necessary for his happiness—perhaps even for life.

Taffy resisted, for the slightest of moments, trying still to free her arms, but then relaxed against him. Her mouth softened under his. Her lips parted.

Distracted, Malcolm loosened his hold. Her soft arms slid around his neck, pulling herself closer and mating their bodies mouth to knees.

He caught a brief glimpse of something moving in her eyes before her lids closed over them. Malcolm went into shock as he felt her tongue touch his lips and then invade his mouth in the brashest possible manner. Passion poured into the kiss with the force of oceans at the turning tide.

Every part of his body went rigid.

Taffy bit lightly at his lower lip and he realized that in that instant the situation had turned about. His shy lass was playing with *him!* Ravishing him, as he had teasingly suggested. He shuddered with unanticipated pleasure, pulling her in tight.

He wanted to demand of his modest lover where she had found the audacity to kiss in this manner. The kirk had always preached against such displays, and the women he had known had been affected by that. But Taffy was acting . . . He couldn't think of a word that meant both *indecent* and *arousing*.

Whatever his previous teachings believed or approved of, his body loved what she did. Excitement at her bold invitation fired through him. Her fearless kiss made his senses blaze. Her hands felt like live coals laid up on the tinder of his body. The firestorm it ignited within him was a shocking contrast to the cool stream of water washing down his back.

His body ignored the water, reacting instead to Taffy's touch. His sex thickened, heated, grew stronger. As had happened the day that Taffy rescued him from the Campbells, he could feel some wild part of himself slip free of his stern control and come surging to the fore, where he had to wrestle with the impurest of impulses.

And the impure impulses were winning. He could not stop them.

As quickly as possible, he moved her from the slippery wet rocks. Malcolm managed to stagger perhaps an arm's length away from the falls. He would contemplate later what there was about this woman that was so arousing to this inner beast in him, what it was that his lust could gain the strength to throw off his hard-learned voice of reason.

"Taffy, lass?" he heard himself growl, his fingers tangling in her dripping hair, turning her face up to his.

She answered with a small moan that was both question and agreement.

"Ye shouldna be shy with me *ever*. We were meant tae be as one." Even as he said it, Malcolm knew that the reassuring words were superfluous. Taffy was not acting like a woman who was overcome with modesty. She seemed to sense the same hand of destiny that was now upon him and her own inner beast was awake and on the prowl.

He leaned back against the dry rock's rough face and pulled her to him, melding her softer flesh into his own. The contact only inflamed the lustful beast and made it want more.

Taffy didn't notice. All her previous worry about witnesses had been driven from her mind. Her sole ambition was to assuage the hunger prowling through her body, tightening her skin, weakening her knees, burning her alive. It was stunning—wonderful—to let all restraints slip and do what one wanted. She could not envision turning away from this world of feelings and sensations. She couldn't imagine why she had shut her eyes against it before.

"I'm not feeling at all shy," she assured him in return, as her hands traced up his flank and over his shoulder blades until they encountered the hot stone that cut into his back.

"These walls are so hard," she muttered, tremors rippling through her body as she pressed into him. "I might hurt you."

"Nay." The sharpened rocks at his shoulders should have been uncomfortable with their combined weight forcing them into the stony ledge, but he didn't feel a thing beyond the lustful fire consuming every inch of his flesh.

"Hurry," Taffy suggested, riding the wave of the licentious euphoria that had swept over her brain. It was a desire so strong she had no words for it.

Hard hands clamped around her waist, lifting Taffy into the air until they were pressed loin to loin. His hips moved and they both groaned.

A stray spray of ice-cold water hit Taffy's back, shocking her into some semblance of intelligence. The wet stones near the falls would be dangerously slippery and there was a lovely bed of grass nearby.

"Malcolm." Taffy tried to wiggle free of his iron grip.

"Aye?"

"Malcolm, love, not here. It isn't safe. We have

to move. *Duine!*" Taffy bit his ear lightly to get his attention. She could tell that he was nearly beyond understanding her in any language. His pulse hammered against the bronze flesh of his throat. "We have to lie down before we fall down."

His only answer was a growl and the scrape of his teeth along her neck. He tested the taste of the flesh stretched over her collar bone.

"Malcolm!" Her light smack sounded very loud on his wet skin. He paused his nuzzling. His usually gray eyes were dilated to complete blackness and eerie shadows were moving about in them.

"Taffy, lass, there's no call tae be striking me," he complained. "I cannae feel it anyway. Greedy woman, ye'll be seen tae this time, I promise."

"Malcolm, *duine*—pay attention. We have to move from these stones. Please—" She stared directly into his turbulent gaze. Her hands made a gentle frame at his cheeks. "You don't want to hurt me, do you?"

"Nay!" he denied immediately, his eyes finally focusing on her own.

"And you want to be seduced by me, don't you?"

As a reply, Malcolm turned swiftly from the water, still holding her firmly around her waist, her tender feet well up off of the stony ground.

"Lie down," she commanded in a shaky voice. "There. On the grass."

He complied by kneeling in the patch of velvety green, but did not recline, preferring instead to drag her back against his lap and resume their kiss.

"No, lay back, love," Taffy instructed, resisting his arms' gentle but relentless pull. "It is my turn now."

"Yer turn?" He stared at her.

"Yes. I want to make this decision. To direct this."

"The decision 'tis made. The direction is set. Ye needn't worry, lass. I know where we are going."

"Malcolm, please." Taffy willed him to understand. "I have to know that *I* can do this."

Bemused and frustrated by the delay, he nevertheless did as she commanded, lying readily as she laid an urgent palm on his chest—and then nearly sat up again as he felt her hands on his heated flesh and her weeping hair raining water down upon his abdomen as she stroked and tickled and kneaded. He arched unwilling into her touch.

"I have been like a leaf, too, blown about by everyone's whims," she said softly. "And I did not mind because I had no path of my own. But now I know what I want. Oh, sure. I was willful. But I've never made the choices that truly matter, or so it seems now."

"Taffy, lass?" he croaked, his resolve to listen

to her words tested by the feel of her hands upon him. His most primitive instincts were roaring for permission to take what they needed and search for the meaning behind her actions later.

"I want you, Malcolm. More than anything in the world." She kissed his stomach. "And I want to stop being moved about by others' wills and conveniences. So I must be strong enough to choose my own course."

"And this will give ye strength?"

"Yes. This gives me strength."

"I do not understand ye, lass, but do as ye will." He gritted his teeth and prepared to be patient. "Talk all ye like. I'll listen."

She smiled, her expression a mixture of elation and impishness.

"Don't worry, I'm done with speaking," she assured him. "It is time to act."

"Aye? Then please do!"

She laughed softly at the mix of annoyance and desperation in his voice. Teasing him was irresistible.

"I heard about this interesting method from a French woman who moved to New York. She said that one did not need a saddle and bridle to enjoy riding a man. I didn't understand what she meant then."

"A French woman?" But he didn't protest anymore as she lay down on top of him and returned to his mouth where she began to nibble, responding instinctively to the roll of her hips that settled him into their cradle.

"Of course, she said that she usually used a crop as well."

"A crop," he repeated. Then the import of her words arrived in his foggy brain. "*Ride a man!* Ye brazen deil! Yer teasing me now, ye heartless wretch."

"Only a little," she said, laughing.

In an instant, she was rolled beneath him. The tides surging through his body could wait no more for jokes or exploration. *Ride him, was it? And such brash kisses!*

"Yer a wanton woman today, lass. And taking chances with yer teasing. I could pin ye here and devour ye an it was my wish."

"Yes," she answered, flexing against his hard palm. Her skin felt prickly and feverish. She snagged two handfuls of his hair and tugged. Her eyes remained wide open. "Yes. I am. And *I* want to do this. Now."

"Then 'tis my pleasure to serve ye, lass,"

Malcolm fitted himself against her. He surged once and Taffy's long legs wrapped around him. Her hands wound into his hair, pulling his mouth down to hers with the strength of some new and urgent need.

Malcolm ceased attempting to understand her puzzling aggression and decided to simply enjoy the experience of making love with this now truly passionate female. In his experience, women were usually passive—obedient. Especially the Sassenach. But something had changed in Taffy during this last night.

Then he couldn't think anything at all. Taffy had tightened against him and cried out in enjoyment. He set his lips to hers and drank her in. It was shocking, this demure beauty taking such open pleasure in coupling! She had been affectionate before, willing certainly—

Then the ecstatic trembling that had overtaken Taffy came to him. A last surge into her and Malcolm stopped being shocked and instead flew over the edge of the precipice where his body had been continually hovering since Taffy came into his life. He buried his face in her golden hair and gave a muffled roar as the healing heat poured through his battered heart and mind, and sent his lustful inner beast in a contented state back to its lair.

Eventually, time restarted itself in the corrie. The grass regained texture. The waterfall resumed playing its watery chorus at normal volume. A gentle sun caressed his skin. But still, Malcolm did not move.

"Malcolm." Taffy's voice was worried. She smoothed down his damp hair. He seemed far too quiet, and she was concerned that he had perhaps passed out. Heaven knew that she had left her own mind for a while there and had aspic where once her bones had been.

"Aye, love?" he finally asked in the laziest of voices, turning his head back and forth as he rubbed his face in her tresses and tangled the wet locks horribly.

"Are you well?" The question sounded idiotic but she wasn't sure quite what else to say. She had never attacked a man before and wasn't at all certain how he was taking it . . . or she was taking it. He had probably been shocked at her behavior. She was, herself, well-nigh reeling with astonishment.

One didn't need a saddle and bridle to enjoy riding a man? What monster of wickedness had said that?

"I am quite well. And ye, wanton creature?" he asked, echoing her thoughts. Malcolm raised up on his forearms and stared down at her blushing face. Plainly, he was amused rather than offended. "Have ye proven yer mettle?"

"Yes, thank you. I mean, I am fine," she replied, falling back on good manners.

In point of fact, she wasn't at all certain that she was *fine*. How could she be *fine* when she had just been the victim of overwhelming, wanton, abandoned compulsion? And the pleasure which had come of it . . . It seemed almost impossible to reconcile what she had been taught of the normal feminine impulse and what had happened to her.

On the other hand, she felt strong and contented. And though that was not ladylike, it *was* wonderful.

"Taffy." Malcolm looked suddenly very serious as he played with a lock of her hair.

"Yes?" she asked reluctantly, not wanting to spoil her tentative sense of balance, and not prepared to think any more until she had slept.

"I wish us tae marry. I know a priest, an Irishman. He'll do this for us. I'd take ye tae an Anglican—an I knew one—and be married there, but there is nobody I can trust here. Not wi' yer life."

Taffy closed her eyes, trying to shut out returning reality. She wasn't ready to again confront the danger of their situation.

"Is it that ye are hide-bound, lass? Not wishful of marrying a man o' some other faith."

"No. Of course not."

As Malcolm remained silent, waiting for some further answer, she finally cracked open one lid and studied her lover's expression.

His dark hair was thick and smooth and fell carelessly around the tanned face, partially hiding his prominent ears. His slightly arrogant— but entirely exciting—mouth was, for the moment, unsmiling.

But most compelling of all these attributes of

countenance were his fey eyes, fringed with the thickest lashes any human had ever possessed. It was a face that was vivid with life, sober for the most part, and very intelligent.

Taffy's skin still prickled and there was a hunger inside, but something else as well. A babe, she was sure of it. For its sake, if not for her own, she should do as he asked. It was only some notion of the rituals of courtship from her previous life that made her hesitate.

"This would please you?" she finally asked.

"Aye. It would."

"Very well, then. If it's safe," she added, laying a palm against Malcolm's smooth cheek. "I don't want you to take any risks."

"Fear not, lass. I'll take no chances with ye or the bairn," he vowed.

Taffy's eyes widened.

"You—you're certain that there is a babe?"

"Aye." Malcolm laid a hand over her belly. " 'Tis a wee girl with yer golden hair and my eyes."

Taffy exhaled slowly, assimilating his words and conviction.

"And does she have your ears?"

"Nay. They're great pointy things. She takes them from her mother."

Taffy's lips trembled. So, it was true then.

And she was supposed to walk away from this man? To return home to—*what?* Her father? Her former life of empty socializing? And how empty it would be! For she would have no one except her babe to share it with. And they would be ostracized for her being husbandless.

And yet, she couldn't stay here, could she? Running away from Campbells and Covenanters, and all the other human carnivores who roamed this damaged land. Their only times of peace would be these moments they had snatched in these strange, magical oases provided by the still-folk.

Taffy turned her head, looking at the beautiful water, which spilled from the gray rock, feeling the unnaturally delicate grass woven into a blanket beneath them. Above them, the sun filled a clear, azure sky. At the mouth of the cavern, Smokey lay sleeping, filling the autumn air with gentle snores.

"Could we not stay here a while?" she asked, speaking her thoughts aloud.

Malcolm smiled sadly.

"Aye, we could. But the day would come—and soon—when we could never leave at all."

She turned back to look at him.

"What does that mean?" she asked, touching the hard lines that had appeared suddenly at the side of his mouth. A touch of cold fear went through her sternum and pricked her heart. "Why couldn't we leave?"

"Ye recall yer fairy tales, lass? Of what happens

tae men who go tae visit among the still-folk? The fiddlers who come and play for a night. The giddy maids who stay for the length o' one reel?"

"They are gone for a hundred years, the stories say," she whispered around the growing tightness in her throat. Tears of exhaustion and frustration began to pool in her eyes. "They turn to dust and die when they go home."

"Aye."

"And it's true?" Taffy could feel the scalding salt trails as the tracked down her temples and joined the water in her hair.

Malcolm brushed one of the burning tears with the pad of his thumb.

"Ye had two-hundred and forty-four years tae use on the day ye arrived."

"And now?" The question was barely audible.

"I cannae say. Less than ye did. Soon, the still-folk will have to send ye home or ye'll never leave at all."

She stared at him for a moment and then her heart burst out in speech: "And what of you? Malcolm, what will happen to you? Can you still go to America and rejoin your family? Or is it too late for you to return?"

He hesitated, then spoke the truth. "I ken not."

"What do you think will happen?" she pleaded. "Tell me! Will you have to stay someplace like this forever? You can still leave, can't you? Or will you be old?"

There was a long silence while Malcolm stared down at her with his tragic, fey eyes.

Taffy rushed into speech, trying to negate the awful silence.

"I could stay with you! We could be happy. We could build a house—"

"That is no' possible, lass. Ye and the bairn are needed elsetimes," he said kindly. "Though I wish with all my heart it wasnae so. I would give anything tae stay wi' ye. Here or anywhere."

"I won't go and leave you with these horrid faeries! They can't force me to go!" Her voice was a whisper, but fierce.

"Dinnae worry, lass. I wouldnae stay wi' the still-folk. I ken now that such would be no life at all."

Understanding what he meant, Taffy rolled on her side and wept in grief and frustration.

"Lass." Malcolm rolled her into his arms. Her tears were scalding on his bare chest. Her sobs were an agony to endure until he heard what she was actually saying.

As her creative cursing became clearer, Malcolm gave a low whistle.

"And where would ye have learned such words, Taffy, lass?"

Taffy rolled over, her face and voice vehement. Malcolm was enthralled. He'd seen such expressions of grim determination staring at him from behind a row of enemy pikes on the field of bat-

243

tle, but never from a naked woman lying in his arms. The changes that had come over this lass in her time with him had transformed her into a queen.

"I have had enough of being manipulated! I won't stand for any more! I am going home!"

"Aye, lass. Soon."

Taffy drew back her hand and smacked his bicep.

"You are coming with me. And I don't want to hear another word from you about dying or what happened to other people in fairy tales! We aren't other people. We are MacLeods. It's not the same for us. The faeries are powerful, able to work magic on us—well, they can just bloody well find a way to send you home with me."

Taffy sat up and glared at the bushes in the glen. She raised her voice.

"Are you listening to me? I won't go back without him! I won't have this baby alone, either," she threatened, suddenly realizing that she actually did have the power to reach down inside and snuff out the new life growing there.

Malcolm's eyes dilated at her words and he flinched in protest.

He was not the only one affected by the intimidation. Sudden dark clouds boiled up in the sky overhead, covering the sun in a gray pall.

Taffy wanted to assure Malcolm that she would never carry through with her threat, but didn't dare do more than take his hand and squeeze it reassuringly.

"I don't care if you loosen the storm of the apocalypse on me! I won't move one step from this corrie until you tell me that Malcolm can go with me! No more coy games! Answer me now!"

There was a sudden absence of light and a black veil fell over them, encasing them in a night so black it had no stars or illumination of any kind. There was a sudden patter of many rushing feet.

"Nay!" Malcolm was on his feet in an instant and had Taffy gathered close. An odd glowing silver of the *sgian dubh* in his fist was the only light at hand. "Ye'll not force her tae do anything against her will. So help me, ye come nigh of her and I'll cut her throat!"

"Kill me, Malcolm," she ordered, none of her inner terror showing, though the power of faerie magic was dancing all over her skin. She understood that he was threatening them and making a bluff they would never call. She added to it: "If they come near us, kill me."

There was a long pause at her words and then great shifting in the black around them, one heave of wind that sighed low, and then the sunlight began to bleed back into the world.

It was immediately apparent that they were no longer in a protected quarry. There was still a mountain behind them, but the passageway was closed. So fine was the seam that it might never have been opened to let them through.

The waterfall was also gone, but in its place was a small loaf of bread and Malcolm's skin of water. It had been refilled.

Malcolm took his *sgian dubh* from her throat. His hand tremored.

An unhappy whine led them to Smokey who was sheltering under a dried and dusty shrub of wiry heather. His tail beat happily when they called to him, and he rushed immediately to their side.

Feeling the dog's fur on her bare legs recalled Taffy to the fact that she was still naked, and she looked about quickly, half-expecting the enraged faeries to have taken her clothing with them.

But her clothes, including her missing chemise, were waiting in a tidy pile, looking as clean and new as the day she had received them from the dressmaker's hand. Malcolm's plaid was likewise neatly folded, his sark crisp and laundered.

"I thought maybe they would be angry and vengeful," she whispered.

"Yer daft lass, to threaten them like that!" Malcolm pulled her tighter against him. His heart was thundering and his torso was lightly sheened with sweat. He laughed once. It was a sound more horrified than amused.

Taffy raised on tip-toes and found his ear. Pressing close, she breathed: "I didn't mean it about the babe. I just wanted to get their attention."

Malcolm snorted. His hands were urgent as they examined her for hurts.

"Well, ye've got it." His voice was thick.

"Do you think we can sleep now?"

He hesitated then said: "Best we eat whilst food is here. Then ye can have a short rest."

"And you?" she asked, suddenly weary enough to collapse on the stony ground, uncaring of her naked state. It was a sure sign that some magic had been done in the dark. Always, she was exhausted when faerie magic came too near.

"I think it may be prudent that one of us is awake tae keep an eye on things. Yer threat was the most serious one ye could have made, lass. They will steal ye from me do they have a chance, and they can keep ye prisoner in *Tomhnafurach* until the babe is born."

"I wouldn't go," Taffy assured him, though her lids were growing heavy. "They couldn't make me."

"Eat, lass," Malcolm said, handing her a chunk of bread. He didn't bother to argue about what the faeries could do if they chose to, or what would happen to her if they kept her imprisoned for that long. "We'll be needing our strength. If the still-folk are angered enough, they may not allow us the shorter paths through the forest."

"But that would put us in danger. They don't want that, do they?"

"They don't want you endangered. About now, they might well be happiest tae see me spitted on the end of a Campbell pike, though. They likely consider that I have betrayed them!"

"They wouldn't dare!" Taffy said, appalled enough to speak with a mouth full of food. The bread was completely tasteless, as though the still-folk were no longer bothering to use glamourie on the fare they provided. "What will we do if they decide to be vindictive?"

Malcolm shrugged and took up his own piece of the loaf.

"We'll do what I planned tae do before. We are going tae see a priest and be married. 'Tis more urgent now than ever."

"It is? Why?"

"Because, though they may still attempt tae take a married lady, it makes the kidnapping much harder tae complete. The still-folk fear the power o' the church's incantations. It is not something they understand, but magic all the same. It makes them wary."

Malcolm picked up his plaid and shook it loose.

"Wrap up, Taffy lass, and have a wee sleep. We must away as soon as the sun has set."

Taffy didn't argue, for it was beyond her power. Whatever had moved over them in the dark had been vast and draining, and she had no choice but to surrender to healing sleep.

Chapter Ten

Taffy awoke in Malcolm's arms and watched silently as the sun fell over the western horizon. She was much refreshed in both body and spirit, and felt prepared to resume their journey.

Malcolm, too, seemed ready to travel, even though he'd had no chance to sleep. But since the safety of true darkness had not yet embraced the land, he kept them lingering within the shelter of the hill waiting for night to fall.

Taffy reflected, as she washed with a dampened handkerchief, that she had rapidly become accustomed to tending to toiletries in Malcolm's presence. Before her trip down the faerie's road into this land, she had rarely so much as drawn off gloves or scarf in the presence of any man other than her father. Yet now, she bathed in plain sight of her lover and even allowed Malcolm to comb and braid her hair. Years of constraining etiquette had slipped away from her as new experiences enlarged her world, and she was beginning to have troubling doubts about her ability to resume the rigid standards of behavior worn in her previous life.

They ate another small meal of the tasteless bread and water, which they shared with an unenthusiastic Smokey. And then, despite his earlier skepticism and teasing about training for combat, Malcolm showed Taffy the proper manner for striking out with her fist. He made her practice hitting at his hands until he was certain she had mastered keeping her wrists locked and straight when she jabbed at her target.

"Good. Now hit harder, lass. Ye'll no' get more than one blow at a man. Best it be a ferocious one."

The next punch she delivered with enough force to earn a grunt of approval. Striking out again and again, Taffy reflected that learning the art of fisticuffs was yet another process completely at odds with all other training she had ever had, which said that ladies did not strike out in anger—or for any other reason.

But Taffy determinedly put aside her childhood admonitions against women using violence to defend themselves. It might be that this lesson would unwoman her, ruin her feminine charm for other gentlemen of her class. But the usual skills of polite requests for aid to obliging gentlemen, and modest acceptance of adversity until such an obliging gentleman came along, might have served in her own sheltered world when such persons were readily available, but they were of no use in this one.

No longer caring so much for her parent's horror of her occupation—after all, had she not already suffered the *fate worse than death* and found it to be not a terror but something profound and wonderful?—she went at her task with a will. Defense against a deadly enemy was no longer some abstract thing—a tale culled from an adventure novel about worlds across the sea. In this place, on this night, danger was near. She could sense it waiting all around them.

Malcolm at last declared her proficient in fisticuffs and then insisted upon a course of instruction for himself in the use of her rifle. She sensed that he found the weapon somehow distasteful, but he yet insisted upon learning about it.

The lessons were quickly accomplished, for Malcolm had used a flintlock before and understood the principles of projectile weapon. The only real difference was the manner of loading the rifle, and this was easily learned for the weapon was of simpler design.

Combined with his keen eye and fast reflexes,

Taffy knew that the Winchester could be put to formidable use. Especially in the dark, when then enemy would be handicapped by their lack of sight. It wasn't sporting of her to rejoice in this fact, but she did. Their enemies were legion and they needed every advantage against them.

Malcolm's last act, before leaving their suddenly bleak haven, was to draw his dirk and cut a short twig of rowan, which he sharpened to a point.

He put up his knife and, approaching her, took her chin in hand and turned her head aside. He jabbed the twig through the stubborn jean up at the edge of her left collar until it was well secured in the warp. He then carefully wiped his fingers clean of sap.

Taffy looked questioningly at him.

"The still-folk have no liking for rowan," he told her. "Keep this near tae hand, but dinnae be touching it unless ye are in need, for it stings our flesh."

Taffy touched her collar near the hand-length stick and then nodded at the compromise. Cold iron would stop them, too, but it would also bring them death. Rowan could inflict a painful wound, but probably not a fatal one. What she used to defend herself would be her own choice, she knew, but was grateful to Malcolm for providing her with an alternative to the rifle. She didn't want to kill any of the still-folk. They were, she was coming to accept, some form of distant kin.

Night fell abruptly, snuffing out the last ray of sun. There was nothing left to do but go on. In silence, they shouldered their gear and struck out on the nearest southward path.

The way down from their hill was a grim little trail that wound tortuously through a spiny thicket that had never known a woodsman's axe. The flora did not actively molest them, but it was of a most hostile aspect, and Taffy found herself treading the dark pathway with extra silence and care and searching the shadows for some sign of the beast that she sensed was stalking them whenever they were away from the faeries' magic shelters.

Malcolm, too, moved like a wolf on the hunt: sniffing at the air, keeping to shadows, embracing the complete silence of the night. He and Smokey moved in tandem, two of a kind as they prowled the darkness.

Their extreme caution proved worthwhile, for presently the smell of torches reached them. Thus far, such had always meant Campbells.

Sensing Malcolm's deep perturbation, Taffy closed the distance between them and pressed close to his side. She jerked her head at the path ahead, questioning if they should go on.

Malcolm laid his lips against her ear and breathed: " 'Tis the priest I spoke of, Father Feehan, who lives in yonder croft. He has unwanted visitors."

The smallest of moans hung in the thin air, telling Taffy of the dangers Malcolm had left unspecified. She shuddered involuntarily.

Always, it seemed, they had arrived too late to help anyone at the mercy of the Campbells. But this was different. They were hard upon the scene, and this time the person in trouble was someone Malcolm knew.

Taffy turned her head, and after brushing her lips across Malcolm's stern mouth, she sought out his ear.

"Can we do nothing to help?" she breathed, hefting her rifle with hands that still smarted from her repeated practice blows.

Malcolm pulled back, assessing her in the moonlight. She had to wonder what he saw. Trees loomed strange and twisted in the silvery light. The night sky was an ocean in which the moon had drowned and spread its light across the celestial seas. The piper looked both dark and grim in the black shadow, and she felt equal to his angry mood. Days of frustration were gathered at her back as well, urging her to some action against the monsters that hounded them. She knew the impulse could only be stronger in Malcolm, and worried for a moment at it affecting their judgement.

"We shall see," he answered, more with his

mind than with physical speech. He touched her gently on the cheek before pulling away and resuming his hunter's stance. "I'll no' be putting ye tae risk. Stay ye back a pace and make no more noise than a mousie before a cat."

Malcolm set a course uphill where they might easily survey the corrie. They crept to the edge of a small escarpment, and easing around a stand of gorse, Malcolm was able to peer down at the one room croft at the base of the hill.

He could not tell if anyone lingered within the walls of the hut, but there were half-a-dozen men outside, all ranged about a captive staked to the ground.

The prisoner's robes of office were plainly seen in the moon's bright light, and Malcolm breathed a word that Taffy had never heard, but nevertheless fully comprehended. She filed it away for future use. Dreading what more she would see, she crept closer to the edge and looked down.

Father Feehan was bound, hand and foot, to pegs driven deep into the ground. One of his captors held the priest's head bent well back in the crook of his powerful arm. A stick had been placed between the old man's jaws, canted at a sideways angle, forcing his mouth wide open.

As they watched, one of the other men lifted a hunk of peat from the fire kindled on the bare dirt before the croft's narrow door. It glowed red and evil, skewered at the end of a pronged stick that looked for all the world like a giant fork.

"Lost the fire in yer belly, Papist?" a harsh voice demanded. "I can put it back for ye afore ye meet yer Popish God."

Taffy divined what they intended and was filled with outraged horror. This demanded immediate action, regardless of what danger it might place them in.

"Malcolm!" she breathed, reaching for the rifle. One glance at her lover's face told her that he also meant to intervene.

She looked down again. Father Feehan lay exhausted and silent as his tormentor approached, but that wouldn't last, not once the embers were forced into his mouth and pushed down into his stomach.

"Give me the weapon, lass," he ordered.

"Malcolm, maybe I should be the one to—"

"Give me the weapon."

Frustrated, Taffy nevertheless complied. She was a better than fair shot, but Malcolm's eyesight was still superior in the dark.

"Be careful, love," she whispered, handing over the fearsome weapon, and wishing with all her heart that it was a cannon that would blow the evil creatures below straight to the hell in which they belonged.

"This may be a trap, lass. For those sympathetic to the cause. And they may have Sassenach flintlocks. Go down to the bottom o' the slope and wait for me." Malcolm threaded hard fingers through her hair and kissed her briefly. He looked into her eyes with a gaze that was as black and turbulent as she had ever seen. This night, there was no love moving in his pupils, only death.

But she did not fear the shadows there. They were only reflections—complements—of what was in her own heart and soul.

"Have your *savage-trainer* close at hand, lass, and yer rowan. Scream and hit hard if any o' the Campbells come by, and stab any still-folk who come next or nigh o' ye. *Cu*, go wi' her."

Hearing the sound of rough laughter from below, Taffy didn't waste time in argument. She slid quickly and quietly down the hill and into cover of the stunted trees. Smokey pressed close to her side as she waited, his hackles on the rise.

Taffy flinched as the Winchester spat and then spat again. There were confused cries boiling up in the air and the sound of running feet. There was more rifle fire and steadily less screaming. Finally, the breach clicked down on an empty load.

Realizing then that she had the ammunition belts, Taffy started out of hiding, racing back up the hill.

"*Hsst!* Toss it up, lass," Malcolm instructed, not bothering to lower his voice. Taffy shrugged out of a belt and made the awkward uphill throw.

Malcolm reached for his own belt and returned her toss, planting his dirk in the soil near her feet.

"I'll keep watch from here and shoot any who come tae the glen. Go down and cut the priest loose. If he cannae walk, leave him. Be swift, Taffy lass, we have little time tae spare. I sense others nearby."

Mentally, Taffy protested the harsh order to leave the wounded priest if he could not walk, but she wasted no time in an argument of ethics. The sounds of gunfire would bring others to the scene. Campbells, covenanters, Gallowglas—there were so many who might come, and they were all potential enemies.

His dirk taken up in her left hand, her right was awkwardly encumbered with the silver knuckles. The long knife was warm to the touch, comforting in its protective power.

Knowing there was not an instant to spare, she turned and sped around the hillock, running at a reckless pace along the narrow pathway that led to the clearing.

There was a patch of deeper shadow waiting at the ledge's base, cloaked in thin shrubbery and hidden from the moon. Her quick eyes saw movement there—a wild boar! She was sure of it.

Smokey gave a low snarl and tried to overtake her, but there was no room on the trail. Warned more by instinct than by sight, Taffy put on a burst of speed and leapt for the creature she sensed lurking behind the screen of leafy branches on the right of the trail.

"Malcolm!" she yelled, not as a cry for aid but rather a call to battle.

She had only a moment to gather impressions before she fell upon her quarry.

It was a man there, not the beast or even faerie she had half-expected, but he was still so inhuman a creature that she never thought to turn aside her dagger. He rose like a nightmare, pouring out malevolence as a storm did rain. He was dressed in the robes of the clergy, but she could imagine no one less suited to them. There was hate in those little, piglike eyes that looked up at her—and rage, endless and soul-consuming. Malice for her and all living things gleamed in his wrath-distorted face, and his lower jaw thrust up in jagged tusks.

Clenched in his right hand was a dirk of cold iron, and there were traces of blood upon it.

Instincts took hold. Knowing a wound from his knife would be fatal for her babe, if not for herself, she parried his stabbing blade away with the edge of Malcolm's silver dirk, and without hesitation sank her silver knuckles into his gut.

Momentum carried her past him, spinning her into the open space beyond the trees.

"Taffy!" Malcolm shouted.

She landed unevenly on the packed earth and fell to the ground. But with a new agility of body that had come with the other gifts of the still-folk, she was able to roll immediately to her feet and turn about to face her foe.

There was no need for haste. Smokey had followed immediately upon her heels and done the job he was trained to do. Her attacker was lying dead on his back. Part of his neck had been torn and bled profusely while his throat was crushed in Smokey's powerful jaws. The hound didn't hold his prey long, just until it ceased all struggling. But it was an eternity to witness, and Taffy knew she would be haunted by the horrible image until her dying day.

There was sudden movement all around her, then. Taffy spun about with feral speed. One man, she might have fought and won, but in that next instant there were many bodies circled around her. She wondered, even as she tensed to leap at the nearest arrival, why Malcolm had not fired the rifle at them, as he could surely see them from his place on the escarpment.

Her answer was short in coming.

"MacColla!" Malcolm shouted, his footsteps only sporadically coming into contact with the earth as he came flying down the path she had just traveled. "Keep yer men back from my wife!"

"Your wife?" said the giant who came to an abrupt halt a safe pace back from Taffy's dirk,

261

which she realized she was holding in a battle-ready position. Smokey was crouched beside her, silent but likewise radiating warning at the strangers who ringed his mistress.

"Aye! Well, she shall be as soon as I get Father Feehan back upright." Malcolm stopped just outside the circle of men who stood about Taffy, the rifle lowered, but hand still upon the trigger. He was breathing hard but managed to say gently: "Taffy lass, it's safe now. We're among friends. Ye can put up yer blade. Go o'er and cut the father free and see tae his hurts. *Cu*, come away tae me."

He was lying that they were among friends, and Taffy understood that what Malcolm really wanted was for her to step away from these people so that she would not be hurt if he was forced into firing his gun. She tried to behave as though she believed Malcolm's words, but it took all her will to lower her weapon.

"Certainly," she managed to say, tucking the dirk into her skirt's concealing folds and standing up from her half-crouch. Bile was rising in the back of her throat, and she feared for a moment that her quaking knees would give way. But her days of passing in and out of faerie magic had served her well, and she was able to fight back the weakening impulses.

"A Sassenach lady, is she?" MacColla asked, making no effort to detain Taffy as she slipped by him, though she felt his eyes on her face.

She walked quickly to the priest, keeping her gaze well away from the dead that littered the glen's floor. Moonlight had drained the scene of much of its horror. The tiny patches of blood from the wounds opened by bullets showed simply as black stains. Almost, she could believe that they were just more night shadows. But her new eyes showed her that some of the stains were still growing and gleamed with the sheen of once warm gore.

"Aye. Sent from London," Malcolm lied.

"Is she the one who got you safe from Duntrune?"

"Aye," Malcolm answered after a moment. "Ye've heard of her?"

"And of little else. The tales are outlandish. I thought them mostly lies and faerie tales." Taffy felt the MacColla's calculating eyes again resting upon her back as she knelt by the priest.

Colkitto! she thought, amazed, and then shuddered. The great MacColla of the Irish in the flesh. He wasn't handsome and daring as she had expected from her reading—he was terrifying.

Taffy slipped the silver knuckles from her shaking hands and secured them in her pocket. Using great care with Malcolm's dirk, she began sawing through the cords that fastened Father Feehan to the ground. The rope had bitten deep and his hands had turned from dark red to nearly blue and were greatly swollen.

Still, that was a minor hurt compared to what they had intended, and she was relieved that no greater aid was required, for she was certain that Malcolm would not linger in this place to nurse the priest—no matter how wounded the man was.

"Father," she said gently. "I shall have you free in a moment."

"Aye, lassie," he croaked in a broken voice. He sounded awful, but Taffy was relieved that he was conscious and there was intelligence in his eyes. She feared that perhaps some of the burning peat might have been stuffed into his throat before they arrived, or that he was so deep in shock that he could not speak.

Taffy listened with half an ear to the conversation being conducted between MacColla's men and Malcolm. It sounded perfectly cordial, but after so many days on the run, hiding from all people, she found their proximity to this man and his soldiers to be disturbing.

Smokey presently joined her, standing at guard while she cut the last rope. He, too, seemed less than happy to be among the strangers, but didn't bark or whine.

" 'Tis the black bitch's tame cleric, Markham, your woman and hound exterminated," Mac-Colla said. He sounded vaguely pleased. "He escaped his rightful judgement from the sassans, but found it here."

"Aye, I see his shauchled thumb," Malcolm answered. "Damn his black soul."

"Do you see it, piper? I didn't, not until I looked for it. We thought we were chasing a boar who attacked and killed two of my men. Instead, we have discovered Markham and his filthy band. All of them dead." The voice was neutral. Then: "That is an interesting weapon you have. It came from your Sassenach lady?"

"Aye."

"Is she the one we spoke of before on the ship?"

"Aye. She is." Malcolm was equally uninflected in his reply, but this very lack of emotion in his rich voice was disturbing.

Not knowing why, but very uncomfortable with the turn in the conversation, Taffy decided to intervene before there was any more talk of boars, or her, or the strange weapon she had brought with her to this time. Gone was any desire to spend time with one of Irish history's great figures. There was something very dangerous shimmering in the air that surrounded the Isleman. She could sense it as plainly as the new storm that was approaching.

"Gentlemen," she said, rising. Her tone was as proper as a lady taking tea with the Royals, and as commanding as any who had been born to the purple. It took an effort to meet the MacColla's eyes with an assumption of ease and calm, but she forced herself to return his gaze unflinching. "I believe that Father Feehan could use some immediate assistance."

MacColla stared at her a long moment and then finally nodded. Two of his men stepped over to help the priest to his feet. They handled him gently, but the slight old man still had to bite back the sounds of anguish that came when his swollen ankles first took his body's weight.

Taffy, though she wanted to help, remained well back from the Irish soldiers who watched her with curious eyes. She circled the other men who stood waiting and came up on Malcolm's left side. She longed to reach for him, but didn't make any move to distract him. His own posture spoke of battle readiness, suggesting that he too felt the tension in the air.

She did her best to ignore the body lying on the ground behind them, and the MacColla's hypnotic stare, which was trying to examine her mind and peer into her heart. She had the intuition that he would have been able to see her clearly were it not for the lingering cloak of faerie magic that had been thrown over them.

"Father?" Malcolm called softly. "Are ye badly hurt?"

"*Malcolm the Pipes? Is* that yer voice I hear?" the priest asked, peering into the shadows where they stood. It was one of the pools of blackness that the torchlight did not illumine. Malcolm had chosen it deliberately.

As the priest approached, Taffy was careful to shake her hair over her ears. Malcolm's, she noticed, were already concealed.

"Aye, Father. That it is."

"And how are ye, lad?" Father Feehan asked, walking gingerly in their direction. His face was lined with pain, though he made an effort to smile.

"I am well, Father," Malcolm replied. "But I am in need o' yer help."

"In that great a hurry, are you, piper?" the MacColla asked softly. His men, well versed in his ways of battle, did not fill the air with idle conversation, so everyone could hear the exchange and wonder at its meaning.

"Aye. That I am."

"What do ye need, lad?" the priest asked, his voice growing stronger.

"This lady, Taffy MacLeod, and I wish tae be married."

"Now." It was not a question. The priest looked from Malcolm to her and then back again. He nodded his head. "A MacLeod is she? It would be my joy."

There was a brief ripple of surprise that passed through MacColla's men.

"I am not certain that we have the time, piper. We left the Campbells stirring not an hour past."

"There is time," Malcolm said firmly, daring anyone to doubt him. "An yer concerned, send a scout on ahead tae be sure of the way, but I tell ye that no Campbells are there yet."

The two men, towering over the other soldiers, stared at each other in an awful hush, engaged in some contest of will that Taffy did not understand.

"We will begin at once," the priest said, breaking the apprehensive silence. "Someone fetch a torch. I cannae see a blessed thing. And drag that body away before he bleeds on the bride. Sorry, lass, that there is no English orange blossom for to bridal yer hair."

"That's all right, Father," she assured him. She couldn't imagine any bridal trappings in this horrible place. It would be sacrilegious.

The soldiers looked to MacColla, and receiving no contradictory order, went to do the priest's bidding.

"We've no time for a Mass," Father Feehan told Malcolm, *sotto voce.*

"It doesnae matter, Father."

"The lass is a Catholic?"

Malcolm hesitated.

"No, I am not," Taffy said quietly, worried, but the priest merely nodded.

"Dispensation for a mixed marriage can be granted in a grave situation. I believe that this circumstance qualifies. Ye'll do as your husband bids ye and study his religion later, will ye not?"

"I shall strive to do whatever Malcolm asks," was her qualified answer, which brought a slight smile to Malcolm's lips.

"Very well. You." The priest gestured to MacColla and a second soldier. "Stand here. Ye'll be the witnesses."

With that, the priest launched into a hurried Latin prayer. Distracted by the MacColla's continuing scrutiny, Taffy followed few of the priest's words, though her Latin was fair enough to understand him. She did recognize the admonition to Malcolm that "husbands should love their wives as Christ also loved the church."

She repeated the phrase and was dimly surprised to realize that this wasn't a question she had thought to ask of Malcolm in their time together, so caught had she been in her own turmoiled emotions. But she did wonder about it now. He was fiercely protective of her—and certainly loverlike—but did he actually *love* her in the way the priest meant? And did it matter if he did not?

Taffy looked inside with her new sight and found that it did matter, at least a little. However, such thoughts couldn't be allowed to interfere with what needed to be done.

She sighed. And why did they talk of obedience for the woman, rather than asking that she promise to love in return? That, she knew, would not be a difficult thing for her to swear, as she surely did love this man.

As if sensing that her thoughts had wandered someplace unpleasant, Malcolm twitched her cuff with a long finger. She rejoined the priest's words at the part of the ceremony about "for this cause shall a man leave his father and mother, and shall cleave to his wife, and they shall be two in one flesh."

But that made her think of her own parent and his likely reaction if—*when*—Malcolm was presented to him. Her lover was not at all what her father had in mind for a son-in-law. He expected her to marry a gentleman, which by his definition, was some sort of an indolent, wealthy fop who would squire her to socially approved amusements and occasionally sire heirs upon her.

Taffy looked at her groom. Malcolm was not at all indolent or foppish in body or in mind. He acted toward her with what her father would feel was an ill-bred familiarity, and a total disregard for what the conventions of her age said was the proper treatment of the weaker sex by the stronger.

While he was tender with her, he did not behave toward her as if she was of frail health or slight of reason.

Nor did he make any fuss about the protection he offered her, though she knew that it was a princely gift as he was going against the will of faeries he must have previously seen as friends— even as kin—in order to protect her from them.

And though they had been thrown together in a situation beyond the social pale, he had never taken unfair advantage of her—Taffy paused at that thought and then smiled slightly. Her father wouldn't agree with her about that, either. He would not consider that she was able to give informed consent to the intimacies that had passed between them. But she knew otherwise.

Added together, this catalogue of practical virtues made Malcolm more of a gentleman than many of her contemporaries who put their gentility on and off with the whims of the moment and the social station of those with which they interacted. Malcolm's beliefs and behavior were not donned only when he put on his plaid or drew a weapon or came to her bed. He was always himself, true in every circumstance.

But more important than all that, she loved him. It was this circumstance that made him the only husband she would ever have.

This time it was Father Feehan who cleared his throat and stared at her warningly, perhaps knowing that the bride's attention had wandered. Malcolm closed one eye in a slow wink and squeezed her hand. Aware of the MacColla's watchful eye upon them, Taffy shook off her pointless reverie and made an effort to pay greater attention to what was being said.

There came an awkward moment when Father Feehan asked for a ring, but Taffy reached into her pocket and produced her silver knuckles.

Both Father Feehan and MacColla stared incredulously at the length of silver, but Malcolm's smile told her that he was not upset with her unorthodox solution.

"Well, lass, wi' four rings, ye'll be well and truly wed," the priest said, hastily blessing the weapon that had saved her from Lady Dunstaffnage's demonic cleric.

The fit was uncomfortable on her left hand, but Taffy left the mongery in place until the ceremony was over.

Father Feehan offered hurried congratulations, but MacColla and his men were already on the move and the priest had wisely decided to go with them.

The great man paused for a moment as his men faded back into the stunted wood. His gaze was thoughtful as it passed over them for a final time.

"You'll not come with us? Though you are a piper, a man of war, and we have need of you?"

"Nay," Malcolm answered. "I was a piper, but my calling has changed. There are others wi' greater need than yers. Our path now lies south."

MacColla nodded.

"You still have plans to *travel*, piper?"

"They were never *my* plans," Malcolm answered. He smiled suddenly. "My wife thinks otherwise. We'll see shortly who has the greater will. Any road, tell them in Glen Noe that in spite of the stories, *Malcolm the Pipes* died in Duntrune. Let him rest in peace."

MacColla's eyes flicked over Taffy. She knew that he could not see much in the dark, but she still had the impression that he had catalogued every aspect of her face, bearing, and dress.

"Your own battle will be an interesting one, piper. Good luck to you both, for you shall need it in the lands you plan to see."

Malcolm nodded.

"And to you, Colkitto," Taffy said softly. She found herself adding some hurried advice. "Stay away from Lord Inchiquin. In fact, don't go back to Ireland at all next year."

The MacColla's expression turned quizzical.

"I think I shall still have plenty of Covenanters to kill for the king in the year to come. They are still all about, as are the Campbells. And, piper, though I do not approve of what you do—or even *what* I suspect you *are*—I still thank you for your message. It saved the lives of many of my men." The Irishman smiled briefly before turning away.

"He doesn't believe me," Taffy said sadly, as the legend's footsteps retreated into the increasingly restless dark.

"It's his destiny, lass. There's no escapin' it."

273

"Oh, hogwash!" she said irritatedly. "You Celts are all too damned mystical for your own good."

Malcolm laughed softly and pulled her into his arms. His eyes blazed with sudden joy.

"I do believe that the reason ye were sent tae me is that the burden o' life was too heavy without some laughter tae lighten the load."

"And you find me amusing?" she asked, a little disappointed that he didn't declare his love for her, and a lot breathless because she was always short of breath when Malcolm was near.

"Aye. And bonnie." Malcolm's warm gaze seemed to cover her like a cloak, warming her clear to the soul. Down came his mouth to cover her lips and a tide of sweet fire swept over her. Leaning into him, she gave herself over to the warming flames, which purged all doubt and fear.

"Ah, wife!" he said, turning his face into her hair. "Ye tempt me past all reason. But we must away."

"Wife," she repeated, the fact still an alien one. How could one speak of being a wife when there had as yet been no talk of love?

In the distance, thunder crackled in warning. Taffy groaned and leaned her head against his chest.

"Again?"

"One would think the Campbells would have tired o' chasin' us through the rain." He laughed shortly. "But nobody said they were keen o' wit, just bloody stubborn."

Disappointed, Taffy nevertheless accepted that there was no time for sweet words or deeds between them. Indeed, the notion of sharing their love in the defiled glen was repellent.

"So we go south?" she asked, in a voice made steady by effort. The growing roar of thunder told of the storm marching swiftly overland. Smokey whined once and then barked sharply.

"Soon. But first we go west a bittock."

"You don't trust anyone," she said, thinking of the lie he had told the MacColla.

"Untrue, Taffy lass! After all, I trust ye."

The praise was nearly as warming as the most romantic declaration of love. *Nearly*.

Chapter Eleven

Taffy sighed as she spied the now familiar opening in the mountain stones. The mouth in the hill was only a narrow shadow of darker hue cracked a shoulder's-breadth wide in the black wetness around them. It didn't look like the entrance of a cave, but she was coming to recognize the faeries' resting places.

"Ye should no listen tae yer weariness, lass. It will tell ye tae despair," Malcolm told her as he set a hand on her shoulder.

"I am too tired to despair," she answered, stepping boldly into the cavern, confident from past experience that it would be uninhabited. A small frisson passed over her skin, but after the uncleanliness of the place where they'd intended to maim Father Feehan, the magicked cave seemed to her almost wholesome.

"Too weary are ye then for being a wife?" he asked, stepping close behind her and putting comforting arms about her waist.

Taffy leaned back into his heat and sighed with pleasure.

"I could probably be persuaded to do my duty," she replied. This time, there was no blush.

"I'd not have duty doing desire's work," he answered, bestowing a kiss on her ear. "For desire should live between man and wife rather than duty."

"I agree. I just wish that for once it could pass between sheets on a bed," she said wistfully. "It would be so novel."

He squeezed her quickly, and then with a show of the strength that always left her amazed, he lifted her onto a stony ledge.

"We've a bed. 'Tis just made of rock instead of hide. I'll build a fire so our linens may dry." He picked up her heavy skirts, testing the fabric for dampness. The worst of the rain had passed them by, but she was still more wet than dry. "Ye'll regret it else, for ye'll chap yer tender skin on this cloth. 'Tis tough as sail canvas."

"I might regret it anyway. This rock is cold." But she didn't believe her words. She might dislike the hard ground, which would leave bruises, but better that than to lament a lost opportunity to be in Malcolm's arms. It was only there that the horrors of this world were completely cleansed and she forgot that time was closing in upon them.

Too, she knew from experience that making love would give her the energy—and probably provide ample discomfort—to remain awake while she kept her lonely vigil. It was Malcolm's turn to rest and she had every intention that he should have some sleep this night.

Perhaps she was being over-cautious by setting a watch. The still-folk were apparently continuing to act as their friends. But what had passed in the stone corrie was still fresh in her mind and likely in theirs as well. She would take no chances on their trying to steal her away from Malcolm while they slept.

As Malcolm lit their small fire, Taffy slid from her perch and went to stand beside an uneasy Smokey. The hound was squinting at the dawn sun rising up through the rain and sighing morosely.

She sympathized. The light, though muted by silvery showers, still hurt her eyes, and she wondered if she would forever more love only the moon, and always shun the sun's harsher light in its gentler favor.

"It is bright, isn't, boy?" she said, laying a hand atop his brindled head, and trying not to see Lady Dunstaffnage's cleric clasped in the powerful

278

jaws, which were but inches from her own body.

Smokey sighed again and closed his eyes on the fire in the sky. For a moment, the beast leaned against her.

Taffy sighed, too. The dawn also meant that another night had passed, bringing them to another faerie shelter and ever closer to their destination—the barrow—and the time when she would have to return to her world.

Close in pursuit of that thought came the inevitable worry that perhaps—in spite of her threats—the faeries would not find the way to return Malcolm with her, and that he might be lost forever as dust on the low road that they would have to travel to her home.

"No. It won't happen," she muttered.

For how would she bear it if he was taken from her? No matter what conventional wisdom said about the healing properties of time, she knew that there would be no forgetfulness for her heart or mind. Separation of their bodies there might be, but division of the heart and mind and soul was not possible as long as she had her memories of him. The rational mind might recognize the passage of hours, days, months—even the long years—that were supposed to bring healing indifference, but her heart would never be whole again if he was taken from her. It would not forget that once it had been completed—no, not even in an eon would it fail to recall that once it had been joined to its other half.

The apprehension of this fell chance was a heaviness in her breast that threatened to crowd out this time of peace and rest. Taking Malcolm's advice not to pay heed to weariness or despair, she resolutely turned her stinging eyes and thoughts away from the harsh red brilliance of the new day.

"Ah!" There was a wealth of satisfaction in Malcolm's voice. "We've been forgiven, Taffy lass."

He turned and in his hands was a wooden tray, which held a loaf of bread, a small ball of cheese—and her flask!

"Is it—?"

"Aye. There's water in the cave as well. Cold for drinking and a bit in there is a hot spring for bathing."

"Truly?" Some of the apprehension melted away. The still-folk surely would not have made them so comfortable if they were enraged by her demands.

"It is. And there's some dried grass tae make up a bed, so ye'll no' be resting on the hard stone. Which is well, so delicate as ye are," he added, a betraying gleam in his eye.

"It is very well," she agreed, taking a seat near the tiny fire. "Especially as I have decided that it is high time that you *rested* on the floor instead."

"Aye? Well, then, if ye mean to pin me down, best ye have a meal and regain some strength."

Taffy accepted the offered bread, smiling smugly at the challenge laid before her.

"I don't think I shall need any particular strength to overcome you. You haven't slept in a long while and it is a simple fact that women are the more cunning sex."

"Cunning, are ye? In what manner?"

"Well, to begin with, I shall ply you with drink," she said lightly, taking the flask and uncapping it. She passed it beneath his nose as if wielding a bottle of smelling salts. "Not enough to leave you sotted. Just pliant."

Getting no reaction from her ploy, Taffy dipped a finger into the flask and then drew the wetted tip across Malcolm's lips.

She was warned by a twitch beneath the sensitive finger pad, but she had no time to escape before finding herself captured in his teeth and his tongue laving her into shivers.

The fey eyes watched her involuntary shudder with undisguised pleasure and his mouth curved into a wicked grin. He released her finger.

"Ye needs must be quicker, Taffy lass, if ye are tae take me unawares."

"I think that perhaps a bit more whisky is needed," she said, setting the bottle to her own lips. She was careful not to swallow, for it would make her sleepy, but she sheened her mouth with the potent drink. "And I never said that I wanted you unaware."

Being careful of the fire, she crawled over to Malcolm. Her hand at his chest urged him to lie back, and when he obliged, she stretched herself over him as a blanket. Her body was taut and balanced and she did not worry about crushing Malcolm beneath her weight. She had learned from experience that she would not bruise his agile body on the hard floor.

She set her mouth lightly to his, moving over him with feigned leisure, ignoring her racing heart as she raised herself slightly with her lower arms so that she might arch fully into him.

Malcolm made a sound that was midway between a groan and laughter, and clasped her about the waist, urging her to find her seat.

The task was greatly hampered by the folds of her wet skirt, which had them tangled like a winding sheet.

"Bloody hell," she muttered, frustrated by her trapped legs.

" 'Tis not enough tae be bold, Taffy lass. One must also use a wee bit of strategy," he said, rolling to one side and reaching for her blouse's buttons with dexterous fingers. He grinned at her.

Taffy smiled back, pleased with his playfulness, and charmed as ever by the sight before her. His hair was drying and the dark locks fell in waves about his face. His sark was plastered as close as skin to his broad chest, and its lacing conveniently at hand. He was more beautiful than she had ever seen him.

"What are ye thinking, Taffy lass?"

"That firelight becomes you."

His eyes widened slightly.

"How plain ye have become, wife. How bright yer spirit. It fair dazzles me that ye can speak so clearly of what ye like."

"You told me not to hide," she reminded him.

"So I did! And good advice it was."

He touched his lips to hers, tasting carefully of the last traces of whisky upon them. Like her, he kissed without haste, allowing them to enjoy the sensations of building lust.

His fingers were unhurried as he undressed her, removing first her blouse and then unfastening the ties of her chemise. He took his mouth from hers long enough for his eyes to follow his hand's path as he pushed her damp skirts from her legs. The journey from thigh to ankle was a lingering one as he enjoyed the exquisite feel of her bared skin, calves to thighs, over the curve of waist to the softer pillows of breasts.

Beneath his hands, her nipples tightened, bringing another smile to his lips as he read the signs of desire that changed her body. Taffy did not mind either the scrutiny or his outward pleasure for she, too, felt the familiar joy that came from a complete joining. Malcolm was her first and only love, and now husband in fact as well as in spirit. It was right to celebrate the union and wash away the ugly memories of what had passed the night before.

Her hands tugged his plaid loose and then moved over his skin, touching him as she wished, reveling in the feel of skin on skin, marveling at the difference that desire wrought upon them, his body becoming more hard and powerful, hers softer and yielding.

Malcolm watched her exploration, memorizing her expressions as he created a perfect memory, painting the moment with all its glorious emotional colors in the most personal corner of his mind. Her blushing skin, her golden hair spread in a wild halo, her eyes beckoning without shyness; all this went into memory's portrait where it might be treasured in the days to come.

He cupped her chin and said softly: "Ye'll never ken, lass, what delight ye have brought me. Ye've pulled me away from blackest despair."

"I know what you mean to me," she answered softly. "I think I can guess how you might feel."

"I pray that I have brought ye joy in equal measure, wife, but doubt o' it being possible."

He kissed her then without circumspection, allowing need to overtake him and desire to ride him straight to its coveted end.

Taffy lifted her arms and wrapped him tight. Her legs she wound about him, too. She could move but little, but she could feel—and did, with every bit of delicate flesh that touched Malcolm's own. The friction made her squirm and arch. His lips upon her neck and then her ears were nearly scorching. The path of kisses sent her nerves dancing.

She squirmed and arched and even pleaded, but still Malcolm would not give her what she needed.

"Malcolm!" she groaned, beginning to tremble. Her body knew an actual ache and her loins yearned to clasp about him. "You are a heartless—"

Another kiss silenced her complaint. A last move of hips saw them finally joined. She gloried as he moved against her with telling urgency, the hard stone of their marriage bed completely forgotten.

Finally, there came the splintering of mind and body and the shower of sparks rained down upon her.

Malcolm went into the fire then, too. He released his own pleasure with a hoarse shout that was more elemental in tone than the music of his normal voice, and partially collapsed upon her.

"Sleep, love," she said softly, touching his hair. "I will watch for us."

Malcolm rolled to his side, and pulling his plaid over them, obeyed her command.

Taffy turned her face away from the growing

light and watched the shadows of wind-swept trees outside the cave dance upon the wall.

Nightfall saw them traversing the wildest tract of pathless moor. Malcolm had begun the evening in a cheerful mood, whistling a traditional *pibroch* while they bathed and he belted his plaid. But as they went into the world and the new moon wheeled overhead and began its descent into the day, he became quiet.

Taffy, too, felt uneasy. Small whispers of energy passed repeatedly over her skin, soft and unpleasant as dewy cobwebs on the face. But though she looked, she saw no sign that the still-folk were near. For once, no storm clouded the sky. There was no shadow stalking them. The plants behaved as they should, and they even disturbed a flock of doves who were nesting in a gnarled oak tree. Everything looked normal, peaceful even.

But Smokey and Malcolm were again moving like beasts of the hunt, quartering back and forth across the trail, so she did not attempt to lull herself into a tranquil, inattentive state.

Dawn brought them without mishap to yet another cave, but unlike the others where they had passed their days, Taffy felt a fierce aversion to entering the new shelter's large interior.

"It isn't a faerie cave, is it?" she whispered.

"It was. Something grievous has happened

within it." He closed his eyes and began some inner communion. After a time, his eyes reopened and he shrugged. "I cannae feel that there is any present danger. Do ye wish tae go on a bit?"

Taffy considered the suggestion. A part of her wanted to do just that, but she was hungry and tired after her night of missed sleep. And a quick look inside the deep cavern did not suggest that there was anything physically threatening within its stone belly. There was simply an unpleasant atmosphere radiating from the cave's black mouth, which could well be caused by her new sensitivity to some previous visitor's upsetting the faerie spells that guarded it.

"No, let's rest here. There is no guarantee that there will be better shelter and it is getting light."

"Aye. Well, then, I think I must walk a deasil and make the place fit for the still folk to again inhabit. Else it shall be a long and unpleasant night." So saying, he stepped into the cave and circled it thrice around, whistling some eerie, if not quite musical, tune as he did so.

With each pass by the cave's mouth, the atmosphere within grew clearer, until with the third turn, the worst of the unpleasantness had dissipated.

Taffy and Smokey entered eagerly then. The sun had crested the hills, and they knew that just as they were favored by night, the daytime belonged to their foes—Campbells and Covenanters and human carnivores of every stripe.

They settled into rest, but though Taffy was very tired, her sleep was troubled first by evil dreams where she and Malcolm were pursued by a faceless, relentless evil. She woke, only to find a peculiar and realistic vision of a long, black crack opening in the back of their cave.

Taffy stared at it, horrified. Inch by inch, the opening grew, silently—and there were many pairs of eyes peering out at them from the black beyond.

Malcolm! Where was he?

It took a mighty effort, but she moved her head, inch by inch, until she could see him sitting with Smokey near the mouth of the cave. He stood with her rifle in hand, his head cocked at a listening angle as he stared out into the bright outside.

Taffy tried to speak, tried to waken herself that she might give warning that someone was coming—and not from outside the cave but from within—but a strange stillness had settled over her, paralyzing her limbs and voice. It was a magic more powerful than she had ever encountered or imagined.

"Waken, lass! We are attacked!" she heard Malcolm shout, as he raised the rifle and fired out into the brightness outside the cave.

His words and the rifle's loud report freed her

of the dream paralysis, and she rolled to her knees, prepared to rush to Malcolm's side. But in that moment, several tall, lean bodies swarmed inside the cave through the crack in the back wall and leaned down over her, grabbing her arms with long, white hands.

"Malcolm!" she screamed, trying to reach for the rowan thorn jammed into her collar, but there were too many hands upon her. They were not cruel grips that held her, but they were relentless as they dragged her toward the ominous black crevice at the rear of the cavern.

She saw Malcolm turn and raise the rifle in their direction, but he hesitated to fire, and then it was too late.

"Taffy!" he shouted, his eyes wild, leaping toward her. But behind him came two soldiers, and then four, iron swords in hand. They were checked a moment by the cave's darkness, which was as muffling as any blindfold to human eyes, and that allowed Malcolm to gain another leaping pace away from them.

"Malcolm!" Taffy strained with every fiber in every sinew, but she couldn't break the hold upon her limbs. How had these Campbells found them? Had the still-folk led them here to serve as a diversion for when they meant to steal her away?

"Lass!"

Taffy saw half the still-folk who had come for

her turn about and drop to the floor on bended knee. Their long white hands slapped down upon the stone in front of Malcolm, and before the echo had reached the ceiling, another giant crack had opened in the floor.

As though overpowered by the sudden blows, the ground canted crazily and Malcolm and the soldiers—and even the still-folk who had kneeled to open the ground—tumbled into the black crevasse that tore the cave's floor.

Taffy saw one of the faeries catch Malcolm with his long, pale fingers hooked into a claw, and grab for purchase on the stony ledge. For a moment the two clung, hanging at the edge of the deep pit by the strength of that one pale fist.

The still folk who had her shackled paused for a moment, as though considering whether to rush to their comrade's aid and risk her escape.

Malcolm looked past his rescuer and up to Taffy's face. His eyes were wide and black as he addressed her.

"Be strong, lass," he said, the voice in her ear implacable. *"Donnae give in tae fear. Ye must keep yourself whole, yer thoughts strong, so I may find ye again."*

"Malcolm!" she cried, unable to obey, her fear a sickness spreading through her heart like freezing water that replaced her own blood. "Don't let go!"

The floor shifted again. A panicked wail filled the air as several soldiers plummeted further down into the depths of the crevasse, and the terrified echos made the cave tremble.

"Promise me, lass, that ye'll be strong! That ye'll not be magicked."

"Malcolm," she whispered, too frightened of further shaking the collapsing cave to overcome the hands restraining her.

"Promise me, lass! Ye must fight and live!"

"Yes. If I can," she answered. Then, fiercely to her captors: "Help them!"

But before they could move, there was another deafening crack of breaking stone. The ledge gave way and the clinging faerie and Malcolm both disappeared into the same black maw that had swallowed the soldiers.

Neither of them cried out.

"Malcolm!" Taffy screamed with all the force in her lungs, as though her voice might defy cruel gravity and call him back to her.

A horrible new howling tore the air of the cavern and a trembling, wild-eyed Smokey, spurred by his mistress's thwarted will, leaped recklessly into the void after the piper.

There came another abrupt silence, followed by more splintering of stone from overhead.

"Nooooooo!" she screamed, as her captors caught her up and dragged her into the tunnel at a dead run that had her feet skimming over the ground.

She was still screaming for Malcolm when the stone wall snapped shut behind her and the cave collapsed in upon itself.

Chapter Twelve

Ever after, Taffy's memories of the period that followed her exodus from that cavern were nightmarish and hazy. After Malcolm had toppled into the abyss and his voiceless presence was abruptly ripped from her, she had passed from acute anxiety about his welfare into a furious hysteria where she wailed his name over and over. The sound of her voice was a violent concussion in the confined space of the tunnel into which they'd escaped, and it seemed to shake the walls around her, and loose a smell that was half earth and half living trees which had been sundered. The stink of bleeding sap prevailed.

Even as she fought against her invisible abductors in the smothering dark, she knew that she was being half-dragged and half-carried down another faerie road. Her eyes were wide open, but through her streaming tears she could see nothing more of her surroundings than several points of dancing golden light, like torches being carried at a great distance on a foggy night.

She grieved without cease, but after her throat had been rasped raw, she stopped calling for Malcolm and fighting so vigorously. She calmed enough to realize that she was not being taken back upon the road that brought her to this time. Unlike that journey, when she had traveled from her time to Malcolm's, there was no sound around her, except the eerie padding of nearly silent feet slapping on hard stone.

She was minimally relieved to know that they were not returning her home yet, and she tried to pay attention to her surroundings. But strive as she might, Taffy could see no one in the dark, not even great shadows moving against lesser ones. Foiled by the lack of light, she recoursed then to her other senses, and from her sensitive ears she deducted that the echoing noises about her came from such a multitude of directions that she must be in the midst of a party of enormous size.

She had screamed herself into a voiceless state and wearied her body, but she still continued to periodically try and free herself. There was always the hope that she might return to Malcolm.

In the meanwhile, she continued calling for him with her heart and mind, hoping against the evidence of her eyes and ears—and the silence in her mind—that he might still live.

But her captors did not allow her to escape, never relenting their hold until she finally collapsed from her exhausting struggles and went limp, and it seemed to her that somehow they were muffling her thoughts and appeals to her love.

When she hung heavily in her living shackle, which had not loosened their pitiless grip no matter how she struggled and pleaded, the raiding party finally paused in their hurried travels.

She sensed that they had met up with another band of still-folk and were exchanging news. As her body folded in on itself, they released their hold on her arms and stepped back from her.

Do not run.

Taffy ignored the alien voice in her head. She was no sooner freed from her living bonds then she summoned a last bit of strength and clumsily attempted to run back through the darkness to where she had last seen Malcolm.

But before she was more than a step away, something viney tangled about her ankles, and her hobbled legs gave way beneath her.

She put out her arms and screamed again—this time with fear for her child—but without any sound coming from her ruined throat.

There was a breath of displaced air and someone caught her about the waist before she hit the floor. Her rescuer lowered her gently onto the ground and after a moment padded away.

There was a quick whisper of voices that sounded more like the rustling of leaves than human speech.

The padding steps quickly returned to her side. Rather than continue to drag her along in her now supine state, as she half-expected they might, someone untangled her hobbled legs, and before she could kick out, she was taken up in one of her captors' arms.

Taffy thrashed feebly and tried to speak with her broken voice, but was held tight against a narrow chest with limbs that were whipcord lean and impossibly strong. Struggle feebly though she did, those arms allowed her no leeway, except what she could achieve by movement of her neck.

The journey resumed. The black went on for what seemed miles, but eventually began to change in tone, taking on a reddish hue. Occasionally, a breeze would pass over the party and a stray lock of her abductor's hair would brush over her face. It was insubstantial, soft . . . not *human*.

And yet, in a way, her captor was also familiar. And it was the comfort of this familiarity that allowed her to drop down into kind oblivion

when a soft, dark breath whispered to her: *Sleep,
lady, do not fear.*

Fear? she thought. She did not fear. Grief
would kill her before anything else could.

Nay, thou shalt live. And with those words
some comforting swaddling was drawn over her
brain and she let go of consciousness in favor of
the veil of forgetfulness that was offered.

When Malcolm opened his eyes, it was to a blackness so near complete that he was not certain
that he had truly awakened. It took a moment for
him to recall what had happened in the cave.

"Taffy?" he asked immediately, even then
knowing that she was not there.

Head swimming, he groped about for a moment with clumsy hands to look for the faerie
who had grabbed on in an attempt to save him
from a fall into the void. His senses told him that
he was alone, but still he searched for a body and
also to assure himself that the floor about him
was where it was supposed to be.

Presently, feeling nothing but firm, cold stone
around him, Malcolm slowly and cautiously rose
to his feet, then continued his investigation of the
rough face of the wall before him.

There was a pungent smell of fresh sap in the
air, dying quickly with every breath he pulled
into his lungs. The odor explained why he was
alive and the faerie was not lying broken beside

him. The deepest roots of the ancient trees had lifted up through the mountain's stone at the faeries' command to save them, even at the cost of damage to their subterranean limbs.

"Tapadh leibh," he thanked them in the old tongue.

Malcolm tried to orient himself, but it was difficult in the dark when his swimming head said that the tunnel was turning and his eyes could not lie to his other senses. He could only guess at where he was and what direction to travel. *Tomhnafurach* was to the south. It was the largest of the fairy strongholds and the nearest. That was the way he would go.

Still, he hesitated to leave his place without the certainty that he was moving truly toward Taffy rather than away. It was entirely possible that she was being carried to one of the smaller *shians*. Seeking confirmation of his plan, he went into the corner of his mind where Taffy dwelled and searched for her presence.

Nothing.

Taffy? he asked automatically, hunting for her with his full attention.

Taffy lass, where are ye?

He peered south and called again. And then again.

When there continued to be no answer, he became alarmed and then nearly frantic that he couldn't discover a trace of her mind.

Always, he had been able to find her when he looked. Now there was nothing, not even an echo of her thoughts that he might follow.

Night was falling above him, he sensed, and taking hold of his fraying patience, he waited for the sun to leave the sky. The night belonged to his kind, faerie kin that he was. He would be stronger then, he assured himself, able to track her.

Malcolm refrained from pacing, but only with great difficulty, as his nerves demanded that he start after her immediately.

Until this hour, some part of him had always resisted the pull of the still-folk's magic. Just as a part of him had been closed off to his father's kin for their hostility to his faerie blood, so too had part of him been kept from his mother's un-human kind. But he fought the ancient magic no longer. If faerie magic would take him to Taffy, then he would surrender to the pull and embrace it with his whole being.

Darkness. Malcolm felt it settle upon the world.

Taking a deep breath, he turned inward again and looked out through the window in his mind. He began hunting ruthlessly for his wife.

Ah! He had her. He couldn't speak to her because she was deep in sleep, a dreamless state that was so drugged as to seem near death.

He gave thanks that she was still in his world,

that the still-folk had not yet placed her beyond his reach in some other time.

He tried next to rouse her with a soft call, growing impatient and demanding when she failed to respond. For some reason she clung to her coma with desperation, as though terrified of waking.

Taffy, lass, awake, he pleaded—needing to touch her alert mind so that he could assure himself that she was well, not wounded, bespelled, or drugged with some dangerous faerie decoction.

Malcolm frowned as he concentrated, again feeling the birth of alarm. The last glimpse he'd had of her, she had been in the still-folk's keeping. They should have got her safe away from the band of Campbells that had invaded the cave.

But perhaps they had been caught in the shifting earth that caused the cavern floor to give way and were somehow trapped in the ground. Perhaps the faeries had deadened her senses so she would not panic.

Horrified that Taffy might also be lost, alone but for her captors and terrified in the thick dark of the underground, he strained outward with his mind, striving with all his will to know more of her circumstance.

Again, with the new effort, he was able to push past barriers and see through the window in his mind.

She was well, he saw—just exhausted and under a calming spell. The still-folk were carrying her sleeping body to *Tomhnafurach*.

One of her guardians felt very familiar to Malcolm, though he could not say just where he had encountered this faerie before.

"Taffy, lass," he whispered to her, this time gently and deep in her mind where dreams were made. "Ha'e I no' told ye tae listen not tae yer despair? Ye'll break yer heart for sure."

Malcolm?

The touch was tentative, weak, sluggish, and wrenchingly disbelieving.

"Aye, Taffy, lass. 'Tis yer husband."

"You are a ghost again, Malcolm," she cried, her brain painted with black grief as she struggled toward wakefulness. "You are lost! Lost!"

"Nay, lass. I am well," he assured her. "The still-folk are taking ye to *Tomhnafurach*. I shall find ye there. Soon."

"Malcolm, love, come to me, even if you are but a ghost . . ." The thread was growing fainter as Taffy slid back toward comforting oblivion.

"Sleep then, lass," he told her, wanting to cling to the sweet brush of her thoughts, however despairing, but fearful that such prolonged anguish might be damaging to her. He said soothingly: "Rest and heal, Taffy, lass. I shall be wi' ye soon."

He wasn't certain how he would keep this promise, lost as he was in some forgotten faerie maze, but Malcolm knew that he *would* find her. Or he would die trying.

When Taffy awoke, she was curled on her side resting near a tiny streamlet that seemed almost to sing as it danced over its bed of sparkling crystal pebbles. Her fingers told her that she lay on cerements of soft green velvet. Her nose breathed happily of the faint scent of living moss and heather.

Someone had bathed her face, for chilling droplets still clung to her skin, cooling the fever of her tears, which had swollen her eyes to mere slits.

She rolled slowly onto her back and looked up into the sky. It was a perfect light blue, cloudless, but unnatural in its stillness. Not a swallow, thrush, or blackbird used these untrue heavens, or disturbed the silence with their summer song.

Tomhnafurach.

Yes, that seemed right. She had heard Malcolm's ghost whispering to her that she would be taken here.

So, this was the faeries' kingdom, where they dwelled beyond the call of human habitation, buried a fathom deep within the sheltering earth.

Aye, child.

Curiously unalarmed, Taffy turned her head and studied the tall, lean man seated beneath a giant flowering chestnut. He was dressed in a modest cloak of green camlet spotted carelessly with a spray of spent heather blossom. He had an aquiline face—unlined but definitely lived-in. It was a face of seeming youth, but his eyes, silver and fey, were very old. And wise. Yet she had learned not to be deceived by the trappings of pretty faerie magic. Nothing about the still-folk was ever at it seemed.

"Do I not appear sufficiently benevolent?" the faerie asked in a soft voice, shaded with the music of every song that had ever been sung. It was so beautiful! So very like Malcolm's voice that had she any tears left, she would have wept. "I could slump and age if you would find an old man less frightening."

"I'm not frightened," she croaked. And it was true, for there was nothing left to fear.

The man frowned at the harsh rasp of her voice. He rose gracefully and went to the stream. Taking a silver dipper from out of his pocket, he ladled up a small measure of water and then came to kneel at her side.

"Drink, child. Mend thy voice."

Feeling how the magicked waters had drawn the swelling from her skin, Taffy gladly swallowed the healing potion, forcing the cold liquid past the tight muscles of her tender throat.

"We feared for thy life, child. And that of your babe. Would thou grieve this man so violently that you endangered both your lives? Even when he commanded otherwise?"

"I have no life anymore," she whispered, her voice already growing stronger. Perhaps it was the magic water, which held the waiting despair at bay as they spoke of her husband. She knew it was still out there, ready to wrap its icy arms about her heart and drown her in its endless sea as soon as the protection was withdrawn from her senses.

"And your daughter? Is she to have no life either?"

Daughter?

Taffy laid a hand over her belly and stroked it gently.

"Then so too must thou live, child."

"Will you keep me here?" she asked, not caring particularly what the answer might be.

"Only if there is no other choice." The chestnut shivered at his words and blossoms rained down, dancing in the still air to some unseen tune.

Taffy watched the flowers twirl overhead and then said: "It's very pretty here."

"Aye, when thou looks upon it with your new eyes. But what says thy heart, child?"

Taffy looked up at the empty sky where tiny blossoms flew upward without any breeze.

"That it isn't real."

"And couldst thou live forever in such an unreal place?"

"I don't know." Taffy swallowed. Her throat was nearly healed.

"I believe that in time it would disturb thee. And given centuries, small cankers grow into terrible wounds. Thou wouldst not be happy here, daughter."

"Centuries?"

"Aye."

"I shan't be happy in my world either," she told him. "Not now."

"Thou art certain of that?"

Taffy nodded once.

"I was not happy before. It was only that I didn't know it then."

The faerie tipped his head to one side and studied her for a long moment.

"That is often the way of your kind, to be born, to live and die without ever truly awaking. You walk in beauty, but see it not. Thou art surrounded by music, but thou dost not hear it."

"I was afraid," she explained, sitting up slowly and drawing the cloak about her. She was not cold but needed comfort. She pushed her loosened hair behind her ears, for once uncaring that they showed. "We all are, I think: the women I know."

"What didst thou fear?"

"Everything." She waved a hand at her surroundings. "The entire world. But mostly I feared to fail in my—my *external* life."

"The life thou hast shown to thy family and friends."

She nodded.

"And all of society."

"Ah." The faerie nodded.

"So fearful was I of that failure that I never once thought to question if I was faulting my spirit—my heart. If I was compromising my . . ." She trailed off, unable to find the words.

"Your soul?"

"Yes, but I don't mean the soul that goes to Heaven—the one the church talks about. I mean—" she paused, frustrated at her inadequacy at finding the words she needed.

"Your *internal* life," the faerie suggested. "The part of thee that hears the music of the waters there and sees the sunshine dance when it glints in the shallows and weeps for the beauty of it. The part that seeks the quiet of the forest rather than the chatter of men. The part of you that loves passionately, even when the mind has been taught that such love should not be."

"Yes, that's right. But I have started to feel otherwise in the past days. Malcolm changed that. He showed me—" Taffy stopped and looked deep into the faerie's ancient, silvered eyes. "Who are you, faerie? You seem familiar to me."

"My name is Tomas." The man smiled. His face was covered in a radiant beauty.

"Tomas Rimer?" she asked, feeling the vague

306

stirrings of awe. Some of her senses were awakening.

"So have some of your kind called me."

"I'm honored," she said, and then laughed once at the polite conventionality of her words. It was only a small sound, her brief laughter, but somehow it rolled the tide of waiting grief further away from them.

Tomas laughed, too, setting more chestnut blossoms flying into the blue crystal sky.

"Come, daughter, tell me now of this internal life thou hast found. Tell me of our son, Malcolm. And then I shall play you a song. One of happiness, or love, or forgetfulness—whatever thou desires. I can givest thee complete oblivion to all that has passed in thy visit to this age, an thou wishes it."

"I don't know if I can tell you of Malcolm," she answered after a long moment, waiting fearfully for grief to overwhelm her at the mention of his name. But when the dam held she went on: "I can speak many languages, have read all the great love poems—"

"Of human creation."

"Yes, of *my* people."

Tomas did not bother to correct her, but she sensed his inward amusement at her continuing denial of kinship to his kind.

"And thou hast sung many songs. But thou hast never written thine own? Why not, child?

Thou had songs within thee. All MacLeods of faerie blood do."

"I don't know." She shrugged helplessly at the
question, dropping her hands into her lap.

"But then, for all thy reading and thy blood,
thou hast been raised with an impoverished vo-
cabulary in an often cruel land." He looked up
into the heavens above them as though he could
see past them and into her world.

"I fear so. Though it was not so cruel as this
one."

He nodded and returned his gaze to her face.

"The human world was ever an ungenial one
for female poets. Still, while one lives, so mayest
one learn. Make the attempt now, daughter, to
tell me of your thoughts and feelings—and I shall
write for thee thine very own song to fit thy lyr-
ics."

There was a shiver overhead and Taffy stared
up into the branches of the chestnut tree, not terribly surprised to see the feline she'd met in the
forest lounging there, its large, orange head resting on folded paws.

"Hello, cat."

The feline smiled in a very human way.

"It's simple. I love Malcolm," Taffy said directly, looking back at Tomas, and recanting the
last of her parental teachings which said that she
should never speak of such vulgar things as her

feelings for a man. "And I believe that he loves me, too."

There was a loud whine in the darkness and then a sharp bark.

"*Cu?*"

A moment later, Smokey came trotting out of the dark, snuffling with his nose to the floor as he searched for his master in this black place of strange smells and confusing byways.

"So ye found me, hound," Malcolm greeted him, pleased to have some company in the lonely blackness. "Let us see if yer nose can sniff out yer mistress, since mine own efforts have failed tae find the path."

But Smokey only sat on the floor and whined apologetically.

"So she has no' been this way? Well, I didnae expect this task tae be so simple. It never is when the still-folk are involved." Malcolm patted Smokey's head. "Come then, *cu.* Let us be off tae the south, and we'd best hope we shall no' be needing a mattock or spade tae dig our way out, for I have little hope that any have been carelessly left about for us tae use."

Smokey rose eagerly to his feet and waited for Malcolm to point the way.

" 'Tis a pity that Taffy is still bespelled, for 'twould be easiest if there was a voice tae follow the—" Malcolm stopped abruptly and slapped a palm to his head. "And the devil take me for a fool! There *is* someone whom we may follow."

Smokey whined and thumped his long tail twice against the wall.

"But we must go softly, *cu*. I dare not frighten the bairn after her mother's grievous hurt." Using the greatest care, Malcolm cracked open the door in his mind where he had once glimpsed the child.

"*Mo nighean*," he whispered low and soft, calling to his daughter in the tongue of his ancestors. "I am with ye now, little one. How fare ye and your mother, child?"

There was no verbal reply, for the babe was but barely formed, but she sensed her father's presence and answered him with her tiny mind.

She was in a garden now, so far away from him. Her mother was troubled, not herself, and the babe wanted the reassuring touch of her father's attention now that Taffy's was withdrawn.

I am here, daughter, he said soothingly.

The babe turned in the womb and smiled happily.

Da?

Here.

Malcolm turned south and, hands stretched out before him, began trotting toward the tiny voice that called happily to him. His daughter's tiny mind was a beautiful clarion call.

Chapter Thirteen

Malcolm was accustomed to traveling in the dark and moving along the faeries' obscure trails, so he did not easily lose his sense of direction. But the path to *Tomhnafurach* was not straight and it was intersected many times by broad tunnels that felt to his sight-deprived senses every bit as likely as the one he traveled. Since he could not afford to be led astray on a false trail, he had to pause and assess each one he came across, which was exhausting to his faculties and ate away at his small store of precious time.

The journey through the mountain could not truly be endless, for a part of Malcolm was keenly aware of the stars shifting in the skies overhead and bringing the dawn ever closer, but it was difficult for his body to make sense of the passage of time or distance he had traveled in the unchanging dark of the tunnels.

He was somewhat relieved when the trail ceased descending into the bowels of the mountain and began a steady ascent toward the human world above. Doubtless the unpleasant notion of imminent death was all in his imagination, but the press of all the weight of the earth over his head was oppressive to the spirit and made the night-black atmosphere seem darker than the grave.

Soon there were fewer intersections to confuse him, and he had just put on a burst of speed when suddenly the uphill path turned back downward. Malcolm was at once disappointed and concerned by the event. With cause, he discovered, for just three paces on, he trod in a streamlet of icy water that clutched at his brogues with icy claws that wriggled quickly into the skin of his feet.

Instantly Malcolm halted, urging his gloomy hound to do the same.

He laid a hand over Smokey's muzzle and then stilled his own labored breathing. The sudden drop in temperature had the perspiration of his labors beading instantly upon his fevered skin, making him feel not only cold but clammy.

As soon as he had ceased his panting, he began listening carefully for a clue about how deep and wide this underground pool might be. The noise was rather confusing as echoes rebounded off of echoes in the vast space that had opened around him.

The water was not deep, he decided after a long moment of concentration, at least not near his feet. There was a drip from the unseen roof, marking the edge of the wet as it fell with the soft pings of an arrhythmic clock. It had not the low tone of water droplets plunging into a deep body. Yet—

Malcolm breathed in, casting his tired mind out yet again to look over the water.

The pool was enormous, freezing, and at one end there was an unpleasant boiling, which troubled the water. The aquatic disturbance hadn't the sound of a spring filling a pond, but rather of something vast draining rapidly—as from the bottom of a stone sieve.

Recalling the hollow sound of the cave's rotten floor splintering beneath his feet, Malcolm decided that he had had enough of falling for one day and the watery noise was one he preferred to avoid if at all possible.

Smokey whined softly, his troubled call echoing in the immense space.

"We must go on, *cu*," Malcolm said, stepping cautiously into the subterranean lake. He could not hold back a grimace of discomfort. The waters at the heart of the mountain were as cold as they could be and yet not be ice.

Smokey hesitated.

"Come away, *cu*. We've no other choice."

The dog shivered. He whined unhappily at the frigid temperature of the water that lapped at his paws, but the dark was worse even than the unseen lake, so he followed his master into the freezing wet—complaining all the way.

Tomas played for Taffy on a pipe, a tune to gladden the heart and told of all the wonderful things about Malcolm that she had been unable to articulate. They'd had a day of music and verse, poems that set the stars afire and made mist burn. Chronicles of long-ago kings had been sung, as well as stories of worlds long since passed away. The faerie's exquisite voice took the worst of her grief away and made her glad that she had known, if only for a while, the joy of being in love.

So beguiled and distracted did she become by the song that she scarcely noticed the passing of the hours in *Tomhnafurach*—and was completely unaware of the decades that flew by on fleeting wings above them.

There, in the human world, the rebellion ended. Lady Dunstaffnage died and became dust. Kings were crowned, they reigned and died and others replaced them. Wars were fought, railroads and steamer ships were born, and her father and mother also came into the world.

But for Taffy, the events that marked the history books of the human world passed by unnoticed, buried under the sweetness of the faerie's musical spell.

Malcolm, afire with impatience and roused by a growing disquiet, again picked up the pace of travel. His lungs burned from trying to draw nourishment from the dark cavern's air, and his eyes ached from staring at the nothingness about him.

A tiring Smokey protested their haste, for he did not care for the increasingly stagnant atmosphere either, nor the foreign smells that were increasingly riding on its odd oily currents. But Malcolm could no longer afford to spare his lungs, or to be cautious of hazards like snags in the floor, or low arches that might be waiting overhead. He did not slow for Smokey's whines, even though they were now running through a darkness that had no equivalent this side of oblivion.

Soon, Smokey ceased his fruitless complaints, cowed by the new changes he sensed in the atmosphere. In the distance, there was a knocking, an unnerving cadence whose vibrations traversed the very stones beneath his feet and filled the breathless air about him with painful concussions.

Malcolm felt it, too. He was also alarmed because his daughter's voice was growing increasingly more distant, and he knew that while time in *Tomhnafurach* was passing slowly for Taffy and the bairn, in the world beyond, the tides of change were roaring by like a river in spate.

Even in his own world, he felt the shadowy lights of dawn stealing over the land. His time was running out. Soon, Taffy would be taken to a door that led into her world and she would be sent beyond his reach. And he would not be able to follow.

Already, she was traversing the road back to her time. And though he tried again and again to reach her thoughts, he was defeated by the powerful faerie spells woven about her.

How far and precisely where Taffy went she could not say, for she paid scant attention to the direction she and Tomas were walking as he showed her the lovely gardens where so many unknown species of flowers grew.

It was, in fact, only as they left the river of *Tomhnafurach* far behind that some of the veils began parting in her mind, and she realized that they had been traveling along the same road for some extended period of time.

"Didst thou enjoy the romaunt, child?" the faerie asked, his voice a pleasant and soothing murmur that would not wake a baby. Nevertheless, his question lapped at her brain.

Had she enjoyed her romance? *Her romance?* She looked in question at Tomas.

He said: "There often comes a time when the wheel turns and the change shall either snuff out the embers of passion, or else fan them to a blaze. If thou must remember, now is that time. Else say the word, and thou shalt forget that thou knewest love."

The words reverberated in her mind. Taffy, still walking—though more slowly—didn't answer. Layers of swaddling were gradually unraveling from her brain, and she became aware again of the tiny life inside of her. Laying a hand over her abdomen where the child stirred restlessly, she made an effort to concentrate on what was causing the babe's agitation.

After a moment, she stopped in her tracks, momentarily disbelieving the babe's sad message, then turned to look at Tomas Rimer.

She blinked the worst spell from her brain and saw the faerie then with her human eyes, a creature of potent magic, ancient and unchangeable. He was beautiful, but also strange and dark and terrible.

"Malcolm is *alive*," she said accusingly.

Tomas pulled on his chin with thumb and forefinger and watched her awakening senses with cool interest.

"Aye," he agreed. "He is."

"Take me to him," she demanded.

"I am." He looked down at her hand, which cradled her belly and shook his head. The still-folk man sighed. "So he found the bairn and tracked thee that way? Our son is determined and clever. It makes thy choice all the more difficult, child."

What choice? Again, Taffy didn't answer. She was reaching out with her mind, trying to find her husband. Wherever he was, it was a place so distant that she could scarcely sense him.

"You lie. Malcolm isn't anywhere near here."

Taffy took another step back from the faerie and drew in a deep breath. Her nose, much keener than when she had entered *Tomhnafurach*, was able to pick out the faint scent of smoke that clung to the air around her with its sticky, dirty fingers. It was not the windborne remains of peat fires that drifted by, but the smell of coal. The smell of her time.

Malcolm might not be far from her geographically, but chronologically he was almost two hundred and forty-four years away.

She turned about slowly, looking at the scenery with disenchanted eyes that saw beyond the bordering flowers that hedged the path they were on. She was shocked to find that they had traveled down a narrow gorge whose walls were split with exact precision by what she now recognized as sealed faerie portals.

How had she failed to perceive all this? Was Tomas Rimer's glamourie so strong that it blotted out all her senses?

Their present path pointed toward a deep defile that ended on a narrow ledge, and at its edge sat a great granite door chased with wrought silver. As she watched in trepidation, the great stone shivered to life, and she became aware of a slow pounding in the earth beneath her feet.

"Where is *Malcolm?*" She swung back around and faced the waiting Tomas. Her hands reached for her rowan spike, only to find that the weapon had been taken from her at some point when she was unaware. Her voice shook with anger: "I will not leave without him."

"Thou must," he said simply. "Thou hast no more time. Thou must leave now, or leave never."

"Then I choose never," she said flatly, ripping the last of the clouding shroud from her brain so that she was again in full possession of her senses.

"A poor choice, my child, and a potentially cruel one." Tomas's fey eyes no longer twinkled. His voice was still beautiful, but now it made her shiver with fear.

"And *your* choice isn't?"

"Mayhap." The faerie shrugged. His failure to

answer her more completely caused her unease to grow stronger.

"Explain this to me, Tomas. I don't understand. What do you mean my decision is cruel?" she asked reluctantly when he still did not answer. Though she was angered, she was also fearful that he would use his voice to work some new magic upon her reason and trick her into leaving Malcolm forever.

Or worse yet, he would slay in her the hope for Malcolm's survival that had been so newly reborn.

Tomas's eyes were as beautiful yet blank as highly polished silver. "Our son is lost in the tunnels beneath *Tomhnafurach*."

Taffy's heart clenched at his words. She reached out again for Malcolm, trying to discover if what the faerie said was true. Alarm burst within, showering her with burning sparks that further cleared her mind of any doubts she may have had about her feelings or what she needed to do.

"Then we must find him. At once!"

"Thou cannot, child. He fell into the old tunnels from the cave where we took you."

"Then we'll go back there and get him."

"The entrance to the cavern is now gone, crushed under the hill's weight."

"You could open it again," she insisted. "I

know that you could. You open doors all the time—*in* time, even."

"Nay. We have no need to visit that time and place again. And to do so would be to place us all in peril. There are soldiers waiting there, hovering outside."

Taffy grappled with his words, weighing them for truth and reluctantly believing him to be sincere in his assessment of the danger.

Tomas nodded an affirmation at her thought.

"That way shall never be reopened. One by one, we have closed our doors to the human world, shutting out the ways of egress for humankind." He gestured at the walls around them, at the dozens of doors shut seamlessly into the fabric of the mountain.

"If that cavern was the entrance to a tunnel, then there must be an exit somewhere," she reasoned with growing desperation.

"There is. But the only remaining door from that tunnel opens into your time."

"When in my time? Now? A year? The day I die? When?" Her heart began to pound. It was partly nerves, but there was also some powerful magic beginning to disturb the air. It shimmered and sparkled with a cold fire.

"This very afternoon. Before the sun has set in your sky," Tomas promised.

Taffy thought about this. She also recalled Malcolm's story about faerie trickery, and was not inclined to entirely trust this being.

"Why did you not tell me this before, Tomas? Why did you let me grieve for him as one dead?" she demanded, her suspicions plain.

The faerie sighed.

"Because I cannot promise you that Malcolm will arrive in time. I thought it kinder to take most of the painful memories away."

"Why *wouldn't* he arrive?" Taffy demanded as she patted her stomach, a gesture done as much to reassure herself as the daughter who was growing steadily more agitated at her mother's upset.

"Because the road is confusing, black as death, and in poor repair. As we speak, it is collapsing, being swallowed by the mountain."

Taffy focused her senses on the trembling beneath her feet. The temblor was distant but growing stronger, rolling through the earth at a relentless pace.

She stared at Tomas with horror.

"And you left him there? Alone in the dark?" she whispered. "What sort of inhuman monster are you?"

"An unhuman one," he answered, with a brief flare of black dilating his eyes. His voice had all the cold of the howling winds of winter. "But not so monstrous as we deliberately placed our son there to die."

"I don't believe you," she whispered, causing the faerie's eyes to flare again.

"Believe this, lady, we will close that road forever this afternoon. *Your* kind have come too close to us with their pawing over the bones of the dead. We can wait no longer. Malcolm will escape today, or he will escape not at all. That is truth, and thou must accept it. If need be, I shall take these memories away."

Taffy shook her head in angry refusal.

"Never. I will never let you back into my brain!"

"Child—"

"Just answer me one thing. Why did you bring me here?" she demanded, both furious and terrified for Malcolm. "Why make me fall in love Malcolm if you planned all along to kill him?"

"Why art thou here? That babe in thy womb shall be our presence in the future. None of us could endure long in the world where thou lives. To survive now, we must retreat into the *shians* and wait for another age—one which is more conducive. Yet some of our blood must walk this earth as we did in times before humankind came to our lands with their savagery and cruel iron. Otherwise, we will not find our way back. You and your babe are our legacy. Malcolm too was our legacy—and we wished some joy to our son that he might awaken to who he truly was and decide how he wished to live."

Tomas looked to the sky and then pointed at the door.

"No more questions. Open it, child. Go forth to thy destiny. Malcolm shall join thee an he may."

"No. Not yet." Taffy shook her head, trying to absorb what the faerie had said and quiet the confusion that was engulfing her brain. All around her, magic was rising in the air. "I must know."

She called again for Malcolm but he did not answer.

"Wouldst thou have Malcolm arrive in your time, alone? Unversed in the dangers of that world? Condemned there until death without his love—the woman for whom he sacrifices everything? He is staking all on this throw, can you not do the same? Art thou so heartless as to do this to the man thou hast professed to love?" The faerie pressed her, bombarding her with questions that invoked guilt and fear.

"I hate you! I must hate you," she said to herself. "You're cruel and heartless and you'll deceive me if you can."

Tomas pointed again at the door. His eyes had gone black and his face was taut and blank.

"Now, child. I can still time no longer." The faerie's voice was urgent.

Feeling the ground rumble beneath her feet,

Taffy staggered to the granite slab, which marked her path home.

Malcolm are you there? she cried one last time.

Are you coming, lass? A voice asked faintly.

Her heart contracted.

Yes. I'm coming, Malcolm.

She reached out a reluctant hand. The touch of the moon metal in the archway beneath her palm sent a tingling through the veins of her trembling hands, up her arm, and went into her heart. Unable to stand the feel of pure faerie magic passing through her body, she pushed on the slab with her full weight.

A long-fingered hand appeared beside her head and lent its great strength to her endeavor, shifting the massive stone.

The door ground slowly opened under their combined efforts. In front of her was a wavering image of the cemetery at Kilmartin looking much as it might if seen through a defective looking glass.

"Go," Tomas urged, his voice no longer harsh, but still strained. "My blessings with thee, child. Make haste. This door shall not remain open for long."

Taffy looked back once at the ancient faerie, standing under the light of an unreal sun, and her heart turned over with remorse. If what Tomas said was true, then the faeries had been forced into their magic world because humans had taken the one above from them. The terms of their survival *were* cruel, but the still-folk had not set them.

"I don't hate you, Tomas. And I'm sorry," she said, stepping through the door. Pushing through the magic barrier was a labor. "Good-bye."

Good-bye, whispered the wind as the mountain closed behind her with the hollow sound of old stone marrying itself to its own kind.

Dizzy and slightly sick, Taffy stood swaying in front of the familiar barrows of Kilmartin. She had spent so many days with her camera here, and yet it seemed so long ago.

Taffy stood trembling in every limb, unable to believe that she was actually back in her own time, safe from Campbells, Colkitto, and Covenanters, but without Malcolm at her side.

Had she made the right decision about leaving *Tomhnafurach?*

Sick and uncertain, she looked up toward the heavens, trying to judge the hour—and year—by the sun.

Branches of one of the few remaining trees in the cemetery scarred her view of the sky, but the strong sunlight that flooded through the leaves was the golden fire of midday.

"He didn't lie about that," she murmured, putting a hand to her brow, which was beaded with cold sweat.

It was too early for Malcolm's arrival, but she still looked about with anxious eyes, trying to judge from which tomb he might emerge.

Her hunt was not a long one, as the faerie door was apparent to her trained eye, and also well marked by the neatly ordered pile of her missing possessions; her rifle, sacks, and even her camera were waiting in front of an undistinguished mound.

She stared at the weapon, too tired to be angry at what it implied. If the faeries had found the rifle and returned it, then they could also have returned Malcolm. Couldn't they?

"Tomas, you're a lying, evil faerie."

Then she saw another gift from the still-folk. Pipes. They had saved Malcolm's pipes and brought them to this place! She took heart at their sight. It had to mean that the still-folk believed that Malcolm had at least a chance at survival.

Weakened by her passage through the magic portal, and nearly sick with the mixture of hope and terror that churned in her brain, Taffy dropped to her knees beside the piled goods and closed her eyes against the harsh sun that beat upon her.

Her vigil had begun and she would not move until . . . until Malcolm was there, or there was no more hope.

No hope. She wondered how long that might be.

She was gone! Malcolm could find not the slightest trace of either Taffy or the bairn.

Noooooooooo! he shouted with his mind, causing the stones around him to rumble ominously with the added strain.

It could not be too late! He would not believe that. But even as he swore it, the first seeds of doubt sprouted in his mind, setting down their roots, and starting the process of draining his will to live.

Smokey, who had run ahead of his master, began an excited barking that pierced his self-absorption. Relieved to have his dark mood interrupted, Malcolm went forward swiftly to join the hound.

He soon discovered why Smokey was in ecstasy. Their narrow path ended abruptly in a stone slab that marked a faerie door.

"And the devil swallow it sideways," he muttered to the hound, running his quickening hands over the stone, seeking a latch or bar.

The beast continued to bark and snuffle, and Malcolm understood why. There was the faintest pencillings of light outlining the door. And in the air there hung a faint trace of some unknown smoke.

Malcolm? The question burst upon him, full of

alarm and healthy vigor. Was it coming from the other side of the stone?

"Taffy, lass!" he shouted, dropping to the floor, and trying to be heard above Smokey's enthusiastic howling. "Hush, ye brainless *cu*! I cannae hear a thing!"

Malcolm, open the door! Hurry! Day is nearly gone. Tomas said the road would close forever at the end of day.

Malcolm obeyed readily, again running his hands over the surface until he found what felt like an old lock. Behind him, to punctuate her fearful statement of time running short, the tunnel gave a heart-rending groan and swayed alarmingly.

An apprehensive Smokey began a frantic effort to dig his way free.

Is Smokey there?

The hound howled another greeting and redoubled his frantic pawing.

Malcolm's fingers explored the lock hurriedly. Its key was gone and the metal rotted, freezing the tumblers in place. Swearing roughly, he pulled out his dirk, and using the pommel, he pounded on the latch, trying to coax it free of its moorings.

Behind them, the tunnel shrieked and a length of ceiling fell to the floor with a deafening clap of tearing air.

Malcolm!

329

He could feel her fear as though it was his own.

"I'm coming, lass!" he assured her.

But the air was growing unbreathable and the mountain was coming down around him. There was no time for delicate coaxing. He could only hope to smash the lock completely and use brute strength to force the door.

"Get back, *cu*." Malcolm instructed the hound and then struck for his life, putting his whole might into the one blow.

The assaulted lock clattered obligingly to the floor, but the shifting mountain settled heavily on the frame, snuffing out the tiny thread of light that had guided him, and refused thereafter to loosen the door no matter how he pushed against it.

The tree, Malcolm. By the door! Make the tree pull out its roots! There will be a hole and you can crawl through the wall!

Malcolm felt to the right of the lock and found the gnarled, hairy growth of ancient tree roots. Reaching down inside the well of ancient knowledge where faerie magic was made, he found the power he needed to work a spell and commanded the old limbs to shift themselves in the stony soil.

For a long moment nothing happened. Then the tree's knobby ropes trembled and then began to slide from their earth-bound moorings.

It's working!

Behind them, the tunnel gave forth another

boom, and particles of dust filled the air with a choking cloud of stinging sand. Malcolm laid hold of the transshifting roots and, taking a last breath, allowed himself to be pulled into the earth.

No sound could overpower the rumble of the collapsing mountain, but Malcolm could feel the faithful hound digging beside him with frantic haste. He wondered if they would escape or if both of them would be buried alive while Taffy looked on.

He shut his eyes and lips to the stony soil and ceased breathing. If this was death, it was a cruel one—and if rebirth, twice as harsh as the first had been.

Then, when the eternal blackness of death seemed inevitable, familiar hands were about his wrists, his wife's new strength adding itself to that of the falling tree. He heard Smokey give an exuberant howl and wriggle free of the strangling earth.

Then he, too, was pulled out into the new world, and opened his caked eyes to witness the death of the sun and the eternal closure of the faerie's deadly portal as the ancient burial mound sank into the earth and vanished forever.

Chapter Fourteen

"Malcolm!" Taffy threw herself on top of him, heedless of the clotted earth that covered his clothing and the frantic hound who laved her face with a sticky tongue. She didn't even the feel the heaved-up stones, which bruised her knees on their rough edges.

"Taffy, lass," he croaked, closing his arms about her in a fierce grip. His tired body came instantly alive and he began to cough the bad air from his lungs. After he had caught his breath he said: "I thought I wouldnae ever see yer bonnie face again."

"You still aren't seeing me," she said, tears spilling over her lashes and raining down on his filthy cheeks. She made a stab at brushing the worst of the soil away, an effort happily aided by an exuberant Smokey who tried to worm his way between them. "How can anyone so dirty look so wonderful?"

A white smile split his muddy face and he tucked her wild hair back behind her ears so that he might better examine her.

She looked tired, bedraggled, slightly swollen by crying and—utterly wonderful! He pulled her close again, and then feeling for the first time the accumulation of leaves and sap stuck to her back, he looked past her at the rest of the world.

Night had overtaken the land, making it soft for his eyes. The terrain was at once familiar but also very different. This world was a less wooded one, but that was only the beginning of the differences that clamored for his attention.

He breathed deeply. The atmosphere seemed expectant, waiting for his explorations. It was also, while far from tranquil with the sounds of many night birds and bats filling the air, a night that was filled with peace. There was no smell of burning crofts, no clashes of ringing steel. Had a lasting peace between the Scots and Sassenachs truly been called?

Taffy stirred and then raised herself up to a sitting position. She pulled the equally filthy Smokey close and gave him a brief hug.

"You must want a bath," she said, looking from

the muddy hound to her dirty husband. "And a meal. And to sleep for a month."

"Aye," he agreed, sitting up slowly. His body was healing, but still very much aware that it had been dragged through a mountain. "But all in their good time, lass. Show me first this new world of ours."

"Well, this is the cemetery at Kilmartin," Taffy said, rolling to her feet and offering Malcolm a hand. He took it, though he did not need her assistance to rise. "Not precisely paradise, is it?"

Malcolm nodded. Through the dark, he could see not only the ancient barrows of Kilmartin, but in the distance he could make out a rail-fenced cemetery where the recent dead lay beneath ornate stones.

He stared in wonder at the writing on the tombs. Though knowing what to expect, the dates still amazed him: 1847, 1872, 1881.

"I kenned that we had traveled," he said at last. " 'Tis in the air. This is the same wind that ever blew, but now I sense in it a new gramacie. And the birks are gone."

"Yes," she said sadly. "That birch was the last one growing here. What you smell is coal. It feeds machines as well as fires."

They looked at the uprooted tree that had saved Malcolm from death. It stretched its dying limbs up toward the night sky, shivering even though there was no breeze.

"It wouldnae have survived the mountain's fall," he said consolingly, but went to lay hands upon the trembling roots until they ceased to quiver.

"No," Taffy shivered. Nothing living could have survived the mountain's fall.

Malcolm came away from the tree and quickly wrapped his arms about her. He pulled her to the comforting heat of his body.

"You smell of earth," she told him.

"Aye and less pleasant things, as well. But it shall wash away soon enough. Now, when was the last time ye ate, lass, that yer so near tae swoonin'?" he asked with tender practicality. It made Taffy smile.

"I don't recall. Not since the cave, I think."

"Then I'd best be hunting up some supper." He released her reluctantly.

"There's no need," she answered, smiling happily. "We are not far from the inn. It is perhaps an hour's walk from here. Let me gather our things—Oh! Malcolm, they brought your pipes, too."

"*Mo pioban?*" he repeated. "I didnae think tae see them again."

"They're here," she said, catching his hand and leading him to the familiar pile of belongings.

"I have my lyart reed as well, so I may play for ye now." He gave one of his rare and beautiful smiles.

"I look forward to that—as long as it isn't the song you played at Duntrune. I never want to hear that piece again."

"Nor I, lass. That sadness is behind us. Well, let us be off then." Malcolm stooped and shouldered the packs and rifle, leaving the camera to its mistress's care.

The moon rising up slowly in the sky gave a soft, velvet light to the gloom about them.

"The inn is west," Taffy began. Then: "Oh! Malcolm, look! There's a plate in the camera. Someone has taken a photograph."

"Mayhap the faeries sent ye a present."

"I wonder what it is a picture of," she murmured.

Malcolm laughed softly at her familiar distraction with her favorite tool. He could understand it, having much the same love for his pipes.

"We shall discover it presently," he promised, turning west and starting across the disturbed earth. His feet sank slightly into the loose soil and leaf mold that was all that was left of the faeries' sunken portal.

Taffy hurried after him, order happily restored to her universe.

The gloom of night thinned away as they neared the inn's brightly lit windows.

"Are all men so forswunk here?" he asked, noting the high level of activity in the yard and the shadows of people within rushing about in confusion.

"No, they aren't." Taffy took a deep breath. "Likely, they have discovered that I am missing and are going out to search for me."

The two looked at each other and started to laugh.

"Well, they would have had a long hunt. But what do ye plan tae tell them."

"That a barrow collapsed with us on it." She stopped laughing. "My father will have fits."

Malcolm ceased laughing.

"We shall tell him that we are man and wife, and then there shall be no sin in our being together so late at night.

"It isn't my being with you that will anger him. It is the collapsed barrow."

Malcolm looked skeptical of her conclusion.

"But I shall most certainly tell everyone that we are married," she assured him, for the first time feeling nervous about what they were to do.

Smokey wagged his tail, ostensibly in support of the idea. He could smell the odor of cooking meat and was anxious to get to the place where it was coming from.

"Very well," Taffy murmured, and the three bedraggled companions walked into the light that lined the yard, causing all activity to stop.

"Tafaline!"

Her father strode out from the group of men

337

and stopped a careful pace back from her muddy body. His expression was a mix of relief and horrified disapproval. Displeasure seemed dominant.

"Hello, father. This is—" she began, only to be interrupted.

"What on earth has happened to you, girl? You look a fright!"

"I got married and had a mountain fall on me," she snapped, suddenly angry. His reaction was what she had expected, but still it enraged her. And having faced murderous Campbells, her father's petty wrath held no terror for her. "Now, I need a bath and—"

"What mountain? Not one of the barrows!" he demanded in a tone of greatest horror.

"Yes, a barrow," she confirmed heartlessly.

Taffy watched as her father clutched at his head, and she felt a little ill. The faerie had been right; this man, at least, was not her kind.

"Have I taught you nothing?" he asked. "How could you be so careless—"

At that, Malcolm took a step forward. He was an awesome sight by lantern light. Tall, well-knit, strongly made, and with an aspect of unknown danger about him. His expression as he looked upon his new father-in-law was a less than kindly one.

"I am Malcolm MacLeod," he said in a hypnotic voice that contained only a trace of Scots in its depths. There was a ripple of surprise through the men who had been preparing the search parties. "Your daughter, *my wife*, has been close to death this night. She is hungry and tired, and we both need tae bathe. Your questions will have tae wait."

As if to underline Malcolm's point, Smokey also came forward into the light, his posture mildly aggressive as he took a position in front of his mistress, growling low at Davis.

Taffy watched without sympathy as her father divided his attention between the aggressive males of two species, and concern for the damaged barrow. Of her, he seemed to think not at all.

Finally, when the silence around them had grown unbearable, he made up his mind which statements most required his attention.

"Your *wife?*" Taffy heard him ask.

"Indeed. My wife."

Taffy's daughter shifted inside her as she felt her father's annoyance with this stranger. The babe had grown greatly when Taffy passed through the faerie door and she had stepped between times. There, for an instant, the clock of the ages had been loosened upon her.

"We married four months ago," she said, giving the earliest possible date for when she and Malcolm might have met and married, and drawing her father's attention back to herself.

She felt Malcolm cock a mental brow, but he did not question her statement. In faerie time, who knew how long ago they had wed? And she could never explain that their nuptials had happened on a summer's night two-hundred and forty-four years in the past. That was a bloodstained occasion of which she would never tell anyone—except their daughter.

"Malcolm is a piper," she explained with ready invention. "He has lately been in service in Her Majesty's armed services in India. We met when he was home on leave after an injury."

"Bloody dangerous place," her father said, the first glimmerings of approval in his voice. He strongly favored the imperial notion of bringing English enlightenment to heathen lands.

Having just been in the midst of such enlightenment, Taffy did not share his opinion. She did not however say so in front of their audience. She wished to conclude this discussion quickly and gain the privacy of the inn before anyone noticed the oddity of Malcolm's clothing beneath the thick mud that covered it. Very few highlanders wore such long plaids anymore.

"Malcolm sent a cable, but there was difficulty tracking me down. When I finally received it just after dinner, I started off for Kilmartin to meet him. Unfortunately," she said, rushing the story a bit as she was getting cold, and she had recalled a wonderful explanation from her days in America that would explain what had happened to the barrow. "There was a sinkhole that opened under our feet. I am afraid that the barrow collapsed into it. We were lucky to escape with our lives. From here forward, great caution will have to be used in the cemetery. The ground may be unstable in other places."

"Certainly!" her father agreed, finally horrified enough at her description to show some concern for his daughter. "But Taffy—my dear! Why did you not tell me of your marriage? Four months— and not a word to me!"

"I did not want to disturb your work with outside concerns." Aware of the intense interest of their audience, and the fact that Malcolm would need coaching in his role of military piper before conversing with the locals at any length, Taffy began walking toward the inn, hurriedly constructing the rest of her tale.

"We did not know whether Malcolm would survive. Right after our marriage he succumbed to a fever that had been troubling him for weeks—and I was sent away for fear of harming the baby."

"You—you are—" Her father's voice lowered as he strangled on the words he would never have willingly uttered in public.

"Pregnant. Yes." She said clearly, leaning heavily on Malcolm's proffered arm. Sensing his amusement with her father's tongue-tied speech, she pinched his forearm lightly. "But all is well now, as you can see. I am sorry that this has been such a shock."

She uttered the last sentence as a concession to her father's stunned silence. And she truly was sorry that she had been forced to be so abrupt with her news, but she decided that it was best to get all the unpleasantness over with at once.

"We shall likely be going back to the States soon," she announced, stepping through the fascinated throng of lantern carriers. She spared a small smile for Jamesy who was looking back and forth between her ears and Malcolm's with alarmed speculation. "Malcolm comes of a restless breed, and I think that America will suit us well."

"America," her father repeated in failing accents, falling in behind them. Taffy looked back briefly. He seemed to be shrinking in stature with every step they took toward the inn.

Ahead of them a door was thrown open, letting out the smell of a busy kitchen into the night. Taffy's elderly landlady bustled out into the yard.

"Oh, poor lassie!" she exclaimed, then seeing an even more filthy Malcolm and Smokey standing beside her, stopped in her tracks with her hands clapped to her round pink cheeks. "Ach! What a soss ye are!"

"I fear so, Mistress MacIntyre," Taffy said, leaning harder on Malcolm and doing her best to look frail. It was only partly an act. She was very weary, very hungry, and very tired of her dirty jean dress.

"Come at once," the elderly woman instructed, recovering herself. "Ye shall bathe in the kitchen. The lad may bathe after."

"This is my husband," Taffy quickly explained. "Malcolm MacLeod, late of Her Majesty's army in India."

"Yer husband? And a soldier?" Taffy was glad that she had thought of this tale. Everyone seemed to like it. "Well, he shall have his bath when yer done. And that filthy hound as well. What a strange beastie he is! I've never seen the like. And I'll fetch ye a wee nip of whisky tae warm yer bones while water is heated."

If you only knew! Taffy thought. Smokey's ancient breed had surely been extinct for nearly two hundred years. *No one* in her time had seen his likeness.

"Thank you," Taffy murmured with genuine gratitude for the show of caring that should have come from her father, but hadn't. "We are both very chilled."

It was only an hour later that they managed to close their door to the outside world. Taffy's room was small, but she had insisted that it would do for the two of them for that one night.

Once dressed in clean clothing—Malcolm's

borrowed from a still stunned Davis—they had sat down to dine. Though hungry, they had only eaten lightly of the offered soup, finding the salt flavor overwhelming after the blandness of their previous diet.

Finally, their various immediate needs seen to, they had managed to escape their curious audience who had crowded into the inn to stare and listen while they ate. They retired to bed in Taffy's small chamber.

"Phew!" Taffy leaned back against her door, wishing it had a bar.

"Aye!" Malcolm agreed, drawing the shutter over the window. He did not bother to light the lamp. "Yer father was beginning tae bestir his thoughts and ask questions of me. And that Jamesy man was casting a strange eye o'er my face and ears."

"He isn't stupid—my father," Taffy said, coming away from the door. "Just very involved in his work. Actually, we will have to be careful of Jamesy, too. He knows all the local legends, including yours."

"Including *mine*," Malcolm repeated and then shook his head in bemusement. He began to strip off his borrowed clothing, starting with her father's trews, which Taffy could tell he did not like.

"Well, you and Colkitto are rather large legends in these parts," she explained, also removing her briefly donned clean apparel.

"I dinnae feel legendary. Except perhaps when ye look at me," he added, raising his gaze to her body. He noted at once the slight changes that had taken place; a thickening at the waist and slight swelling in the breasts. "Then I feel like a king—with ye as my queen."

Taffy blushed, but did not cover herself with a nightrail.

"Well, you certainly look the part of a legend," she said, walking the paces that were between them and wrapping her arms about his lean hard waist. She rested her head upon his breast and listened to the reassuring beat of his heart, keeping time beneath the cage of his ribs and impressive muscles.

He touched her hair.

"It occurs tae me, Taffy lass, that yer likely as large a legend as I am."

"What?" she looked up, startled.

"Did ye no' hear the MacColla talking o' the wild stories of a Sassenach lady come tae rescue me?"

"But . . ." She thought about the strange looks Jamesy had been giving them. "Dear heaven above! Perhaps you're right. Well, that's all the more reason for us to depart on the morrow."

There was a slight pause.

"Aye. We'll depart on the morrow."

Taffy stared into Malcolm's eyes, trying to read

what was there. For the first time since their re-union, he was holding something back from her.

"What is it? What's wrong?" she asked with alarm. "You don't think that the still-folk will try and stop us somehow?"

"Nay. Their door is closed now," he assured her, gathering her close and then laying her on the narrow cot. "They willnae interfere, nor would I think they'd want to."

"Malcolm?" she coaxed.

"Did I no' hear ye wishin' for some coverpanes and a proper bed? Behold! Yer wish is granted." He lowered his lips to hers. His kiss was coaxing and hungry, and feeling the anticipation building in her own body, Taffy decided to let her questions rest until later.

His hands slipped over her hips and he pulled her into his body as he carefully fitted them onto the narrow cot. He looked down at her pale breasts and then gave a sigh.

"So bonnie," he murmured, sliding down her to set lips to her nipples, which he laved tenderly.

Taffy arched, pressing closer. Her head swam giddily as she rubbed against the man she knew and loved so well. Malcolm paused long enough to look up and smile at her. As always, the sight of his rarely expressed happiness made her heart turn over in her breast.

Malcolm's clever fingers moved up the edge of her legs and then slid slowly to the soft flesh of her inner thighs. Though loving the feel of her beneath his hands, he did not dawdle there, so great was his desire to find her warmth and make a place for himself there.

"Ah," he breathed with satisfaction when he found her damp and ready.

Taffy shivered, her heart thundering in her chest so hard that it interfered with her breath. Her body, always sensitive to Malcolm's touch, was now acutely aware of his every movement and driven wild by them.

She sighed with pleasure as he settled upon her and wrapped her arms and legs about him. Malcolm gently kissed the curve of her jaw, feathered over her cheeks and ears, and then returned to her beautiful mouth. There he plundered happily while the tide of growing desire surged through their bodies.

When uncontrolled shivers wracked her body and her breast and loins were so tight that they ached, Malcolm finally fitted himself against and pushed his way inside her. His hands grasped her buttocks, pulling her closer to him.

"In the time we have left here," he whispered, "I can think of no better place tae be than inside ye."

The breath left Taffy's lungs. Her hands quivered as they moved up and down Malcolm's sweat-slicked spine. Heat was pouring off of him, off of her, melting them both into a state of thoughtless desire where even speech was an impossible feat. The riptide of passion was moving through them, hastening them toward their goal.

He moved in and out of her with increasing speed until their bodies writhed. Such intensity of need and desire could not be long sustained. Taffy felt as though her lungs had stopped moving, that her heart was going to burst in her chest.

He rolled his hips against her, and with that the passion became too much to bear. Crying out, Taffy was catapulted into fulfillment.

Malcolm's hoarse shout said that he too had let go of this world.

Slowly, Taffy regained her senses and she could feel the aftermath of passion being wrung from Malcolm's body. After a few moments, his muscles finally unknotted and he gradually subsided upon her.

Taffy, feeling fiercely protective and suddenly shadowed with worry, touched him gently. Her hands were tender as they stroked up and down his back.

"Love?" she whispered.

"Aye?" Malcolm turned onto his side, bringing her with him, refusing to uncouple them.

He looked into her dark blue eyes framed with tussles of silky honey hair. They still carried the sparkle of the incandescent joy they had shared, and he hesitated to speak any words that might dim them with worry. He wanted to spend this night lost in the depths of her pliant body, reveling in her sweet-scented skin and looking at the love that shone out of these beautiful, ocean-deep eyes.

The mere sight of her caused hunger to grow in him again. It would not take an effort of mind or body to again lose himself in making love to her. The worry which crouched nearby could wait.

"Forgive me, Taffy lass, but 'tis a greedy man ye've married."

"There's nothing to forgive."

"That was a masterful piece of distraction," Taffy said gently, as Malcolm finally pulled a blanket over them. "But I have not forgotten anything. Well, I didn't forget for long."

He grunted, but didn't answer.

"You may as well tell me the truth. My imagination will run amok else. And if I cannot sleep, I promise, you shall not either."

"I've no mind tae be sleeping this night," he said, meeting her eyes.

"Are you concerned about the future?" she asked. "Worried of what will come when we leave here?"

"Nay. I've no fear of departing this place wi' ye, Taffy lass."

But he did fear the future. Or rather that they

might not have one. Taffy either did not know, or had forgotten what happened to people that had been long in the faeries' world. Her well-being he did not fear for; the faeries would have exercised the greatest care in seeing that she was not harmed. But he had no way of knowing how long he had been lost underground, wandering in the ancient faerie tunnels, and what would happen when the sun rose upon them on the morrow.

There was always the possibility of obliteration by the sun's cruel rays that kept him from being able to plan any of the days that might stretch before them. The only certainty was that they had this night. He would not waste any of their precious time in sleep.

But should he speak to her of his worries? What if sorrow clouded the only time they had and made it bitter and grieving instead of joyous?

"Malcolm, you cannot hide your concern from me. I sense it. Will you not speak to me of whatever is troubling you? Please."

"Let us no' speak of the future until after the dawn has come. Sometimes the light of the sun changes what one may plan."

Taffy's gaze probed his.

"I don't see how. Do you think that I will love you less when I get a look at you in morning light?"

"I bloody well hope not," he muttered, frustrated with himself for being unable to hide his unease and letting it spoil their night.

"And will you love me less with the passage of a few hours— Or do you love me at all?" she asked, her gaze direct. "You've never actually said."

"Of course I love ye," he answered, shocked.

"That relieves my mind." Taffy rose up on her elbow and pushed her hair back from her face. Mane disposed of, she laid a hand along Malcolm's cheek. "Very well, then. Let's have the truth and no more messing about."

In spite of himself, Malcolm smiled at her gentle command. His shy lass had learned well how to straightforwardly order things in life to her liking. He could not help but be pleased that it was so, though it made keeping secrets from her inconvenient.

He wondered, if he rolled her beneath him again, could he perhaps shake her thoughts loose from her tenacious line of questions?

"It won't work," she told him, feeling him stir.

The challenge hung in the air between them.

"And you are a cowardly craven to even think of trying it," she informed him with a glower.

"Aye, that I am," he agreed, running an appreciative hand over her smooth flesh. "But why trouble ye with a foolish fancy?"

"Because it might not be foolish," she answered promptly. "And I do not care for unpleasant surprises. What is there about the sunrise that—"

She stopped speaking, and Malcolm saw realization dawning on her face. Instantly, he pulled her close and began to speak soothingly.

" 'Tis only a chance—an old wives' legend," he assured her.

"It would be just like the faeries though, wouldn't it?" she said, burying her face in his chest. "To spite me for what I said. About taking their child."

"Aye, it would," he admitted. "But this wasnae a faerie plot. They made no devious plan. Mischance brought me here, so I think we needn't fear any trickery from the still-folk."

"But that still leaves mischance," she said, wrapping her arms about him and holding him as tightly as her muscles would allow.

"Aye."

"What happens to people when—when—" He could barely hear the unfinished question, her voice was so strangled and muffled by the linens that she was hiding under.

"They turn instantly to dust. Or salt," he answered, thinking truth kinder than a lie at this point.

"How long until dawn?" she asked at last.

"Only a bit. An hour, no more."

Impossibly, her arms tightened.

"Be at ease, Taffy lass. Strangling me will no' hold back the sun."

"I hate the sun," she muttered, but relaxed her grip slightly. Holding Malcolm's strong body against her own, it did not seem possible that anything as fragile as dawnlight could harm him.

"Well, I've no great liking for this sunrise," he admitted, settling her into her blanket cocoon and turning his gaze to the window. "Try and rest, lass."

"You must be jesting," she muttered.

"Well, worry then as ye may."

"Men!" he thought he heard her say, and he laughed softly.

Chapter Fifteen

The inn was silent as the first faint lifting of darkness appeared in the sky. Horrified, yet fascinated, Taffy turned her head to stare out the tiny widow in her room.

Malcolm was already turned on his side, staring fixedly at the small square of glass.

At first, there was only a soft line of gold penetrating the morning mist to warn that the night's reign was over and day was ascending. But minutes passed inexorably, and it was soon plain that the heaven's powers had shifted. The morning's faint fog would not prevent the sun from climbing over the horizon and mounting the sky.

Resigned and grim, Malcolm gently disentangled himself from their blankets and Taffy's arms, and rose silently from their bed.

Going to the casement, he pulled back the window's half-closed shutter. Taffy quickly followed after him, wincing at the unpleasant chill of the bare boards on her naked feet.

Together, they stood at the window. Watching, waiting, hoping. . . .

Forerunners of the true sun shot up into the sky, a halo of beautiful golden light that touched the eastern firmament end to end. Stars winked out—thousands at a time. The fog burned away, and the gates of heaven opened to admit the sun. It was beautiful—and horrible—to see.

Neither of them flinched as the fiery ball crept over the land and rose in the eastern sky. They did not move back from the tiny window as the fingers of burning sun approached, though Taffy could see the pulse in Malcolm's throat hammering his flesh with brutal force, and her own heart was likely to fail from its frantic thundering against her ribs.

Up the gray-stone wall, the burning fingers crept, rising higher by the moment as they painted the building with flaming light.

Colder than she had ever been, Taffy slipped a trembling arm about Malcolm's waist and moved closer to his living, breathing warmth.

It couldn't end this way! Malcolm was here— real! The stories they had heard were nothing but folktales. Legends. Stop! She called to the sun. *Stop for just one more moment. . . .*

Ignoring her, the heartless golden dawn crept coyly over the windowsill and reached hungrily for Malcolm's unprotected belly.

Nothing happened.

Up it crept onto his chest making his dark hair glint with red fire.

But nothing else happened.

On it went to touch his face—chin, lips, cheeks, and eyes—and all the while he stood unflinching, not even lowering his lids against the cruel light.

Up it went and spilled golden light all over his unbound hair.

And still nothing happened.

Finally it reached beyond him, touching the walls and ceiling with golden radiance.

Taffy released a pent-up breath and slumped against him.

"Thank heavens," she began and then jumped in alarm when the kirk's bell began to toll. Recalling that a church's chime was the other thing that killed those returning from that faerieland, she waited an eternity for the last knell to sound.

Silence fell.

"Nothing happened," she whispered in near disbelief, as dawn firmed its hold in the sky and the inn began to stir around them.

"Nay." Malcolm started to smile.

"Oh, thank heavens!" Taffy wrapped her arms around him and began to cry weakly.

"Taffy, lass?" he asked, his smile dying, as he pulled her close into his body and began stroking her naked back. "What is wrong, love? Is it the bairn?"

Malcolm searched quickly and found his daughter sleeping peacefully. She, at least, was not upset with the dawn, for which he gave silent but heartfelt thanks.

"No. I'm fine—truly! It is just that I have been so afraid and so very tired. I just can't believe that we are actually safe. That the still-folk kept their word and let you come." She sniffed pathetically and looked about for a handkerchief.

"Well, ye shall fear no more, lass," he promised, scooping her up in his arms and returning her to bed where he dried her tears with the corner of the laundered sheet.

Taffy snuggled against him, allowing all the ugly dread to drain away and her tears of relief to dry up.

"Lass, ye've conquered Campbells, Covenanters, Colkitto's army, and even the sun—"

A polite scratching at the door interrupted him.

"A moment, *cu*," Malcolm called softly. "I didnae think the hound would stay away so long as this, even wi' his upset at the bath."

Taffy gave a watery laugh as she recalled

Smokey's look of hurt reproach when he was summoned to the tub for a much needed bathing.

"What shall we do today?" she asked with a small yawn as she nuzzled Malcolm's chin.

"Sleep," Malcolm said promptly. Then, as his stomach rumbled: "And eat."

He tucked her carefully beneath the blankets and then went to the door to admit Smokey. The hound had felt his mistress's worry and came up immediately to offer comfort and protection.

Malcolm patted him gently on his brindled—and now clean—head. "Yer a loyal beast."

"And make love?" Taffy asked sleepily, also patting Smokey as he turned to her and thrust his damp muzzle beneath her hand.

"Aye. That as well." Malcolm finally pushed the hound aside and slipped in beside her, tucking himself into the narrow cot like a spoon. "And play my pipes. I must write a new song about our adventure."

"And tomorrow?"

"Whatever we wish, love. We've the whole world to see, Taffy, lass. And plenty of time tae see it."

Taffy smiled sleepily at the propitious truth. They *had* the world—and time.

Exhausted though they were, together they watched the sun until it was well up in the sky. And only then, when the luminary giant had completely cleared the horizon, did they close their weary eyes against it.

`Slipping toward a deep, healing sleep, they let their thoughts mingle, and began dreaming happily of what would come.

Likewise content, Smokey made a quick check of his little mistress, resting inside her mother's belly. Then he also went to sleep.

Far away in *Caislean na Nor*, Tomas Rimer smiled at the picture in his auguring bowl before brushing the image away with a delicate finger.

Their daughter had been prevented from making a potentially dangerous visual record of their sacred lands, but she had not been sent away without a memento. When she thought to examine her picture box, she would find a small gift there. The babe she carried would be able to see the faerie *mathair* who had fallen in love with a mortal MacLeod and given birth to their line. Malcolm's grandmother.

And though they did not know it, both Malcolm and Taffy would have a little more than the average human lifetime to enjoy her world, raise their babes, and write beautiful songs. The effects of their time in the sacred glen would be with them for years to come.

"Long life, my children," he said quietly. "And much happiness upon thee."

Epilogue

Bishop Mapleton sat in his study, watching the clock on his desk and feeling happily amazed. The dreaded hour had come and gone and there had been no playing heard in the battlements. It seemed that his exorcism had finally done the trick. Or perhaps it was taking the piper's bones and burying them at the edge of the property and setting that massive boulder atop them. Whatever the cause, he was reveling in the silence.

He was so happy, in fact, that the news the archaeologist's daughter had married a piper and the man had come for a visit did not disconcert him.

Night Visitor

He could tolerate a highlander's "agony bags" so long as they weren't being played in *his* castle. He might even pay a call upon the couple and welcome the man to the neighborhood.

RESOURCE LIST FOR
NIGHT VISITOR

Gordon Beresford, Brass Knuckle Museum:
http://www.teknetwork.com/~lyzzard/Brass/brass.html

Keith MacGregor, historian for Clan Gregor, Great Lakes
chapter

Colkitto by Kevin Byrne

What Jane Austen Ate and Charles Dickens Knew by
Daniel Pool (Simon & Schuster)

Where Queen Elizabeth Slept and What The Butler Saw by
David N. Durant (St. Martin's Griffen)

Bardach Albannach, edited by W. I. Watson of The Scottish
Gaelic Texts Society

*The World Guide to Gnomes, Fairies, Elves and Other
Little People* by Thomas Keightly (Avenal Books)

The Celtic Lyre (translation of Gaelic folk songs)

Cothrom (ag adhartachadh na Gaidhlig) Fall 1999

The Highlander (volume 37, No. 2,3,4,5)

Irish Toasts, Curses and Blessings by Padraic O'Farrell
(Sterling Pub. Co.)

Dictionary of Ghost Lore by Peter Haining (Prentice Hall)

Oicheanta Si by Michael mac Liammoir (Lucky Tree)

The Folklore of The Scottish Highlands by Ann Ross
(Barnes & Noble Books)

Scottish Ghost Stories by Elliot O'Donnell (Jarrold)

http://www.velocipede.com/history.htm (bicycle history)

http://costumes.org/pages/timelinepages/1880s1.htm
(costuming)

http://www.emcee.com/~ajmorris/photo/history.htm
(photography history)

http://www.portsdown.demon.co.uk/cal.htm (calendar)

http://www.seanet.com/~efunmoyiwa/MacFie/macfie2.html
(history)

http://www.ndirect.co.uk/~iforshaw/Mag10/10page2.html
(history)

http://www.ndirect.co.uk/~iforshaw/Mag30/page3.html
(history)

http://pbm.com/~lindahl/rialto/SI-songbook1-art.html
(music and photos of Duntrune)

http://hometown.aol.com/skyelander/timeline.html (history)